SICK

by

Brett Battles

Introduction by Blake Crouch

ALSO BY BRETT BATTLES

FOREWORD

The first jolt of interest was the cover...

Ominous gas mask, and the silhouette of a man running across a desert.

Then the title...SICK...one word, powerful, provocative, intriguing...

But it was those first pages that hooked me.

A man roused from sleep in the middle of the night by the cry of one of his children. What parent hasn't experienced that? And, while stumbling toward their child's room in that confused bleariness between consciousness and dreams, who hasn't had that secret fear in the back of their mind, that maybe something is wrong? That maybe their son or daughter isn't merely coming down with a cold, or in the wake of a nightmare. But something much, much worse...

SICK didn't just hook me. It hit me with a devastating uppercut on every primal level as a parent, a father, and a human being.

Brett Battles has fashioned a blistering page turner that is destined to become a classic. This is a novel of paranoia, of fear, of a family blown apart by circumstances none of us could imagine, and ultimately, hope.

This is exactly the kind of novel I love to read, and it reminded me in the very best way of David Morrell's iconic TESTAMENT.

Trust me, you will love it, too.

SICK is absolutely unmissable.

–Blake Crouch, April 2011

1

A cry woke him from his sleep.

A young cry.

A girl's cry.

Daniel Ash pushed himself up on his elbow. "Josie?"

It was more a question for himself than anything. His daughter's room was down the hall, making it hard for her to hear his sleep-filled voice in the best of circumstances. And if she was crying, not a chance.

He glanced at the other side of the bed, thinking his wife might already be up checking on their daughter. But Ellen was still asleep, her back to him. He'd all but forgotten about the headache she'd had, and the two sleeping pills she'd taken before turning in. Chances were, she wouldn't even open her eyes until after the kids left for school.

Ash rubbed a hand across his face then slipped out of bed.

The old hardwood floor was cool on his feet but not unbearable. He grabbed his T-shirt off the chair in the corner and pulled it on as he walked into the hallway.

A cry again. Definitely coming from his daughter's room.

"Josie, it's okay. I'm coming." This time he raised his voice to make sure she would hear him.

As he passed his son's room, he pulled the door closed so Brandon wouldn't wake, too.

Josie's room was at the other end of the hall, closest to the living room. She was the oldest, so she got to pick which room she wanted when they'd moved in. It wasn't any bigger than her brother's but Ash knew she liked the fact that she was as far away from Mom and Dad as possible. Made her feel independent.

Her door was covered with pictures of boy bands and cartoons. She was in that transitional stage between kid and teenager that was both cute and annoying. As he pushed the door open, he expected to find her sitting on her bed, upset about some nightmare she'd had. It wouldn't have been the first time.

"Josie, what's—"

His words caught in his mouth.

She wasn't lying in the bed. She was on the floor, the bedspread hanging down just enough to touch her back. Ash rushed over, thinking that she'd fallen and hurt herself. But the moment his hand touched her he knew he was wrong.

She was so hot. Burning up.

He had no idea a person could get that hot.

The most scared he'd ever been before had been when he'd taken Brandon to a boat show in Texas and the boy had wandered off. It took Ash less than a minute to find him again, but he thought nothing would ever top the panic and fear he'd felt then.

Seeing his daughter like that, feeling her skin burning, he realized he'd been wrong.

He scooped Josie off the floor and ran into the hallway.

"Ellen!" he yelled. "Ellen, I need you!"

He knew his voice was probably going to wake Brandon but, at this point, he didn't care. Josie was sick. Very sick. He needed Ellen to call an ambulance while he tried to bring their daughter's temperature down.

"Ellen!" he yelled again as he ducked into the bathroom.

Using an elbow, he flipped on the light then laid Josie in the tub. He wasted several seconds searching for the rubber plug, then jammed it into the drain and turned on the water, full cold. To help speed up the process, he pulled the shower knob and aimed the showerhead so that it would stream down on her and cool her faster.

Where the hell was Ellen?

He put the back of his hand on Josie's forehead. She was still on fire.

"Ellen!"

He was torn. He wanted to stay with Josie, but the pills Ellen had taken must have really knocked her out, so that meant it was up to him to get help.

"Hang on, baby," he said. "I'll be right back."

He raced into the hall and back to the master bedroom. The nearest phone was on Ellen's nightstand, next to their bed.

"Ellen. Wake up."

He shook her once, then picked up the phone and dialed 911. As he waited for it to ring, he glanced back at the bed.

Ellen hadn't moved.

"Nine one one. What is your emergency?" a female voice said.

He reached down and rolled Ellen onto her back, thinking that might jar her awake. But her eyes were already open, staring blankly at nothing.

He flipped on the light. The skin around her mouth and eyes was turning black, and there were dark drying streaks running across her face from her eye sockets where blood had flowed.

"Nine one one. What is your emergency?"

"Oh, God. Help," he managed to say.

"Are you hurt, sir?"

He touched Ellen's face. It was as cold as Josie's had been hot, and instantly he knew no breath would ever pass her lips again.

"Send help! Send help, please!"

He dropped the phone, not bothering to hang it up. It didn't even dawn on him that he hadn't given the operator an address. He was barely holding on to his sanity.

Back in the hallway, he tried to shove the image of Ellen's cold and lifeless body into the back of his mind. He looked into the bathroom. Josie was still propped up in the tub, the water now several inches deep. He knew he should go see if she was cooling off, but he had to check Brandon first.

He threw open his son's door and flipped on the light. Brandon had one of those beds that were raised in the air like a bunk, but instead of a second mattress underneath there was a desk.

Ash rushed over to the bed. His son was a long lump covered by a Spider-Man comforter. As was the boy's habit, even his head was buried beneath the blanket.

Ash could feel the muscles around his heart tightening. With the yelling and the running and now the light on in the room, he was sure his son should have woken, but Brandon hadn't moved at all.

He grabbed the comforter and pulled it back.

His son was lying on his side, his back to him.

Just like Ellen. Oh, God. Please, no.

Holding his breath, he put a hand on Brandon's shoulder and pulled him onto his back.

His son's eyes fluttered. "Dad?"

For the first time since Josie's cries had awakened him, Ash was unable to move.

"Dad, are you okay?"

Maybe this was the dream part. Maybe this was the final blow. Maybe in a few seconds he'd realize that Brandon's voice was only in his head, and his son was as cold and dead as his wife.

He touched Brandon's forehead.

Warm.

Normal warm.

"Brandon?"

"You're scaring me, Dad," his son said, inching back a little. "What's going on?"

Ash quickly pulled Brandon off the bed and held him tight against his chest as he ran out of the room.

"What's going on?" Brandon asked again.

"No questions right now, okay, buddy?" Ash told him, trying to keep his voice calm. "You're going to be fine."

It was a lie, of course. How would either of them ever be fine again?

He carried his son into the bathroom and sat him on the closed toilet lid.

"What's Josie doing in the tub?" Brandon asked.

"Not now."

The water was nearing the halfway point and was covering Josie's waist and legs. Ash touched the side of her face, hoping her temperature had come down a few degrees.

Not only had it come down, it had plummeted.

No! No, no, no!

He yanked her out of the tub without turning off the water, and began stripping off her drenched nightgown.

"Brandon, get some towels!" he yelled.

"Dad, what's going on? What's wrong with her?"

"Just get the towels!"

By the time Ash had her clothes off, Brandon had retrieved three towels from the cupboard under the sink. Ash used the first to quickly wipe off what water he could, then wrapped the other two around her. Though she was dangerously cold, unlike her mother she was still breathing.

"Get behind her," he told his son as he laid her on the floor. "Hug your body to hers. We need to help her get warm."

Brandon surprised him by not arguing. He stretched out behind his sister and hugged her tight. Ash did the same in front, creating a cocoon of warmth with Josie in the middle. It was the only thing he could think of doing.

"She's so cold," Brandon said.

"I know."

"What's wrong with her?"

"I'm not sure."

"Where's Mom? Does she know?"

"I let her sleep." Brandon would find out the truth soon enough, but at the moment Ash needed him to focus on helping his sister.

Though Josie's breathing was shallow, he could still feel her chest move up and down.

"It's okay, baby," he whispered over and over. "It's okay."

"She's not getting any warmer," Brandon said after a few minutes.

"Just keep hugging her."

They were still holding her like that when the front door of their house smashed open. Ash could hear people running into their living room.

"Who is it?" Brandon asked, fear in his voice.

"I called the paramedics before I woke you," his father said. "Let's just hold on to your sister until they tell us to move. Okay?"

"Okay, Dad."

Ash expected the EMT crew to come into the bathroom at any moment. But when no one appeared, he yelled out, "We're back here! In the bathroom! We need help!"

Footsteps pounded in the hallway, but still no one came.

"We need help! We have a sick girl here!"

Finally, he could hear them approaching the bathroom door. He tilted his head back so he could see into the hallway.

First one person appeared, then two.

But the relief he should have felt was overshadowed by confusion. The people moving into the bathroom weren't dressed in EMT uniforms. They were wearing biohazard suits.

What happened after that was a blur of images.

His daughter rolling out of the house on a gurney under a plastic tent.

Ellen leaving, too, only the plastic that covered her was a black bag.

And people, dozens of them, all dressed in the same biohazard outfits.

He didn't know how long he and Brandon had sat on the couch while all this was going on, but it seemed like hours.

Three things he did clearly remember from after that point.

He recalled being led with Brandon out to a truck that had some sort of isolation container on the back. As they crossed the front yard, he heard another cry, this one not of pain or fear, but anguish. Loud and uninhibited. Looking up, he realized theirs wasn't the only house with an isolation truck out front. There was one parked in front of every home on their block.

The second thing he remembered came several hours later, after he and Brandon had been separated and he'd been put in some kind of cell.

"Captain Ash." The voice came out of a speaker in the ceiling.

"Where are my children?" Ash asked. "They need me!"

"I'm sorry to inform you, Captain," the voice said, still calm, "but your daughter died three minutes ago."

"Josie?" he whispered. "Take me to her! Please, let me see her."

There was no response.

"I have to see my daughter!"

When the voice next spoke several hours later, it was to inform him that Brandon had also died.

That was the third thing he remembered.

2

Dr. Nathaniel Karp stood with his arms crossed, watching the center monitor. There were three other people in the room with him: two technicians and a guard, all of whom had the highest-level clearances within the project.

The feed in the monitor came from cell number 57. Inside the cell, Captain Daniel Ash continued to pace back and forth, his temper seeming to swing from angry to desperate to devastated and back again with each crossing.

Overlaid across the bottom third of the monitor were Captain Ash's vital signs. Dr. Karp noted that the captain's heart rate was elevated, and that his temperature had risen half a degree, but that was understandable given the circumstances. What interested the doctor more was that the captain seemed to be showing no signs of the illness.

The doctor glanced at the other video screens. Seventeen additional cells were currently occupied by neighbors of the Ash family. When they'd first been brought in, they were all like the captain—agitated, but healthy. Now, though, every single one of them was displaying symptoms of infection.

Dr. Karp looked back at Ash's monitor.

So what makes your family different, Captain?

Ash had been as exposed as anyone else when the spray was released on the three streets that made up the Barker Flats Research Center housing area. But it had not affected him at all. Just like it had not affected his son.

Brandon, was it?

The immunity had obviously been passed down through Ash's ancestors, and not his wife's. Preliminary results indicated she was one of the first to succumb. Unfortunately, whatever gene was in play within the Ash family, there was an apparent gender component to it. The fact that Captain Ash and his son had remained immune, while the captain's daughter had not, was definitely something that needed to be investigated.

In many ways, the girl, Josie Ash, was the most interesting. By all accounts, she had gone through the same stages of the infection as the other victims, but not long after she'd been brought in, she had started to show improvement. And now, seven hours later, her temperature was almost normal.

Still, it bothered Dr. Karp. If the immunity affected the sexes differently, any vaccine they might be able to develop from the Ash family could potentially have the same drawbacks. He was sure the female population of the project would be far from excited if they had to go through the same hell the Ash girl had. There was also the very real possibility that, though the girl was now getting better, she might have suffered some internal damage to her organs while the disease had a hold of her. That would be unacceptable.

No, the gender component would have to be identified and eliminated. If that turned out to be impossible, then KV-27a would not be the answer and further testing would have to take place.

"Dr. Karp," one of the technicians said.

The doctor acknowledged the man with a look.

"We've lost the patients in cells 18 and 31. Five other cells are trending toward termination in the next thirty minutes, and the remaining ten sometime over the following two hours."

Dr. Karp nodded once, then looked back at Captain Ash. He was sitting on his bunk now, his head in his hands. His heart rate had come down a bit, and despite the fact they had been pumping the virus directly into his cell since he arrived, there was still no sign he was getting sick.

"Call me if anything changes," the doctor said.

"Yes, sir."

Dr. Karp walked out the door and down the hallway toward the rooms where the children were being held.

As soon as the girl was stable enough, they would move the two Ash kids to a facility outside San Francisco, where observations could continue and the doctor's team could do more extensive testing to determine the source of the immunity. A day, maybe two at most.

Their father, on the other hand, would not be making the trip. A team would continue to keep him under observation there at Barker Flats, waiting to see if the virus broke through and compromised his system. Dr. Karp was convinced it wouldn't, but they had to do their due diligence. If in a week, maybe ten days tops, Ash was still healthy, he would be terminated and his body thoroughly examined

Dr. Karp reached the boy's room first. The guard at the door opened it without being asked, then stood aside.

Brandon Ash was sitting at a small table, an untouched bowl of cereal in front of him.

"You should eat," the doctor said.

"I'm not hungry," Brandon mumbled.

The doctor approached the table. "I have good news."

Instantly, the boy brightened. "My father?"

"Your sister, Josie."

"Oh," the boy said, unable to keep his disappointment completely out of his voice.

"She's getting better. You'll be able to see her soon."

"Good. I'm…I'm glad. But…" He hesitated. "What about my dad?"

Though the doctor was often short and gruff with those who worked for him, he knew how to turn on the bedside manner when needed. He knelt down next to Brandon and put a hand on the boy's shoulder. "I'm not going to lie to you, Brandon, he's not doing well at the moment. But we're hopeful that he'll be better soon, just like Josie."

"Can I see him?"

"That wouldn't be a good idea right now. There are a lot of doctors and nurses working on him, and I'm sure you don't want to get in their way."

Brandon looked down at the table and shook his head. "No. I don't want to do that."

"As soon as you *can* see him, I'll let you know. Okay?"

Brandon tried to smile. "Thank you."

Dr. Karp patted him on the shoulder again then stood up. "Now, eat your breakfast. We don't want you getting sick, too."

3

That night would be burned forever in Ash's mind. He knew there would be no escaping it. His wife, his daughter, his son—all dead. But as utterly painful as that realization was, it was actually the good memories that made him want to curl into a ball in the corner.

Wrestling with Brandon in the backyard.

Reading to Josie as she leaned against him, hanging on his every word.

Kissing Ellen. Holding Ellen. Loving Ellen.

There was a trip they had all taken once that started out badly, but it turned out to be the best vacation they'd ever had. He'd been stationed at Fort Irwin then, outside Barstow, California—ironically only about a hundred miles south of Barker Flats. They'd meant to go to the Grand Canyon but only made it as far as Needles, California, when the van they'd borrowed from a neighbor broke down. Repairs would take several days, which pretty much ruled out sticking to their plan.

The owner of the auto shop was a former Marine. When he found out Ash was in the service, he made a few calls and was soon driving the Ash family the forty or so miles to a vacation house on Lake Havasu his brother-in-law owned.

They spent the days swimming in the lake, the evenings barbecuing, and the nights playing games. Ash became the king of Chinese checkers that trip, while Josie was crowned Miss Monopoly.

One day they even rented a Jet Ski, and Ash took turns taking the kids out on the water. Ellen was a nervous wreck every time she watched them head away from shore, but by the end, even she was smiling and laughing. Ash never did get her on that Jet Ski, though.

She'd claimed someone had to stay on shore in case something went wrong, but he knew that wasn't the real reason. She had a fear of water, something she'd had since she was a kid.

He missed that about her.

He missed everything.

Over a week he had been in his cell, a week of talking with no one but the voice from the speaker, and not actually seeing anyone at all. When he woke each morning, he found a day's worth of food sitting against the wall. He tried pretending to sleep a few times so he could catch whoever was bringing it in, but he could never keep his eyes open long enough. He suspected they were giving him some sort of sleeping drug, either through his food or, more likely, through the air.

The cell that was his world consisted of a cot, a toilet, a sink, and four thick cement walls. The only door was opposite the toilet, but there was no handle on the inside, just a smooth metal surface.

He figured he'd been put in the cell on the chance he'd been infected. It was probably the nearest isolation room available. After all, he'd held his daughter in his arms. Brandon had, too. He'd been healthy when Ash last saw him, but he'd apparently contracted whatever it was before they were taken from the house. So, logically, Ash should be next.

Only, despite the fact that everyone he loved was dead, here he was still breathing.

He felt despair and guilt and loss, but none was as strong as the hatred he felt toward whoever had done this to his family, his friends, his country. There was no way he would ever believe this was not a planned attack. Someone had targeted American soldiers and their families. *Families, for God's sake!* Whoever it was needed to pay.

Perhaps they already had. But if that were the case, no one had told him. In fact, no one had told him much of anything.

Each day, the man on the speaker would ask him questions like: "How are you feeling?" "Do you have any pain?" "Headaches?" Or the voice would give him instructions such as: "Stand with your arms out, then raise them above your head," or "Walk heel to toe across the room in a straight line." He felt like a drunk.

But when Ash asked questions back, they were ignored, and the anger he felt toward the terrorist who'd perpetrated this disaster started to leak a little toward the voice in the ceiling. He just wanted to get out and bury his family. He wanted to sit by their graves and grieve. It was his right.

"Good morning, Captain," the voice on the speaker said.

Ash opened his eyes. It was the beginning of his eighth day in the cell.

"Are you feeling anything unusual? Aches? Pains?" the voice asked.

Ash looked up at the speaker. To him it had become the face of the voice. He could almost see eyes now, and a nose. And, of course, the big round mouth.

The speaker had become his own version of Wilson the volleyball from that Tom Hanks movie, *Cast Away*. Only Wilson had been Hanks's friend. Ash wasn't so sure the speaker was his.

He gritted his teeth. "How much longer?"

"Please answer the question."

"Answer mine first. How much longer until I can get out and deal with my family?"

For more than a minute the cell was silent.

"Are you feeling anything unusual? Aches? Pains?" the voice asked again.

"Go to hell."

"Captain, you are not at liberty to choose whether you will answer the questions or not. It's your duty."

Ash rolled onto his side, as if turning away from the speaker would make it disappear.

As he lay there, he could smell eggs and bacon, and knew a tray with his breakfast was waiting for him by the door. It was the only hot meal he got each day. Lunch and dinner would be in boxes next to it. Sandwiches, most days.

"Are you feeling anything unusual? Aches? Pains?"

The captain let out a snorting you've-got-to-be-kidding-me laugh. "Unusual? Yeah, I'm feeling something unusual."

"Please explain." There was a note of concern in the voice.

Ash just shook his head. If the voice couldn't figure out there was something unusual about his situation, he wasn't going to enlighten him.

"What are you feeling?" the voice asked.

No response.

"Captain, please answer the question."

Ash sat up, suddenly having the urge to eat. He retrieved the tray then returned to his bunk. In addition to the bacon and eggs, there was also a container of orange juice and a cup of coffee. He opened the OJ and downed the contents.

"Captain, if there's a change in your condition, you need to tell us."

Ash lifted the plastic top that covered his plate and picked up his fork. He was just about to scoop up some egg when he noticed a small, folded piece of paper tucked under the bacon. He hesitated for a moment, then placed the lid back down as if he'd decided he wasn't ready to eat yet, and turned his attention to the coffee.

"Captain, are you going to cooperate?"

Ash took a sip of the coffee and made no indication he had even heard the question.

"Captain?"

It was another five minutes before the voice finally fell silent. Still, Ash waited, knowing that after a while their interest in him would wane, and those watching him through the surveillance cameras would no longer be paying as close attention as they had been.

Finally, he lifted the lid off the plate again. This time he grabbed both the piece of paper and a strip of cold bacon. He tucked the paper against his palm, then raised the bacon to his mouth and took a bite. While he chewed, he casually slipped the paper under the blanket.

He ate everything on the plate, even though the eggs had gone rubbery and the bacon had lost much of its flavor. When he was done, he set the tray by the door as he always did, and commenced his daily exercise program.

This consisted of push-ups, sit-ups and running in place, the perfect exercises for the confined man. Outwardly, he maintained an aura of blank detachment, but on the inside he could think of little else but the scrap of paper waiting for him in his bed.

After sixty minutes, he'd worked up quite a sweat. He removed his clothes, then used the cup the coffee had come in to give himself a sink bath. Still sticking to his routine, he toweled off with his shirt and pulled the flimsy cloth pants they'd given him back on.

For the next twenty minutes, he paced the room. This was his cool down, also part of his new daily habit.

As he walked back and forth he began to wonder if he was making a big deal out of nothing. Maybe the paper was just trash, something accidentally dropped there when his food had been prepared. If so, he was getting himself worked up over nothing.

Once his palm touched the concrete wall at the end of his last lap, he returned to his cot and lay down. After a few minutes he closed his eyes, then twisted around so his back was to the vent where he assumed the camera was. As he turned, he slipped his hand under the blanket and grabbed the paper.

Though he kept telling himself that it was nothing, he could feel his heart race as he silently unfolded it. Keeping it close to his chest, he held it out at an angle, lowered his head and opened his eyes.

In the center of the paper, written in pencil, was a single word:

TONIGHT

4

The man running the show in Dr. Karp's absence was Major Frank Littlefield.

The major had left his previous posting three years earlier for a special assignment. After a year in which a whole new world had been opened up to him, the assignment became permanent. It was on that day that the Army—and the U.S. Government, for that matter—ceased to be his true employer. He was a member of the project now, and as such, that's where his loyalties lay.

Major Littlefield was sitting in his office sipping a cup of coffee. Via the monitor on his wall, he had access to all the same feeds as the observation room two doors down, but was limited to watching only one at a time. That wasn't such a big deal anymore since there was just one cell still occupied.

Cell number 57. Captain Daniel Ash.

The captain was taking what had become his usual post-workout morning nap. But this morning there was definitely a change in him, a defiance that had only been a spark in the previous couple of days.

As the major stared at the screen, his phone rang. He pressed the speakerphone button and said, "Major Littlefield."

"I just read your report." It was Dr. Karp. The major had been expecting the call, waiting for it, actually. "Has there been any change in attitude?"

"No, sir."

"What about physically? Still no reaction?"

"None whatsoever, sir."

The doctor was silent for a moment. "I had hoped to give it a few more days, but I think it's safe to assume the results won't change. Where are we with the current dosing cycle?"

"It's scheduled to complete at two a.m."

"All right, we might as well let it run. Once it's complete, pull the plug, Major."

"Yes, sir."

"I want the autopsy performed immediately. Once you have obtained all the required samples, and the body has been eliminated, you and your team are to report to Bluebird."

"Understood."

"Good," the doctor said, then hung up.

As Major Littlefield replaced the receiver in the cradle, his gaze returned to the napping form of Captain Ash.

"Enjoy it," the major said to the TV. "It'll be your last one."

5

Tonight.

It could mean so many different things.

Was it a warning? Was tonight the night they changed the sleeping gas to something stronger? Or was the sender going to try to contact him? *Or* was it just a joke and didn't really mean anything at all?

Ash wasn't sure if he should be looking forward to finding out or dreading it. But there was one thing he couldn't do—stop it from coming.

He kept to his schedule. Eating lunch when he usually ate, exercising again in the afternoon, then pacing until his stomach began to growl, signaling it was time for dinner. Twice the voice had asked how he was feeling, and twice he had ignored it.

When the lights flicked off then back on, he knew the wait was almost over. In ten minutes they would go off and stay that way until morning. Again, he did what he always did, brushing his teeth using only his finger and water from the sink, then relieving himself in the toilet. The only change was the ripped-up note he slipped into the bowl just before he flushed.

As he lay on the cot, he felt tense, suddenly sure the message had been a warning. He tried to stay awake, fearful that if he closed his eyes, he might never open them again. It wasn't that he was scared of death, or that the thought of being with his family again didn't appeal to him. But it was *because* of his family that he needed to live. He had to find who had done this to them. He had to make sure whoever it was had been properly dealt with, and if they hadn't, he had to do it himself. After that, he didn't care.

But then the gas must have come, because his eyelids grew

heavy, and then the next thing he knew someone was shaking his shoulder.

"Wake up, Captain."

The male voice seemed distant, as if it were coming from another room.

"Give him a second," a second voice said, also male and muffled. "The shot takes a moment to kick in."

Shot?

Ash peeled open his eyes, but could see nothing in the darkness. His hand slipped as he tried to push himself up and he fell back onto the bed.

"Easy there, Captain," the first voice said.

Ash turned toward it. "What's going on?"

"Later. Right now we have to get you out of here."

"Out of here? I'm…what?" He knew he wasn't making sense, but they weren't making sense to him, either.

"We can talk later. Right now you need to do exactly what we say and keep quiet."

"I don't under…?"

What was this guy talking about? All Ash wanted to do was put his head back on his pillow and shut his eyes. But gloved hands were under his arms now, lifting him to his feet. As he staggered, someone grabbed him and kept him from falling.

"We'd love to give you a few seconds to wake up, but we don't have time," the second voice said.

Ash looked to his right and could barely make out a dark shadow of an oddly shaped person. Suddenly, he felt an arm wrap around his back.

"Just hold on," the man said, his voice still sounding farther away than it should have been.

They exited the cell into a dark hallway. That seemed odd to Ash. Surely, there should have been some lights on.

"Clear," the first voice called out from the distance.

"We're going to move fast, Captain," the man at his side said. "So keep a hold of me."

As Ash grabbed the man's back, the material of the guy's shirt confused him. It was thick and kind of rubbery. But Ash barely had time to register this before the man began half-pulling, half-dragging him down the corridor. It was all Ash could do to keep from slipping to the floor.

After what he guessed was probably thirty seconds, they mercifully stopped. He heard a knob twist, then a door open, but he still couldn't see anything.

"Straight ahead a couple feet, then we go to the left," his human crutch said.

As they eased forward, Ash asked, "Why are all the lights off?"

"Quiet."

Once they'd made the turn, they picked up speed again, moving quickly down the new corridor and through another door.

"Can you stand on your own?" the man whispered to Ash.

"What? Uh, yeah. I think so."

"Okay. Stay here." The man let go of Ash and stepped away.

"Wait. Where are you going?" the captain asked.

"Don't move, and you'll be fine."

"I don't understand. Why are you—"

A torrent of thick liquid engulfed him from every side, the flow so strong he could hardly breathe. There was also an overwhelming disinfectant smell, which didn't help. He coughed several times and tried to step away.

"Don't," the first voice ordered. "You're covered with the bug. It's either this way or we will be forced to terminate you."

Terminate? Ash stayed where he was.

Soon the spray stopped.

"Remove your clothes and throw them behind you."

Ash hesitated for only a second, then stripped.

Once more the flow commenced, followed by a strong stream of odorless water.

As soon as it shut off, the first voice said, "There's a wall three feet to your left. Follow that toward my voice about ten feet. There you'll find a towel and some clean clothes. Please hurry."

Ash did as instructed. As he was toweling off, he heard the sprays come on again. Judging by the sound, though, it wasn't flowing over flesh.

Decontamination suits, he realized. Like the ones the people who'd come into his house—so long ago, it seemed—wore. That's why the guy's shirt had felt so strange.

The clothes waiting for him were not the flimsy garments he'd been given while in his cell. There was a pair of jeans, a T-shirt, a pullover sweater, socks, and a pair of sturdy but flexible ankle-high boots.

"Ready?" the first voice asked a minute later, no longer muffled by what must have been the hood and mask of the suit.

"Yes," Ash said. He finished tying his last shoelace and stood up. "Are you going to tell me what's going on now?"

"Not until we get out of here," the other voice said.

A door opened, but the lack of light remained unchanged.

The two men led Ash away from the room, one always keeping a hand on the captain's arm.

They'd been fast-walking for nearly three minutes when the guy in the lead let out a very low "shhhh."

They stopped in the middle of the hall.

"Over here," the lead guy whispered.

Ash was ushered through a doorway, into a space that was barely big enough for the three of them. The door then clicked shut.

A moment later, the sound of a single pair of running footsteps rushed by outside without stopping.

"They're going to find out he's gone," one of the men whispered.

"It'll be okay. I'll take care of it," the other one replied. "You get him out of here. You remember the way, right?"

"Are you kidding? This place is a maze."

There was silence for a moment, then, "Okay. I'll show you, but then it'll be up to you."

They headed back into the hallway, picking up their pace to a near run. They passed through two more corridors and made a hard turn to the left.

After another few moments, the one in the lead said, "It's just up—"

Without warning, the emergency lights kicked on.

The guy who'd been holding Ash's arm let go, then ripped something off his head. Night vision goggles. Both of the men had been wearing them. With the lights on, they had become useless.

"Come on," the lead guy said. "We're almost there."

He had a short military haircut and was wearing an officer's uniform with no insignia. The man next to Ash was dressed in clothes more like the blue jeans and sweater he was now wearing, and while this guy's hair was also short, it had a distinct civilian look to it.

They ran down the hallway, took a quick bend to the right, then the lead man skidded to a stop in front of a heavy-looking metal door. As Ash and the other man ran up, he pulled it open.

Chilled air seeped into the hallway.

"Quick, quick!" he said, then pointed at an angle out the door. "Head in that direction. It'll get you to where we were earlier."

"Maybe you should come with us," his partner said.

The first guy shook his head. "I can do more here."

"They're going to know someone on the inside helped."

The lead man's face grew hard. "Go. Now. You don't have time."

He shoved Ash and the other man outside then shut the door.

Ash's escort seemed disoriented for a moment, then he took a deep breath and said, "Keep low, and follow right behind me."

He took off across a wide space of leveled dirt, not waiting for Ash to respond. Though he was tired of not knowing what was going on, Ash was smart enough to realize now wasn't the time to push, so he headed after his rescuer.

The man led him into a narrow ravine that had been carved into the desert. It was deep enough so that they could stand up without being seen by anyone at ground level.

They followed it for thirty minutes, finally stopping when they reached a rocky overhang. There, the man fell to his knees, reached underneath, and pulled out a cloth bag. He unzipped it and removed something.

"Here," he said, tossing it to Ash.

It was a worn-looking leather jacket with a padded lining inside, and a stocking cap and gloves in the pocket. While it was definitely a cool desert night, it wasn't that cold.

"Put it on," the man said. "You'll need it later."

"For what?"

"To stay warm. What do you think?"

Next he pulled out a messenger bag and slung it over his

shoulder. He then shoved the empty cloth bag back under the over-hang. "All right. Let's go."

Ash didn't move.

The man took a few steps down the riverbed before he realized this. "Look, we don't have much time. If you miss the connection, you're out of luck. So let's move it."

"No," Ash said.

The man stared at him. "All right, fine. Then you can stay here and let them find you."

"Why are you doing this?"

The man looked away, obviously not happy. When he turned back, he took a couple steps toward Ash. "If we'd left you in your cell, you wouldn't have woken up tomorrow morning. You were no longer any use to them alive."

"You saved me because they were going to kill me?"

"We saved you because..." He paused, then took a deep breath. "Yeah. That's as good a reason as any. You can either trust me or not, but I can guarantee you one thing. Those people back there..." He pointed in the direction they'd come. "They don't care a thing about you. It's what's inside you that's most important to them. And they can't get to that while you're still breathing. Get it?"

He turned around and started walking, this time without looking back.

Ash stood where he was a moment longer, then followed.

6

Major Littlefield was in the cafeteria when the power went out.

"What the hell?"

He'd made himself a late-night sandwich as he waited for Ash's final cycle to complete. It was already obvious that, once more, the bug would fail to take hold. The captain was as immune to KV-27a as a person could be.

From Littlefield's understanding, the testing of the Ash children was proceeding slowly. But now Dr. Karp would have samples from an actual body he could take a closer look at and hopefully speed up the process.

The plan for that evening was simple. Once the cycle finished at two a.m. and the captain's vital signs remained unchanged, the air to his cell would be slowly cut off and within an hour, he would take his last breath. This method would eliminate any chance of contaminating the body with whatever poison they would have had to use otherwise.

But now the lights had gone off, and the stupid backup power had yet to kick in.

He pulled his radio off his belt. "Control, this is Littlefield."

"Control," a voice replied. It sounded like Brewer.

"What's your power situation there?"

There was a slight pause. "Sir, we're in the dark. Literally."

"Backup?"

"No, sir. Nothing."

Littlefield stood up. "All right, I'm coming to you."

"Sir, where are you?"

"The cafeteria."

"I think you're going to have a problem getting here."

Littlefield pulled his cell phone out of his pocket, using it as a flashlight as he weaved his way out of the room. "Why do you say that?"

"When the power cuts off, the facility entrance automatically locks down until the electricity comes back."

"Well, what about one of the emergency doors?"

"Those can only be opened from the inside."

"Then get off your ass and go open one!"

There was no response for a moment. "The observation room door also locks down. Jones and I are, uh, stuck in here."

"Jesus."

Littlefield stepped out of the cafeteria and jogged quickly toward the entrance to the containment facility. There was absolutely no one else around. Not surprising since Littlefield had been left with only a bare-bones crew of five men including himself, more than enough to deal with the single person under their supervision. The rest of the team that had been at Barker Flats had either left with Dr. Karp and the children, or had relocated to Bluebird already. So with the exception of his team and Captain Ash, there was no one else anywhere on the decommissioned base.

"Are you telling me there's no manual override?" he asked.

"No, sir."

"Well, where are Causey and Ellison? If they're not in there with you, they must be somewhere in the facility. They can let me in."

"Not sure, sir. I'll try to locate them."

Littlefield reached the main door. Sure enough it was locked tight. He made his way around, trying each of the three emergency doors, but they were sealed shut, too.

"Control, have you found Causey or Ellison yet?"

"No, sir. Neither is answering his radio."

A sudden chill ran down the major's back.

"What was the status of Cell 57 when you were last able to check?"

"The captain was sound asleep. Vital signs unchanged."

"Are you sure he was asleep?"

"Absolutely."

That was good, but it still wasn't enough to ease Littlefield' mind. "There's got to be a way for me to get in. Something—"

"Sir?" a new voice came over the radio.

"Who is this?" the major asked.

"It's Jones, sir. I believe if you go to emergency door B, you might be able to get in there."

"I've already tried each of the emergency doors. No go. All closed tight."

"Yes, sir, but…"

"What is it, Jones?"

"Sir, I believe…if I remember correctly, there *is* a manual override outside door B."

"I didn't see anything."

"It's…hidden, sir."

Littlefield began running back toward emergency door B. "How do you know it's hidden?"

There was a pause. "One of the other men, sir. He left with Dr. Karp last week. He found it and showed it to me. We'd used it when we needed a smoke."

That was a potentially serious breach of security. Jones should have known better. It would have to be dealt with later but at the moment, the major could take advantage of the rule-breaking.

"Okay, I'm here," he said half a minute later. "Where is it?"

"If you face the door, you'll see a little panel low and to the right, about three feet from the entrance."

"I see it."

"Open the panel, sir."

Littlefield did. There was a lever inside in the down position, and above it, a series of six tumblers with numbers on each barrel.

"Okay," he said. "I see the lock. What's the combination?"

"Are all ones still showing, sir?"

"Yes."

"Then you just need to pull the handle, sir."

"The combination is all ones?"

"I…think it's just waiting to be reset when the next permanent operation moves in."

Good God. How easily they could have been compromised if someone had snuck onto the base.

He pulled the lever and the door sprang open.

Inside the facility, he couldn't see his fingers even if he tried to poke himself in the eye, so once again he resorted to using his cell phone as a flashlight.

"I'm in," he said as he took off running down the hallway. "I'm going for the emergency power first, then I'll check the cell."

When he got to the emergency panel, his worst fear was confirmed. This wasn't just a simple fault. Someone had tampered with it. Thankfully, it wasn't enough to put it out of action permanently.

He spent several annoying minutes getting enough of it back online so he could engage the backup system. The moment the emergency lights flared on, he began sprinting toward Cell 57.

His radio crackled. "Major Littlefield?" It was Brewer again.

Littlefield raised his radio without slowing his pace. "What?"

"He's not there."

The major didn't have to ask who "he" was. "Are you sure?"

"Yes, sir. The emergency power gave us some limited camera access. Cell 57 is empty."

Littlefield nearly tossed the radio down the hall ahead of him. "Dammit!"

"Sir, where are you?"

"Approaching the cellblock-50 corridor."

"Stop, sir! Stop and get out now!"

The major skidded to a halt. "What is it?"

"The door to Cell 57 is open and the cycle is running again. The cellblock corridor will be contaminated."

The major stared ahead. Not just the cellblock corridor, he realized.

Fifty feet in front of him, he could see the open door to cellblock 50. Soon the whole facility would be contaminated. There was no question his own life was already over.

"Contact Dr. Karp. Inform him that the subject is missing, and that we are conducting a full facility search. Tell him upon completion we'll be initiating Protocol Thirteen."

"What? There's no reason for—"

"Can you access the camera outside cellblock 50?"

"Uh, I think so."

"You should look."

The pause that followed lasted about ten seconds.

"Dear God," Brewer said.

"The main corridor's your only way out, and it's been compromised." What the major didn't have to add was that the door to the observation room was not biosafe-rated. "We're dead one way or the other."

It was nearly half a minute before Brewer finally responded. "I'll call Dr. Karp."

Suddenly, Littlefield heard someone running farther back in the facility. Thinking that it might be Ash, he took off in pursuit, but whoever it was got out at one of the emergency exits before Littlefield could reach them. As much as he wanted to continue tracking the person into the night, in his contaminated condition it was no longer a possibility.

He spent forty minutes searching the building for Ash, but the only person he found was Sergeant Causey. He was lying unconscious in a supply closet near cellblock 30. The major decided not to wake him just to tell him he was about to die.

Ellison, though, was nowhere to be found, making it a pretty damn good bet he'd been involved in freeing Captain Ash. No matter. They'd both be tracked down soon enough. Dr. Karp would make sure of it. Littlefield was just disappointed he wouldn't be there to pull the trigger when it happened.

He walked all the way down to Cell 57 and sat on Ash's cot. He then had Brewer patch him through to Dr. Karp.

"I can't say that I'm pleased," the doctor said when Littlefield finished his report.

"I can't say that I am, either."

"Is that it?"

"Yes, sir."

"Then finish things."

"Yes, sir. I will, sir. Good luck."

Dr. Karp grunted a reply, then was gone.

"Brewer?" Littlefield said.

"I'm here."

"Initiate Protocol Thirteen."

7

Five minutes beyond the rock overhang, Captain Ash and his escort came to a tall chain-link fence. There were several rows of razor wire mounted to brackets across the top, meant to discourage anyone from climbing over.

His guide pulled a small, rectangular device out of his pocket and stared at it for a few seconds before nodding to his right.

"That way," he said. "Seventy-five feet."

As they walked along the fence, Ash caught sight of the building he'd been freed from. It was really no more than a distant, half-lit blob. That surprised him. He hadn't realized they'd traveled so far.

What was even more surprising, though, was that there were no helicopters flying around looking for them, no vehicles racing across the desert hot on their trail, no apparent interest in them at all. Was it possible the Army didn't even realize he was gone?

"Found it," his guide said as he dropped to his knees beside the fence.

The man undid a couple of temporary ties from the chain-link, fence then pulled open a slit that had been previously cut into it.

He shoved the messenger bag through first, followed it, then pulled one of the edges back as far as it would go. "Your turn."

As soon as Ash passed through, the guy hemmed up the fence, then said, "Not long now."

"And then what?"

Ash got no response.

The desert on this side of the fence was no different from that on the other, save for the fact that it wasn't under direct military control.

They found another ravine, this one only deep enough to cover them from the waist down. They followed it for several minutes before they climbed out and veered off to their right. In the sky, there was definitely something brewing in the East that would challenge the night for control before too long.

They walked for five more minutes, then the guide said, "Wait here."

A minute passed. Then two.

Ash was just starting to wonder if the guy was going to come back when—

Light flashed, and a tremendous roar raced across the desert as the ground shook for what seemed like several seconds, knocking Ash to the ground.

He pushed himself up and stared, dumbstruck, toward the middle of the valley. The building that he'd been held in was gone, replaced by flames so bright, his eyes hurt looking at them even at this distance. Above the inferno, a giant cloud of smoke rose into the air, lit from below by the flames.

"You've got to go now!"

Ash whipped around. He hadn't heard the other man return.

"Did…did you guys do that? Did you blow up the building?"

The man glared at Ash for a moment. "We were there to rescue you, not blow up anything. Whatever happened, they did it themselves. Now come on."

"But why would the Army blow up their own building?"

"You think the Army did this to you?" He pointed toward the distant blaze. "The Army *didn't* do that, and they weren't the people who were holding you. You've gotten in a mess here you didn't even realize you'd been pulled into."

"What are you talking about? If they weren't Army, then I need to report in, let them know what's going on."

"You don't get it. Anything you report will get right back to the people who did this to you. You can strike out on your own and find out if I'm right, or you can take the help I'm offering and find out the truth." When Ash didn't immediately respond, the man added, "Don't forget, that guy who helped me get you out was still inside when we left. There's a pretty good chance he just gave his life to save you. So what's it going to be?"

It was all too much for Ash to take in. Not the Army? If not, who were they? And why would reporting in get him in trouble? Almost none of it was making sense. About the only thing he knew for sure was that the man and his partner had gotten him out of the building before it exploded.

Finally he nodded. He didn't have to trust them forever, but for now it seemed like the best option he had.

"Let's go, then," the man said. A few minutes later, they were standing at the edge of a blacktop road. The man pulled the messenger bag off his shoulder and handed it to Ash. "You'll find another change of clothes inside. There's also a driver's license and a credit card under the name Craig Thompson. Don't try using the card. It's just for appearances and won't work. But you'll be Thompson only for the next leg. When you transfer again, you'll be given a new ID. At that point, destroy these."

"Transfer again?" Ash asked.

"There's also two thousand dollars in cash," the guide said, ignoring his question.

"Two thousand?"

"It should be more than enough in case of an emergency along the way."

"Along the way to where?"

The man looked at him for a moment, then opened the flap of the messenger bag and pulled out a seven-by-seven-inches square, half-inch-thick package that had been wrapped completely in brown packing tape. "This is for your contact at your end station. He'll know what to do with it."

"Contact? End station? You're not making any sense."

The man stuffed the package back in the bag then pointed down the road. "A hundred yards that way you'll find an abandoned gas station." He looked at his watch. "In ten minutes, a car is going to stop there. The driver will ask you if you know where the nearest town is. You say it would be easier if you showed them. They'll agree and you'll get in."

"Who is it?"

"I have no idea."

"Where are they supposed to take me?"

"I have no idea."

"So I'm supposed to just trust them?"

"You trusted us."

"I didn't have a choice."

"Seems to me you don't have much of a choice now, either."

"Please. You've gotta tell me what's going on!"

The man looked at his watch again. "You're down to nine minutes. If you're not there when your ride arrives, they won't wait. Then you'll be on your own." He stood up and held out his hand. "Good luck."

Not knowing what else to do, Ash shook it, then watched the man disappear back into the night.

Finally he turned and started jogging down the highway.

8

James Ellison was a dead man, and he knew it.

After guiding Captain Ash and the other man—a man whose name he never knew—to the exit and making sure they got out, his plan had been to return to the supply closet where he'd left Sergeant Causey after he'd drugged the man's coffee. He had a second, weaker dose that he was going to take himself so that they'd both be found unconscious together.

He had been on his way there when he heard Major Littlefield's voice in the distance. He pulled out his radio and turned it up just loud enough so he could listen in on the conversation.

What he heard made his blood turn to ice. The door to cell-block 50 had been left open. He'd been sure he closed it, but apparently the lock hadn't engaged. It was his biohazard suit—it made it hard to hear the click of the latch.

Though Ash and the other man had still been in the facility when the emergency power came back on and the dosing cycle started again, they were so far away at that point, there was no chance the bug could have reached them before they got outside.

He, on the other hand, was toast.

He told himself the reason he needed to get out of there was because someone had to report in the fact that Major Littlefield was no longer in the picture.

His cell phone was in his bag in the observation room, and therefore permanently unavailable, so he would have to find an out-of-the-way pay phone. After he made the call, he could stumble into the desert and die, hopefully from exposure before the bug took him down. That was the best plan he could come up with.

But while the information about Major Littlefield was important, it would also be something the others would learn soon enough without him.

The coming Protocol Thirteen firestorm—*that* was the real reason he turned and ran.

9

The gas station was right where the guide had told Ash it would be. It was an old, adobe-style building with a low concrete pad out front where the pumps used to sit. By the look of it, it had been left for dead a long time ago.

Ash raced across the highway, thinking that whoever was going to be picking him up must already be there, perhaps parked out of sight. But when he got there, no one was around.

Had his ride already come and gone? Had he missed his opportunity to get away from the base? Or, he wondered, had the driver been scared off by the explosion? It certainly wouldn't be out of the question.

Just then he heard a whine, low and from the South. Tires on asphalt. It had to be.

He peered down the highway. Everything was dark. No headlights, no sign that anyone was coming, except the whine.

He didn't see the car until just before it turned off the road, its headlights off. He watched as it pulled in like it was going to fill up with gas.

For a few seconds, he considered making a run for the desert and disappearing. He had no idea who these people were, and had no clue as to why they were helping him. What he did know, though, was getting a ride in a car was considerably better than wandering through the desert.

He stepped out from the building and walked toward the sedan. As he neared, the driver's-side window slid down.

"Morning," a female voice said from inside. She sounded nervous.

Ash leaned down so he could see her. In the darkness, she wasn't much more than a shadow, with shoulder-length hair he thought was probably blonde.

"Could have sworn there was a town around here," she said. "Know of some place I could get a little breakfast?"

"I...I can show you."

His response was a lot less polished than her question, but it served the purpose of identification as her door locks clicked up.

"Hop in," she said.

He moved around to the passenger side. But as he opened the door, the woman shook her head.

"No. In the back."

He hesitated a moment, then shut the door and opened the one behind it.

"Lift the seat," she told him before he could climb in.

"What?"

She pointed at the seat cushion. "There's a latch in the back near the center. Pull and lift."

He did as the woman instructed. The only thing under the bench was the metal body of the car. He looked at her, confused.

She reached under the car's dash. A second later there was a dull thud, and the metal under the backseat popped upward several inches. Not needing to be told, he pulled it open as far as it would go, revealing what could best be described as a storage area. It was identical in length to the back seat, maybe a foot wider, and about two and a half deep.

"Get in," the woman said.

"You've got to be kidding me. I'm not getting in there."

"You get in there or you don't get the ride." She glanced toward the fire that was still burning in the valley. "You're lucky I stopped at all. Please tell me you didn't have anything to do with that."

He started to speak, but she shook her head and held up a hand. "Never mind. I don't want to know." She looked back at the secret compartment. "It's vented, so you'll get plenty of fresh air, and the lining's padded." She grabbed a water bottle off the front passenger seat and held it out to him. "You're not going to want to drink this all at once. You won't be getting out for several hours, so taking a leak can get a little messy."

"I'll just sit in the back seat if it's all right with you." He started to close the metal lid.

"It's *not* all right with me!" she shot back. "I don't know who you are, or why you need to get away from here, but I do know if we get stopped and they find you, I'm going to be in as much trouble as you are. Now you can either get in the hole or start walking. It's up to you."

She stared at him defiantly, the bottle of water still in her outstretched hand.

He looked at the compartment, then at the water, then at the woman. "I don't know who you are, either."

"And you won't," she said.

He stood there a moment longer, then took the water and awkwardly lowered himself into the hiding space. Once he was in position, the woman leaned back and started to lower the lid.

"I didn't start that fire," he said.

"I told you. I don't want to know."

She shut him in.

For the first hour, he was sure they would be stopped at a roadblock and the car inspected. But as the road kept passing a few feet beneath him, he began to think they might have made it away undetected. Eventually, he dozed off.

When he woke again, he could hear other vehicles surrounding them—semi-trucks mostly, cruising at high speeds. He figured they must be on an interstate. Which one, he had no idea. Having just recently been transferred to the Barker Flats Research Center, he didn't know this part of the country that well and had no clue which highways were within a few hours' drive away.

Both he and Ellen had grown up in the Midwest—Ash in Ohio and his wife in Indiana. They'd met at college where he was going through ROTC training and working on an engineering degree, and she was studying to be an accountant.

For him, at least, it was one of those instant attraction kind of things. Ellen had always said it was the same for her, too, but he was never sure if she was joking with him or not. Their bond grew infinitely deeper after her father passed away from a heart attack while they were sophomores. Her mother was already gone—cancer. Several years earlier, Ash's parents had also passed away. No diseases in his family, just bad timing with a tire blowout at seventy miles per hour. His brother was with them, too. Jeff didn't die but, well, the condition he was left in often made Ash wonder if it would have been better if he had.

The fact was, Ash and Ellen really only had each other after that. They were married their senior year, and Josie was born exactly ten months later.

And now here he was alone again, his whole family gone.

He had no idea how long they'd been on the road when he felt the car ease to the right and slow down. Outside, the sounds of the other vehicles grew distant as the sedan came to a near stop, then accelerated again through a sharp right turn.

A couple minutes later, the car slowed once more and veered to the right. The now-familiar hum of tires on asphalt was replaced by the crunch of dirt under treads. Then the car stopped and the engine shut off.

Ash waited, anticipating that the woman would soon release him. A few moments later he heard the seat cushion being lifted above him, but as he waited for the hidden metal flap to open, nothing happened.

"Come on, come on," he said under his breath.

He'd had enough of the secret compartment. It was small and cramped, and though he wasn't claustrophobic, he was starting to sympathize with those who were. It didn't help that since they'd stopped moving, the air seemed to be growing stale, too. He wanted out, and he wanted out now.

He thought about pounding on the lid and screaming, "Open up!" But he had no idea where they were or who might overhear him.

He twisted, trying to get more comfortable. As he did, his shoulder brushed against the lid. There was a click as the metal roof of his box rose slightly in response to the pressure.

What the hell?

He placed his hand on it and pushed upward. A thin seam of light grew along the length of the lid. Though it couldn't have been more than a quarter-of-an-inch wide, it was blinding after hours of pitch darkness. He blinked several times, then squeezed his eyelids together so that only a fraction of the light could penetrate them.

Again, he pushed on the lid. The crack of light grew an inch wider, then two, then three.

He paused, listening for anyone who might be in the car, and letting his eyes adjust to the daylight. Finally, having heard nothing, he pushed the top all the way open and sat up.

For some reason, he thought he was going to find that they were parked behind one of those giant truck stops, and that the woman had just gone to use the facilities or maybe even grab something to eat. But there was no truck stop. In fact, there were no buildings of any kind, just wilderness, broken only by the distant ribbon of the interstate about two miles away.

The car appeared to be parked in a small valley. While there were a few trees here and there, most of the vegetation was lower to the ground. It was what his dad used to call high chaparral country.

A deserted, two-lane road ran out from the highway in his direction, passing the large dirt lot his ride was parked in and heading off into the hills. Apparently the woman had turned off on one of those exits only a handful of locals would use.

The most surprising thing, though, was that she was nowhere to be seen. Where she'd gone, he had no idea. But unless she was crouching right next to the car, he was entirely alone.

He pushed himself out of the box, threw open one of the doors and climbed outside. The air was cool, almost brisk. He reached back in and retrieved the jacket his guide had given him. He was tempted to pull on the stocking cap and gloves, but instead he just stomped around a little to warm up. Then, after a moment of unnecessary self-consciousness, he relieved himself behind the car.

Not knowing what he was supposed to do now, he decided to see if the woman had left the keys. Maybe the idea all along had been for him to take the sedan and get lost. Maybe that's what this had been all about. They got him away from trouble, and now he was on his own.

He opened the driver's door and leaned in. The keys weren't in the ignition, tucked above the sun visor, or lying in the seat. What *was* in the seat, though, was a white legal-size envelope with MR. THOMPSON typed on the front. It took him a couple seconds before he remembered that Thompson was the name on the false

ID he'd been given earlier.

The flap of the envelope was only tucked in, so he flipped it out and removed a single sheet of paper from inside. Like his faux name on the envelope, the note inside was typed. It was short and to the point.

> Wait here. Once it's dark, some-
> one will come for you. Before
> then, burn this and your IDs.
> There is a lighter in the trunk,
> along with some food if you get
> hungry.
>
> Good luck.

He read it twice. It was just another mysterious piece in his ultra-bizarre day. But the mention of food did remind him that it had been almost twenty-four hours since his last meal.

He pulled the trunk release, then moved around back and looked inside. In a brown paper bag, he found a couple of apples, a bag of trail mix, a few energy bars, and three bottles of water. Not exactly the juicy hamburger his stomach was hoping for, but it would do.

There was also one of those long-nosed lighters people used to light campfires and barbecues. But he wasn't really sure if he wanted to burn his IDs. He'd begun to entertain the idea of taking off on his own. If he did that, the IDs could come in handy. He decided to eat first, then figure it out after.

Within ten minutes, he'd devoured both apples, two of the energy bars, and a good portion of the trail mix. The remainder he wrapped inside the brown sack and slipped into his messenger bag.

He moved to the end of the car and stared at the highway for several minutes. At a fast walk, he could get there in no time then hitch a ride to the next town.

What then, though?

Go to the police? Back to the Army?

The man who'd gotten him out of the building had said if he went back to the Army, the people who'd held him would find him again. Ash wasn't convinced there were "people" yet. It still could have just been the Army doing what they thought was best for the greater good. But he couldn't deny something very strange was going on. And if he wanted to find out why Ellen and the kids had been killed, his best bet at the moment was to stay free until he had more answers.

His mind made up, he retrieved his fake IDs and placed them on the ground with the note and envelope from the car. They burned easily, and soon were no more than ash and melted plastic. He mixed what was left into the dirt, then climbed back into the car and waited for the sun to go down.

10

"He's out," Pax said over the phone.

There was no need for anyone to reply. So far, this was only a one-way conversation.

"Grabbed his coat…taking a piss."

Silence again.

"A lot of looking around…checking the car now."

This should be it, Matt thought.

"He found the letter."

Yes. Good. Now what are you going to do, Captain?

"He's read it, and now is checking the trunk. Looks like he's going to eat something."

The silence stretched for nearly ten minutes.

"Looking at the highway again."

Are you walking or are you staying?

"Still looking…still…wait. He's going back to the trunk…got the lighter…he's burning everything. That's a confirm. He's moving back inside and….sitting in the car."

"Janice, Michael," Michael said into the phone. "Pickup is a go. Jordan, get ready to disable the satellite."

Welcome to the team, Captain Ash.

11

The watch Ash's wife had given him on their fifth anniversary had been taken away the night he was put in the cell, so he wasn't exactly sure what time it was when he saw a pair of headlights exit the freeway and head in his direction.

As they neared, he realized they didn't belong to a car, but an old Winnebago motor home. It slowed to a crawl as it turned off the road, then stopped in front of his sedan.

After a few seconds the side door opened, and a man and a woman emerged. They looked maybe ten years older than Ash, and smiled as they walked in his direction. When they neared his car, the woman stopped several feet away, but the man came right up to Ash's window and leaned down.

As soon as Ash lowered it halfway, the man said, "Sorry we're late."

Ash made no reply.

The man rubbed his arms with his hands. "It's a little chilly out. So if you're ready to go, I'd love to get back in the 'Bago."

Ash hesitated a moment. The thought of going it alone once more passed through his mind. But the conclusions he'd come up with before hadn't changed, so he grabbed the messenger bag off the other seat and got out. Immediately, he pulled his jacket tight around his neck. Though it had been cold in the car, it was near freezing outside.

"We've got coffee in the motor home, if you'd like," the man said, then nodded toward the woman. "Janice just heated up a pot before we turned off. If you're hungry we can cook you up something, too. There's plenty of leftover chili from lunch. I'm Mike, by the way."

He held out his hand. Ash shook it.

"Coffee sounds good. My name's—"

"Whoa, whoa, whoa. I already know who you are. You're Sam Wolverton. I'd recognize you anywhere."

Apparently Craig Thompson was out, and Sam Wolverton was in. It was as good a name as any, Ash thought.

Mike and Janice led him over to the Winnebago, then inside where the temperature was a wonderfully bone-thawing forty degrees warmer. Ash slowly stretched his stiff cold fingers then rolled his shoulders, trying to bring his muscles back to life.

Janice pointed at a table in the rear. "If you want to have a seat, I'll get that coffee while Mike gets us back on the road."

"Thanks," Ash said.

He pulled off his jacket and sat down. Between the heat and the feel of movement and the calm exuded by Janice and Mike, some of the tension he'd been holding on to began to ease away.

It's going to be okay. It's going to be okay.

The next thing he knew Janice was touching him on the shoulder.

"You all right?"

He jerked in surprise, then looked up. "I'm fine. Thanks. Just...trying to warm up."

She set a cup of coffee in front of him. "This'll help."

"Thanks again."

The coffee mug had a lid on top that allowed a person to drink without the liquid inside sloshing out while traveling. Ash took a sip. It was hot and delicious. In fact, it was the best cup of coffee he'd had in a long time.

The Winnebago took a turn to the right and began increasing speed. Ash could see they were transitioning back onto the interstate, but he missed the sign so he still had no idea which one they were on.

He took another, longer sip.

"Mind if I join you?" Janice asked from over at the stove.

"Not at all," he told her.

She poured herself a cup of coffee then took a seat across the table from him.

"Do you...do this often?" he asked.

She cocked her head. "Do what?"

"Pick up strangers on deserted roads."

A half-smile graced her lips. "You're not a stranger, Sam. We've known you for years." She lifted her cup and took a drink.

"But we just—"

"We just what? Pulled off the highway so we could stretch our legs?"

He studied her face for a moment. "Who *are* you people?"

"Mike and Janice Humphrey. Your old friends from college."

"I don't care about any cover story. There's no one else around. I'd just like to know *who* you are, and why you're helping me."

"You sure want a lot for someone whose life is being saved."

"How do you know that? I thought you didn't know anything about me. How do you know you're saving my life?"

"How do I know? I don't. It was just an educated guess, and by your reaction, a fairly accurate one. And you're right. We don't know anything about you. But even if we're not saving your life, we're saving you from something. I would think you'd be grateful for that."

"I am," he said quickly. "Very grateful. I'm just...confused. I don't know what's going...what's going..."

His vision suddenly blurred.

"Are you all right?" she asked.

He opened his eyes as wide as he could, but was unable to focus on anything. As he raised a hand to rub them, vertigo raced through his head like a wave. He no longer knew which way was up and which was down. He reached out for the table to try to steady himself, but he missed and fell sideways, dropping onto the floor. Janice was immediately at his side, her hand moving under his head. But her touch seemed distant and disconnected.

"Relax." Her voice was a million miles away. "You're going to be fine. You just need a little sleep."

He tried to speak, to tell her he wasn't fine. That nothing was fine. But his lips refused to move.

A moment later, the unfocused world he'd been seeing turned black.

12

If Ellison had been in a humorous mood, he would have thought it ironic that the car he escaped in belonged to Major Littlefield, but he knew humor would never enter his life again.

The whole time he was hotwiring it, he was sure the major would come charging out and find him, then drag him back into the facility before initiating Protocol Thirteen. But the engine finally roared to life, and he sped away without seeing the major or anyone else.

Just before he reached the far end of the valley, the building exploded, lighting up the sky. Even though he'd been expecting it, it still caught him by surprise. He jerked the wheel to the right and nearly ran off the road.

At least the explosion meant that he was safe for the moment. With the major and the small team at Barker Flats no longer in the picture, anyone the project would send after him was at least a few hundred miles away.

All he had to do was find a pay phone before that.

And torch the car.

And die.

It was an easy enough plan in theory, but after an hour of driving through the empty desert, he was having a hard time keeping his eyes open. He needed to get some rest. He couldn't afford to crash. Not only would he be unable to deliver the message, but anyone who came to his aid would be in danger of being infected.

Just a couple of hours—a nap, really—that was all he needed.

About five minutes later he spotted an old dirt road. He turned onto it and drove far enough that his car wouldn't be spotted from the highway, then crawled into the back seat.

When he woke, the sun was high in the sky. Panicked, he pushed himself up but immediately dropped back down. It felt like his brain was trying to push out of his skull. Even his eyes ached.

More slowly this time, he rose into a sitting position. As he tried to take a deep breath, it caught in his throat and he began to cough.

Ellison was not the kind of man who would delude himself. Sure, he could have pretended he'd only caught a bad cold or maybe the flu. But the truth was he was infected with the KV-27a virus, and unless he had an immunity that worked like Josie Ash's had, he was going to die.

He forced himself to get back behind the wheel. His time was severely limited now. He figured he had no more than two hours to find an isolated pay phone. If he failed to locate one in that time, he would have to forget about the call and concentrate on eliminating his chance of infecting anyone else.

"Should have stayed in the building," the disease in his head said. "Should have let the fire take you."

He ignored it and used every ounce of concentration to keep the car on the road. Even then, he often found himself veering dangerously close to the opposite lane and then overcompensating by weaving back the other way and onto the shoulder. God forbid he came across a highway patrol car. They'd pull him over for sure.

He passed a few possibilities, wide spots in the road with two or three restaurants and a gas station, but there were always too many people around. After ninety minutes, he started to think he would have to give up the idea of reporting in. But then he saw a little gas station along an otherwise deserted stretch of the highway.

Though it looked like it was open, there were no customers out front.

He slowed, then turned into the large dirt lot next to the building, his eyes scanning left and right, looking for...

There.

The pay phone was mounted to a wooden pole a good twenty feet away from the station.

He pulled to a stop and stumbled out of the car, then cursed himself for not having gotten closer to the phone. When he finally got to the pole, he leaned against it and caught his breath. Closing his eyes, he focused on the number, trying to make sure he remembered it correctly. His headache wasn't helping, but once he repeated the number several times, he knew he had it.

He fished some coins out of his pocket, then picked up the receiver and dropped several quarters into the slot on top. His strength waning, he punched in the number, making sure he made no mistakes.

One ring. Two.

Then a *click* and a *beep*.

"This is Ellison," he said. "Barker Flats blown. I repeat Barker Flats blown. Littlefield initiated self-destruct. When the power came back on, the virus they were pumping into the target's cell leaked into the rest of the building. Littlefield and three others eliminated with the facility. Target already freed at that point, but Littlefield discovered the escape and planned to report it to Karp. No confirmation if he was able to do that, but it seems likely." He paused. "I'm...I'm infected, so this will be my last message."

He hung up.

The phone was going to have to be destroyed, too, but that would be easy enough. He would just need to move the car right up against the pole before he lit everything on fire.

He went around to the trunk of Major Littlefield's sedan. Inside he found more than he had hoped for. Not only were there flares that he could use to help get the fire going, but there was also a hard plastic case containing a Colt .45 automatic pistol.

It was a lot more power than Ellison needed, but then again, it wouldn't matter when he pulled the trigger. At least he wouldn't have to crawl out into the desert now.

He stripped off his shirt, then fed as much of it as he could into the gas tank. Once he had the car in position, his plan was to use a flare to light the shirt on fire. He would then get into the car and throw the flare into the back seat to ignite the interior. As soon as he saw the fire catch, he would put the gun to his head and pull the trigger.

What he hadn't counted on were the three sedans that raced off the road and skidded to a stop twenty feet away, before he could get back behind the wheel and move the car into place.

Men jumped out of nearly every door, most with guns pointed directly at him.

"Stay right there, Mr. Ellison."

"They know who you are," the disease whispered in his mind. "They found you. See? You should have just stayed."

"Get back!" Ellison yelled at the men. "I'm infected. Doesn't matter if you shoot me or not. You come near me, your life is over."

None of the men flinched.

"I'm not going to be a problem," Ellison told them, then coughed. "Just let me take care of this, and it'll all be over."

He stepped around the back of the sedan and headed for the driver's door.

"Stop. Now!" someone shouted.

But Ellison couldn't stop. He had to finish.

"Stop!"

Ellison put his hand on the door handle and started to pull it open.

The first bullet caught him in the shoulder, knocking him into the car. The second went through his kidney and exited just below his ribs. He slipped to the ground, rolling onto his back as he did, and ended up looking at the group of armed men.

They parted in the middle, and two new men dressed in protective gear stepped through. Not biohazard suits, though—something different. Then Ellison saw the thin rifles in the men's hands, rifles with hoses attached to one end running around to tanks on the men's backs.

Not rifles. Flamethrowers.

Oh, thank God.

There was a *whoosh*, then short flames flickered at the end of each nozzle.

The two men took a few steps closer to the car and raised their weapons.

"The phone," Ellison whispered as loudly as he could. "Don't forget the phone."

But his words were lost as long streams of flames roared out from each weapon.

"Stop there, stop there," Chuck said, pointing down the road at the lonely gas station.

"Why?" his friend Len asked. They were supposed to be meeting some other friends for a couple nights of camping, but somewhere they'd made a wrong turn. Neither of them could get a signal on their cell phones so using their GPS wasn't an option.

"I gotta go."

"Again?"

"What do you mean, 'again'? That was like two hours ago. I've drank two sodas since then."

Len pulled into the station, figuring while Chuck did his business he could at least find out where they were. As he got out of the car he caught a faint whiff of barbeque. Maybe they were selling sandwiches inside. He could use something to eat.

Chuck raced ahead like his bladder was about to burst.

"Next time, don't drink so much!" Len yelled after him.

Without looking back, Chuck flipped him off as he entered the store. Len reached the door a moment later, and was starting to pull it open when his friend came running back outside. He looked at Len, opened his mouth like he was going to say something, then quickly bent over and threw up on the asphalt.

Len jumped back. "What the hell? I didn't know you were sick." As soon as his friend seemed to finish, he said, "Are you all right?"

Chuck breathed deeply, but said nothing.

Len could see his friend's face was a mess, so he said, "I'll get some napkins." As he reached for the door, Chuck grabbed his arm.

"Don't go in there!"

"Why not?" Len asked.

"The guy's dead. Somebody shot him."

"What guy?"

"The attendant! He's slumped over the counter, blood all over the place."

"Is the person who shot him still there?"

Chuck's eyes widened. "I…I don't know. I didn't hear anybody. Jesus, do you think maybe he is?"

Len glanced around. The only other car he could see was an old truck parked against the side of the store, right where someone who worked there would probably park.

"I doubt it," Len said. "I'm going to go take a look, okay?"

"I don't think that's a good idea."

"Did you check his pulse to make sure he was dead?"

"No," Chuck admitted. "But he looked dead."

"We should check to make sure, don't you think?"

Reluctantly, Chuck nodded.

"Why don't you call the police while I go inside," Len suggested.

"Okay. Good idea."

Len pushed the door open with his shoulder in case there were fingerprints on the handle the police could use, and stepped inside.

Immediately, he covered his nose to block out the overwhelming smell of blood. The counter was just inside on the left. Lying face down across the top was a man with gray hair. There was no reason to check his pulse, though. He was dead for sure. Len could see two bullet wounds: one between his shoulder blades, and one in the back of his head. The cash register was open, and whatever money had been there was gone.

A robbery, out in the middle of nowhere.

"Len," Chuck called from outside.

Grateful for a reason to leave, Len rejoined his friend.

Chuck held up his phone and shrugged. "I still don't have a signal."

Len pulled his cell out. No bars for him, either.

He looked back at the store. There was probably a phone inside, but chances were it was on the counter next to the body, which would mean stepping on the bloody floor to find it. Beyond the fact that doing so wouldn't make the police happy, the creep-out factor was way off the scale, so as far as he was concerned, it wasn't an option.

"We'll have to go to the next town," he said.

"And just leave him here like this?"

Len thought for a moment. "No. You're right. We can't do that. One of us should probably stay."

"I ain't staying."

"Fine. You take the car. I'll stay."

Chuck didn't look happy with that solution, either, but then he started rocking on his feet and said, "I gotta pee."

He headed toward the side of the building.

"Where you going?" Len asked.

"I'm not going back inside!" Chuck disappeared around the corner. But it was only a couple seconds before he yelled, "Hey, Len!"

"What?"

"There's a pay phone over here. If you have change you can call the police."

"You don't need change to call 911."

"What?" Chuck's voice had grown distant.

"You don't…never mind."

Len headed around the side of the building and saw that his friend had moved out into the desert. The phone was off to the right just a bit, hanging on a wooden post.

Good, he thought as he walked over. At least now he and Chuck wouldn't have to split up.

13

Ash woke with a pounding headache.

He must have gasped or something, because a hand was suddenly on his shoulder, rubbing it softly. Then a voice said, "It's all right. You're okay."

It was a woman's voice, but it didn't sound like Janice's.

"My head," he grunted.

He tried to raise his hand to his temple, but his arm would only move a few inches before it stopped. He opened his eyes just enough to see what the problem was. There was a tube or something coming out of his arm, and what looked like a leather strap around his wrist.

He tried his other hand. It moved without opposition.

"Sleep some more," the voice said. "You've been through a lot."

"Are we stopped?" he asked, realizing he felt no motion.

"Stopped?" A pause, then, "Just sleep."

And as if it were a command, darkness overtook him once more.

The next time he woke, his headache was gone.

When he opened his eyes, he realized he was not, as he'd previously thought, still in the RV. Instead he was lying on a bed in a wood-paneled room, soft sunlight seeping in through the window on the far wall.

There was a dresser to his left and an armoire in the corner beyond the foot of the bed. Below the window was a writing desk. All the surfaces were empty.

He tried to prop himself up so he could look out the window

and get a sense of where he was, but his right arm caught on something. No, he quickly realized, not caught. Restrained. Hadn't he been immobilized the last time he'd woken?

Around his right wrist was a padded leather cuff attached to the frame of the bed. The apparent reason for this was the IV line attached to his arm. His left, though, was completely free.

He had no idea what he was being fed from the bag hanging on the stand, but the idea of being both restricted and drugged did not appeal to him. He quickly worked the cuff open, turned the IV flow off, and pulled the tube out of the port on his arm.

His first stop was the dresser to see if there were any clothes to go with the T-shirt and underwear he'd been sleeping in. He found several pairs of jeans, more underwear, socks, and a whole drawer full of colored T-shirts. The bottom drawer even had two dark wool sweaters and a hooded pullover sweatshirt. The biggest surprise was that not only was everything new, it was all in his size, too. He got dressed.

Inside the armoire he found the boots he'd worn during his escape, and beside them, the messenger bag. A quick check of the bag showed that the only thing left was the money. What did he care, though? None of the contents had been his in the first place.

He pulled on the boots, laced them up, and walked over to the window. What greeted him was a surprise. It wasn't the chaparral country where the mysterious Mike and Janice had picked him up, or even the desert. Instead, there was a mix of grassy fields and groves of evergreens. In the distance was a row of mountains.

The only structure in sight was way off to the left and only partially visible. It was big, though. Maybe a barn or large equipment shed. No way to tell for sure.

As for people, he saw none.

Where the hell am I?

He walked over to the door, put his ear against the wood, and listened. In the distance, he thought he could hear a low muffled conversation but that was about it.

He glanced back at the room. He *could* wait until somebody showed up, but he was done waiting so he opened the door.

"Thought I heard you moving around in there."

Directly outside was a hallway about as wide as the room he'd been in. Sitting on a wooden chair against the far wall was a tan-faced man with the gentle creases of someone who'd spent more than his fair share of time outdoors. He had a full head of salt-and-pepper hair and a short mostly-salt goatee. Ash guessed he was in his fifties, early sixties at most. He was outfitted in jeans and a green flannel shirt.

The man pushed himself off the chair. "So how are you feeling?"

Ash glanced down the hallway. "Where am I?"

"You're safe, that's where you are."

"Yeah, that's not really an answer."

The man snickered. "No. No, I guess it's not." He paused. "You're on the Hamilton Ranch. I'm Rich Paxton, but I go by Pax, mostly." He held out his hand. "I help keep things running around here."

Ash kept his hand at his side. "You're the one in charge?"

Pax shook his head. "No, that would be Matt. Matt Hamilton. It's his place. Well, his and Rachel's."

"I want to talk to him right now."

"That's convenient, because he wants to talk to you, too. Supposed to bring you to him when you finally got up. Which I guess is now."

"Let's go," Ash said, ready to follow him.

Pax glanced down at the IV port still attached to Ash's arm. "Should probably have Billy take a look at that first. Get that thing off you."

"I'm fine."

"Sure you are. But Billy's on the way, and it'll only take a minute."

Pax led him through several hallways, a large sitting room, up one flight of stairs, and past a dozen closed doors. Whatever kind of building this was, it certainly wasn't small.

Finally, Pax stopped in front of an open door and stuck his head inside. "Billy?"

"Back here," a voice replied.

Pax signaled Ash to follow him in.

The room was set up like a doctor's office, complete with examining table, cotton swabs, blood pressure cuff, tongue depressors, and all the other medical items you'd expect to find. There was also a computer monitor and wireless keyboard on the counter.

A door on the left led into another room. Since there was no one in the room they'd just entered, Ash assumed this Billy must be in the other.

"The new guy needs his tube removed," Pax said.

"I need a few minutes," Billy called out. "Just have him sit tight, and I'll be down as soon as I can."

"He's not in his room. I brought him with me."

There was the dull thud of a stack of paper being set down, then the sound of footsteps. A second later, a guy a few years younger than Pax entered from the other room. He walked over to Ash, grabbed his arm, and looked at the port. "You shouldn't have done this by yourself."

"No one else was there."

"That's not the point. What about the fluid? Did you close the tube, or is it running all over the floor?"

Ash narrowed his eyes, not liking the tone of the man's voice. "I cut the drip before I disconnected it. I hope that's okay with you."

Billy frowned. "You should have just waited. You have no idea what was in the fluid. It could have been very dangerous."

"Was it?"

"No, but it could have been."

Billy got to work removing the dock from Ash's arm. When it was out, he used some gauze and a bandage to cover the wound. He then looked at Pax. "Can I get back to what I was doing now, or do you have any more emergencies?"

"Have at it. I think we're good."

Billy forced a smile then said to Ash, "Welcome to the ranch." With that, he headed back to the other room.

Ash half expected Pax to give him an excuse for Billy's behavior once they were in the hallway again, but, to his credit, Pax said nothing. He led Ash to a closed door at the far end and knocked.

"Come," a muffled voice said from inside.

Pax opened the door and let Ash pass through first.

It was a big room divided into two areas. The far end was dominated by a large oak desk with a matching credenza behind it, while the area nearest the door was set up with a couch, chairs and a low-lying table. There were several windows, but wooden blinds prevented any clear view of the outside.

The only person in the room was a man sitting in one of the stuffed guest chairs in front of the desk. He was probably about the same age as Pax, only with a little less hair on top and no goatee. Though the man was sitting, Ash could tell he was big. Long legs and a broad chest. Somewhere in his past he'd probably been a high school linebacker. The man had angled his chair so he could watch a TV hanging on the wall.

Ash glanced at the screen just in time to see the Prime Cable News logo in the corner before the picture went dark.

"Glad to see you're up," the man said, rising to his feet. He *was* tall. Six-foot-three on the low end, maybe as much as six-five. His grin was friendly and welcoming as he extended his hand to Ash. "I'm Matt Hamilton. Welcome to the ranch."

Ash hesitated only a second before shaking. "I'm…" He stopped himself, unsure what he should actually say.

"You're Captain Daniel Ash."

"Yes," Ash said with a sense of relief.

"Welcome, Captain. Why don't you have a seat?" He gestured toward the couch.

Ash held his ground. "Excuse me if this sounds rude, but I'd like to know what the hell's going on."

"Of course you would. I would, too, if I were you. What would you like to know first?"

"Let's start with why I am here."

Hamilton shrugged. "Easy enough. You needed someplace safe to hide."

"And what am I hiding from?"

"That one is not so easy."

Ash's nostrils flared as he drew in a long breath.

"Hold on, Captain," Hamilton said. "I'm not avoiding your question. It's just that there are several different answers, and I'm trying to figure out which is the one you're interested in at the moment."

"That's bullshit."

Hamilton said nothing for a moment, then looked at Pax.

"Can you give us a few minutes? Maybe make sure the captain's quarters are ready?"

"You got it." Pax nodded to Ash and left.

Once they were alone, Hamilton said, "You can stand, but if you don't mind, I'm going to sit."

Hamilton favored his left leg as he headed for the couch. He caught Ash looking at it as he sat down.

"I'm told a knee replacement will take care of the problem," Hamilton explained. "Someday, I guess. When I have the time."

Ash walked over. He thought about remaining on his feet, but it seemed a pointless protest so he took the seat across from the couch.

Neither man said anything for several seconds. Finally, Hamilton leaned forward. "By all rights, you should be dead."

A faint sneer grew on Ash's face. "I'm having a hard time believing anyone was planning on killing me. I only went with your people for one reason—to find out who murdered my family and why." He hesitated, then added, "They did get me away from the explosion, so I owe you thanks for that."

"You misunderstood me," Matt said. "I wasn't talking about the fact the order had been given to eliminate you before you woke, which it had been, or about the explosion, which wouldn't have happened if you'd stayed."

"Then what are you talking about?"

"The disease. It should have killed you, too. But it's my understanding that you never showed any effects of the illness. There were seventeen families living at Barker Flats. Seventeen families, all recent transfers to a base that, until two months ago, had been in mothballs. Of the sixteen families besides yours, none had any survivors. So what made you different?"

Ash stared at Hamilton in shock. "None? They're all dead?"

A pause. "They are."

Ash began breathing rapidly, his anger boiling just under his skin. He pushed himself up. "How many people?"

"There were fifty-seven total in the other families."

"Fifty-seven?" With Ellen, Josie, and Brandon, that made an even…"Sixty total. My God." He turned to the television. "It must be all over the news."

Matt hesitated for a split second before saying, "It hasn't been all over the news. There's been no report whatsoever."

"What?" Ash couldn't believe it. He began pacing in the space in front of the door. Maybe the government didn't want to cause a panic. The country took a pretty big hit after 9/11. Sure, everyone had rallied together, but there'd been so much confusion, too. "Do they know who did it? Have they found them?"

Matt took a longer pause this time before answering. "Captain, I will always tell you the truth. That's the promise we make here. Sometimes, though, there are things that need to be held back. Perhaps someone isn't ready to hear it yet, or perhaps the information is just too sensitive. When these situations arise, we won't lie about it and try to cover it up, but the information will not be shared, either." He paused. "There are things you don't know and don't understand. As soon as we're completely sure we can trust you, you will be told. Just not now."

"Trust me?"

"Just like you're unsure whether you can trust us."

As true as the statement was, Ash didn't like hearing it. "What couldn't you trust me with?"

"Is that a trick question?" Matt said. "Okay. How about this? The truth about what happened at Barker Flats."

Ash stared at Hamilton. "Whatever happened *killed* my family! I have every right to know the truth!"

"I would feel the same as you," Hamilton said calmly.

"Then tell me!"

"When the time is right."

Ash stood motionless for several seconds then said, "Mr. Hamilton, I appreciate your hospitality, and whatever you did to help me get away from Barker Flats. There's money still in my bag. Yours, I assume. I'll leave it in the room. I don't have any of my own to cover whatever expenses you might have incurred. I apologize for that." He took a step toward the door. "If someone could show me the way to a main road, I'd be grateful."

Hamilton considered him for a moment, then stood up. "It's late. Spend the night and you can get an early start in the morning."

"You'll lock my door and keep me from leaving."

Hamilton shook his head. "No. If you want to leave, we won't stop you. But we also won't be able to protect you."

"I can protect myself."

Hamilton nodded. "I'm sure you'll do the best that you can. I only ask when they do track you down, you don't mention the ranch or any of us here."

"They won't track me down."

Matt remained silent for a moment, his expression blank. Finally, he said, "I'll have Pax show you to your quarters. If you decide to stay the night, you're welcome to join us for dinner at seven."

Ash answered with a single nod.

"One more thing," Hamilton said.

He limped back over to his desk and pulled a package out of the credenza. It was the same package Ash had been given in the desert. One end was open now. Hamilton reached in, pulled something out, then walked back over to Ash.

"I believe this is yours."

He held out his palm. In it was a watch.

Ash tried not to shake as he lifted it up. It wasn't an expensive brand, but it was priceless to him. He turned it over. Engraved on the back, just as he knew it would be, was:

Happy Birthday All My Love,
Ellen

He had assumed the watch was destroyed in the explosion. He had thought he'd never hold it again. "This was in the package?"

Hamilton nodded.

"What else is in there?"

"That was the only personal item of yours."

"Are you lying to me?"

"I told you, we have no room for lies here."

Ash stared at the watch a moment longer, then put it on.

For the first time since the night that life as he knew it ended, he cried.

14

By the time Len and Chuck found their friends Jimmy and Walt at the campground, it was well after dark but they had the excuse of a lifetime.

They joined the other two at the campfire and recounted the afternoon's events. Chuck played it up to its morbid best, while Len exaggerated his friend's freak-out at finding the body.

"He threw up *everywhere!* If I hadn't jumped out of the way, I'd have been covered in it," he said. "Then he refused to go back inside, like he thought the guy was going to jump up and come running after him."

"Yeah," Chuck said, smiling. Jokes at his expense never bothered him. "Like a zombie, man. Hey, you never know."

Someone threw an empty beer can at him as the rest laughed.

By the time their fire died down to a few coals, they'd retold portions of the story half a dozen times.

"I'm beat," Len finally said, getting up. He swayed a little bit, and had to steady himself by putting a hand on Walt's shoulder.

"Whoa," Jimmy said, laughing. "Drink a little too much?"

Len scowled at him. "Ha ha."

He'd actually had only two, but it had been a long day—the driving, the dead body, the police—so it was a wonder he could even keep his eyes open.

"If you guys are going to stay up, keep the noise down," he said. "I want to get some sleep."

"No guarantees," Walt told him as he popped open another beer.

"You guys suck," Len said.

He headed over to the tent he and Chuck were sharing. As he

unzipped the door, he coughed and then cleared his throat. *Stupid dry desert air,* he thought. He grabbed a bottle of water out of the cooler and crawled inside.

There was a knock at Dr. Karp's door. Without looking up, he said, "Come in."

The door opened and Mr. Shell entered. He was a lean and muscular six-foot-two with sandy blond hair, and a nose that had been broken at least once.

Karp had been expecting him, so he waved to one of the chairs in front of his desk. "Have a seat." Once Shell was situated, he said, "Pleasant trip?"

Shell's mouth moved up and down in a quick smile. "Pleasant enough."

"Any further update on this afternoon's…action?"

Karp had to be careful in his phrasing and tone. Shell was not his subordinate, nor was he Shell's. They worked in completely different branches of the project, their jobs only overlapping when circumstances such as those that happened in the last eighteen hours occurred. Shell was part of the security arm, his specialty emergency situations.

"How much have you been informed of already?" Shell asked.

"That Ellison was neutralized by your team. And the scene was being staged."

"Then you know enough." Shell leaned forward. "What I'd like to do is talk about Captain Daniel Ash."

"Have you found him?"

"Not yet." Shell paused, then set his briefcase on his lap and opened it up. From inside, he extracted a thin stack of photographs and set them on the desk.

"This is an enhanced thermal satellite image," he said, tapping the top photo. "It shows a section of the road north of Barker Flats. It was taken fifty-seven minutes after the loss of power at the facility."

Karp studied the image. There were only two things that showed heat, both very near to each other, and the rest of the image was basically black.

Shell pointed at a thick line just a half shade lighter than the surrounding area. "This is the highway." He moved his finger to the larger of the two bright spots. "And this is a car. As you can see, it's not on the road. We've been able to determine that it is in the process of pulling up at an abandoned gas station. This other bright spot is a person waiting by the building."

He moved the picture to the bottom of the stack. The revealed image was similar to the first. The only change was that the car was now on the road.

"You'll notice the person who had been waiting at the gas station is no longer there."

"Ash?"

"Yes."

"How do you know for sure?"

Instead of answering, Shell laid all the photographs out on the desk. There were eight total, including the two he'd already shown the doctor.

Shell touched the photo to the far left. "Here. That's the Barker Flats facility, seven minutes after the power outage."

There were two small, bright dots in the desert not far from the building.

Shell moved his attention to the next photo. The building was no longer in the picture, but the two dots were still there. "Fifteen minutes after. They've gone just over a mile." The next photo was similar to the last. "Twenty-five minutes. Two and a half miles." Next photo. "Thirty minutes. They paused here before moving on." Next photo. "Forty minutes. They're standing next to the road." And the last photo. "They've separated here. One has stayed where they were, while the other is heading to the gas station."

Karp stared at all the photos. He touched the solitary dot standing by the road in the last shot. "Couldn't that be Ash?"

Shell shook his head. "As soon as Ash reaches the gas station, this person heads three miles south where he is picked by a separate car forty minutes later. It's clear whoever it was knew exactly where he was going. You had Captain Ash under your control for over a week prior to the breakout. Before that, records indicate that in the few weeks he and his family had been living at the base, they had yet to leave. Ash would have no knowledge of this area. The man picked up at the abandoned gas station had to be Ash."

The logic was sound, but Karp didn't like the accusatory tone Shell was taking. "Were you able to follow the car the captain was in?"

"Only as far as the Nevada border. It pulled into the parking garage of a casino there. Once it was out of sight, there was no way to know if it left again."

"I thought these satellites are supposed to be good enough to make out the license numbers on cars."

Shell said nothing for a moment. "In daylight, *if* the angle's right. But it was still dark when the car entered the parking garage. Plus it was a Toyota Camry, the most popular car in the country. So no, Dr. Karp. We lost it." There was a pause. "What I need to know is how troublesome this Ash is. Could he be a problem? Or do we just let him go?"

"What does Bluebird think?"

Shell stared at him. "Naturally, Bluebird is concerned, but they've left it up to me to determine what happens next. So I need to know from you whether you think he *is* a problem, or just someone we can ignore."

Karp thought for a moment, knowing he had to tread carefully. "I would prefer if he were eliminated, primarily because it would aid our research if we had his body. But is he a threat?" He shook his head. "Ash knows nothing that can hurt us."

"Unless your man Ellison told him something."

Though Dr. Karp knew it was true, Shell's accusation annoyed him. "There's absolutely no proof that Ellison had anything to do with Ash's escape. He found out Littlefield was going to engage Protocol Thirteen and ran due to fear. He was found alone in the major's car, for God's sake, not some Toyota Camry. All that proves is that he was weak, not a traitor."

Shell paused a moment before responding. "Doctor, your position within the project is safe. Your skills are needed and you are in no danger. So don't embarrass yourself by ignoring the obvious. The only way Ash could have been freed was if he'd had help on the inside. There is no other way. You know it, and I know it. So drop the bullshit. Is Ash dangerous to us or not?"

Backed into a corner, there was really only one answer Karp could give. "Maybe."

When Len woke up the next morning, he was the only one in the tent. He staggered outside, his head pounding, and found the others sitting at the campfire.

"About time," Chuck said. He stared at his friend for a moment. "How much *did* you have to drink last night?"

Len dropped into the only empty chair. "What time is it?"

"Nine-thirty," Walt said.

"We've been up for two hours," Chuck told him.

Len coughed a couple of times.

"Dude, are you all right?" Walt asked.

"I think I might be getting something."

"Great," Jimmy said. "I swear to God if I get it, too, I'm going to kill you."

"Is there any coffee left?" Len asked.

Chuck poured him a cup and handed it over. "We were just waiting for you so we could hike the dunes."

"I…I don't think I'm up for it."

"Yeah, I can see that."

"You guys go. I'm just going to lie down."

Chuck eyed him for a moment. "Maybe we should just head home."

Shaking his head, Len said, "I don't want to ruin your fun." He tried to smile. "I'll be fine. I just need to sleep it off."

The others protested a bit more, but in the end they headed off for the dunes, and Len crawled back into the tent to rest.

When they got back four hours later, all three of them were more exhausted than they should have been, and two were already sniffling.

Chuck didn't even check Len as he climbed into the tent to take a nap. It wouldn't have mattered anyway. Len had been dead for nearly an hour. Chuck would follow seven hours later, and Walt thirty minutes after that.

Jimmy was the only one still alive, if barely, when the Ranger service found them.

"I'm going to kill him," he kept whispering. "I'm going to kill him."

But, really, it was the other way around.

15

Ash's new quarters weren't quite as nice as the room he'd woken up in the day before, but they were more than adequate. All the clothes that had been in the other dresser had been moved to his new room, as had the messenger bag that surprisingly still had the money inside.

He had slept with the watch on, not a habit he used to have, but one he was determined to start. It had still been on California time when Hamilton gave it to him, but Pax had told him when he showed Ash to the room that it was an hour later here. Where "here" was, Ash still didn't know.

It was because of the watch that he skipped dinner. He was in too much of an emotional state, and didn't want to end up saying something he'd regret later. Pax had brought him a tray of food around eight p.m. and Ash surprised himself by devouring it all.

When morning came, the decision to leave didn't seem as clear as it had twelve hours before. Yes, the conversation with Hamilton had annoyed him, but there was too much he didn't know or understand, and it was clear that many of the answers could probably be found right there on the ranch.

Still unsure of what he was going to do, he packed a few extra shirts, some underwear, and socks into the messenger bag. He then left the bag in the room and went in search of breakfast.

The building he was in was a kind of dormitory just down a wide stone pathway from the main building. It was two stories and held maybe twenty rooms, but if anyone else had been staying there, Ash hadn't heard them. The outside of the building was stone halfway up the first floor, with wooden timbers the rest of the way to the top. It was definitely built to last, but while it had the appearance of having been built decades before, Ash got the sense it was actually recently constructed.

Heading down the path, he could hear birds chirping in the distance, and felt a breeze blowing softly through the tops of the trees. The tranquility of it all was almost overwhelming. It was so at odds with the turmoil going on inside him.

As the trail turned and went up a gentle rise, the main building came into view. It was an impressive structure—old and wooden and huge, with wide, sloped roofs and half a dozen chimneys. It looked like a ski lodge that should have been at the bottom of a hill rather than in a quiet clearing.

There was a workout area off to the left with pull-up bars, sit-up stations, and resistance-training machines. A woman was at one of the machines, using it to work her shoulders. She glanced over at Ash, then quickly looked away as if she'd been caught doing something she shouldn't have.

As Ash neared the main building, he spotted Pax on his hands and knees examining a set of stairs that led up to the wide porch surrounding the structure. When Pax saw him, he got to his feet and brushed off his hands.

"Morning," he said.

"Good morning," Ash replied. "I was wondering if there was someplace I could get some breakfast."

"Sure, sure." Pax turned to the building. "That third door there, that gets you into a short hallway that'll take you into the kitchen. You'll find Bobbi in there. She can whip you up something."

"Thanks." Ash glanced at the stairs. "Is it safe?"

"What? Oh, sure. Just be careful on that second step. The backboard's starting to give a little. I'll have one of the boys replace it this afternoon."

Again, Ash hesitated before moving on. "Can I ask you something?"

"Of course."

"What kind of business is this ranch in? Can't believe you make a lot of money off of people like me."

Pax laughed. "No, that would drive us broke, I think. We have cattle, beef mostly, and a small herd of buffalo."

"Buffalo?"

"You'd be surprised at the size of the buffalo meat market. But Rachel wants us to keep them for historical sake, let them live out their lives here."

"So you only make money off the cattle then."

"When we need to."

It wasn't really an answer, but Ash decided not to push and headed into the house.

Bobbi was a tall woman with short red hair who turned out to be an excellent cook. In no time, Ash was sitting at one of the tables in the restaurant-sized kitchen, working his way through a large plate of eggs and sausage.

"Morning, Rachel," Bobbi said several minutes later.

Ash glanced up. Another woman had entered the kitchen—Rachel, presumably. She was shorter and leaner than Bobbi, and had long silver-streaked blonde hair that was pulled back into a ponytail.

"How about a cup of coffee?" Rachel asked.

"You got it."

While Bobbi filled a mug, Rachel walked over to Ash's table.

"Mind if I sit with you?" she asked him.

"Not at all."

She smiled, took the chair opposite his, then held out her hand. "I'm Rachel Hamilton."

They shook.

"You're Matt's wife?"

She laughed. "Hardly. I'm his sister."

"Sorry. When Pax told me this place was yours and Matt's, I just assumed…"

"Don't be sorry. A lot of people make that same mistake."

Bobbi came over, set the mug in front of Rachel, then glanced at Ash. "And how's your breakfast?"

"It's good. Thank you."

"If either of you need anything, just holler." With that, she headed back to the prep table where she'd been cutting up vegetables.

Rachel took a sip of her coffee then said, "How'd you sleep?"

"Fine," he said. "I appreciate you letting me spend another

night here."

"We've got the beds. Someone might as well use them."

"You do have a lot of space, but I've only seen a handful of people."

"It's an ebb-and-flow kind of thing around here. Sometimes the ranch is packed, and sometimes it feels like just Matt and me."

"Pax tells me that this is a cattle ranch."

She took another sip, then shrugged. "Yeah, we have cattle."

Like Pax, she seemed hesitant to get into the business of the ranch.

"I hear you told Matt you're intending to leave us this morning," she said as he put a piece of sausage in his mouth.

He shrugged.

"I'm sure you have a lot of things to do," she went on. "Starting with trying to find out what happened to your family. If I were you, it would be the first thing I'd want to do." She paused. "But before you go, there are a few things you need to know."

"What?" he said.

"You finish your breakfast first, then we can talk."

He swallowed the sausage, then pushed his plate away. "I'm finished now."

The room she led him to was on the second floor near Matt's office. It was a conference room decorated to keep with the mountain-lodge feel of the place—big pine table, wooden handcrafted chairs, and a fireplace at the far end. There was also a large television hanging on the wall that was currently off.

Ash hadn't even sat down yet when the door opened again, and Matt and Pax walked in.

"Morning, Captain," Matt said. "Trust you slept well."

"I did. Thank you."

Pax gave Ash a nod.

"Where's Billy?" Matt asked.

Pax seemed to take this as his cue. He picked up the phone on a cabinet under the TV and punched in a number.

"Why don't we sit?" Rachel suggested.

While Matt went around to the other side of the table, Rachel took the chair next to the one Ash sat in.

"So what's this all about?" Ash asked.

Before anyone could answer, the door opened and Billy rushed in.

"Sorry," he said. He made his way around to sit with Matt, and placed the notebook he was carrying on the table.

Pax hung up the phone the moment Billy entered, and took the chair next to Rachel.

Matt looked around at everyone, then focused his attention on Ash. "I'll come right to it. We think it would be a mistake for you to leave right now."

"If I want to leave, I'll leave," Ash said, suddenly wary. "You already said you wouldn't try to stop me."

"And we won't," Matt told him. "But I'm hoping what we have to say will convince you to stay."

When he didn't elaborate, Ash asked, "So what *is* it you have to say?"

Matt considered him for a moment before saying, "What happened to the families at Barker Flats didn't occur simply by chance."

"Of course it didn't," Ash said. "It was an attack. Some terrorist organization trying to stir up fear."

Matt hesitated, then stood up. He began walking toward the far end of the room. "How well did you know your neighbors?"

"My neighbors? Not well. We'd just transferred in."

Matt stopped near the center of the table. "Hadn't everyone just transferred in?"

"Well, yes. The base had been closed for a while, and we were there to get it up and running again."

Matt touched a finger to the table. Instantly, a wooden flap rose and disappeared into the surface edgewise, revealing a control panel underneath.

"You're going to want to turn around," Matt said. He hit a button and the TV came to life.

Ash shifted his chair so he could see the screen. Rachel and Pax did the same. The image remained black for a moment, then a picture of a family cut in.

"Do you recognize them?" Matt asked.

"That's Manny…Captain Diaz and his wife. Carol, I think. I don't remember their kids' names."

"They lived next to you, didn't they?"

"Yes."

As Ash stared at the picture, he remembered the scream he'd heard that night while he and Brandon were being led away. It was Carol, wasn't it? And now, if what Matt told him was true, Carol and Manny and their kids were all dead.

The picture changed to one of a man and woman.

"Lieutenant Cross and his wife," Ash said without prompting. The Crosses lived on the other side of them.

Another picture, a couple and a teenage boy.

"The Parsons, I believe." He looked at Matt. "What's the point of all this?"

Matt nodded at the screen. More pictures came up. This time there was no pause for Ash to identify them, but he recognized the faces of many of those he'd seen around the base.

The last image was a collage of all the photos.

"These are the sixteen families that you lived with, the ones that were exposed to the same disease as you and your family. They all have something very important in common."

"You've already told me they're dead."

"There's something else."

The picture of the Diaz family replaced the collage.

"Manny Diaz," Matt said. "His father died when he was seventeen, and his mother a month after he received his commission. He was an only child. Carol Diaz, maiden name Yeager. Mother died when she was eleven, father two years later. She was an only child."

The picture of the Diaz family was replaced by one showing the Crosses.

"Martin Cross. Parents killed in a car accident when he was a freshman in college. He was an only child. Emily Cross, maiden name Vernon. Adopted by an older couple, both of whom died of natural causes within one year of each other while Emily was in high school. She was their only child."

Matt continued to go through the pictures, telling the basically same story every time. The final picture was one that hadn't been shown before.

"Daniel Ash. Parents died in an auto accident when he was

twenty. Not an only child, but his brother Jeff sustained brain damage in the accident and lives in a nursing home. Ellen Ash, maiden name Walker. Mother died of cancer when she was—"

"Stop," Ash whispered. "Please."

The screen went black, and the room fell quiet.

After a few moments, Rachel put a hand on Ash's arm. "We know this isn't easy. But we needed to show you the truth."

"The truth of what?" he asked, shaking her off. "That everyone I used to live around lost their parents? It happens. It's probably not as unusual as it sounds."

"It's not just the parents," Matt said, still at the center of the table. He gestured at the screen. "None of your former neighbors had any close relatives at all. They were isolated."

Ash gritted his teeth. "I have someone."

"You do," Rachel said. "But I think you understand the point Matt is getting at."

He shot her a look, then let out a breath as his gaze fell to the table. "Okay. Fine. So we were all isolated. So what?"

"So that makes all of you the perfect test subjects," Matt said.

"Test subjects?"

"If any of you died, it would be fairly easy to cover that up, don't you think?"

"Wait. Are you trying to tell me what happened at Barker Flats was done to us on purpose *as a test?*"

Matt looked at him, saying nothing.

"That's ridiculous," Ash said.

Matt changed the picture on the screen. Now, instead of a photo, there was an online news article.

"This appeared on a local Ann Arbor, Michigan, news website five days ago," Matt explained.

LOCAL MAN, WIFE DIE IN HOUSE FIRE

First Lieutenant Martin Cross and his wife Emily were killed tragically last night in a fire that consumed their home. Army investigators at the base in South Korea where they lived believe the fire was started by faulty wiring, though an investigation is ongoing.

"South Korea?" Ash said.

Matt brought up two more articles, both for families that had been at Barker Flats. Their deaths were being called accidents, too. One family was said to have died in a car accident in Germany, while the other apparently had been caught in a storm while on a fishing trip off the Philippine coast.

"These are the only articles that have appeared so far, but we have no doubt that within the next three to four weeks, the rest of your neighbors will get their obituaries, too."

"This isn't possible. Someone's playing a game here." Ash shook his head at the screen. "These aren't real."

"They're very real. If you want, I'll take you to a computer and you can search whatever site you'd like." When Ash didn't say anything, Matt hit another button. "Do you recognize this man?"

Ash looked back at the screen. The photo that was now displayed was a head-and-shoulders shot of a man in his late fifties with thinning gray hair. He was wearing gold-rimmed glasses and didn't look happy. It had obviously been cropped from a larger picture and blown up.

Ash's first thought was that he'd never seen the man before, but there was just the hint of recognition—something in the man's expression—that made him unsure.

"I...don't think so," he said.

"Not at Barker Flats?" Matt asked. "Maybe in the distance or in passing?"

Ash studied the photo again, but nothing new came to him. "I just don't know. Who is he?"

"His name is Dr. Nathaniel Karp. He's the man who infected your family."

16

Jimmy was DOA when the ambulance arrived at the Sage Springs Hospital emergency room. The drive from the camping area at the dunes took nearly an hour, but Jimmy would have died even if the hospital had been right next door. Still, the two doctors who were on duty that night, Dr. Fisher and Dr. Morse, made a valiant attempt to bring him back, but to no avail.

Sage Springs boasted a population of only 12,347. And while the hospital was the best medical facility within a seventy-five-mile radius, it was by no means a top-of-the-line operation. That meant the staff it employed, while dedicated, often consisted of doctors and technicians who had graduated at the lower ends of their classes.

Drs. Fisher and Morse were no exceptions. That, of course, didn't mean they lacked the skills to do their jobs. They were intelligent, caring men who, on that night, made a critical mistake.

The assumption they made, based on the information radioed to them from the ambulance, was that the incoming patient was suffering from either a severe case of the flu or pneumonia. Unsure of how contagious the patient might be, they had ordered all staff that would come in contact with him to wear masks and gloves at all times. They couldn't have known it, but the bug was airborne and able to infect new hosts through eyes, ears, and any other entry point to the body, such as a cut. This was unforeseeable, and *not* their mistake.

Their mistake came once they'd pronounced Jimmy dead. Seeing how his body had been ravaged by the disease, and hearing from the ambulance attendants that others at the campground had reported Jimmy and his friends appeared fine earlier in the day should have made them realize something unusual was up. If they had recognized that, they could have immediately declared a quarantine on the entire hospital and limited the deaths to just those in the building.

But when the declaration finally came, it was several hours too late, and the town of Sage Springs paid a heavy price.

Dr. Karp was shaken from his sleep at 5:26 a.m.

Standing beside his bed was Major Ross, the man who served as his military liaison.

"There's a problem," the major said. "We're set up in Conference Room D. Be there in five minutes."

"What is it?" Dr. Karp asked.

But the major had already walked out of the room.

The doctor pushed himself out of bed, swearing under his breath. Ross had never given him an order before. That wasn't the nature of their relationship. But an order was certainly what it had sounded like, and Karp didn't like it.

Just to remind the major who was in charge, he let seven minutes pass before stepping into the conference room. Given that Ross had said "*We're* set up," Karp expected more than just the major waiting inside, but no one else was there.

"What's going on that you couldn't tell me in my room?" the doctor asked.

"Dr. Karp?" The voice came out of a speaker in the middle of the table. The doctor immediately recognized it as belonging to the Project Eden Director of Preparation (DOP).

"Sir, I'm sorry," the doctor said. "I didn't realize you were involved in this meeting. Major Ross gave me no information."

"Because Major Ross has no information," the DOP explained. "He was merely doing exactly what I told him to do."

Feeling suddenly uncomfortable, Dr. Karp said, "Of course," then took a seat a couple of chairs away from Ross.

"Major, have you been able to reach Mr. Shell yet?" the DOP asked.

"He's on hold, sir. I can connect him now, if you'd like."

"Please."

Ross leaned forward and pushed a couple of buttons on the

conference phone. "Mr. Shell, are you there?"

"I'm here."

"Director, we're all present," the major said.

In the silence that followed, Karp wondered if the major had accidentally disconnected the DOP, but then the man's scratchy voice came out of the speaker again.

"At 6:22 p.m. Pacific Time last night, park rangers serving the Mesquite Dunes Recreational Area responded to a call from a camper concerned that someone using the campground had overdosed on drugs. The party in question was seen stumbling through his campsite before collapsing onto the ground. As a precaution, an ambulance was dispatched to the scene. The rangers arrived first, though. What they found was not a camper who had OD'd, but rather one camper who appeared to be very sick, and three others who were lying in their tent, dead.

"The surviving man was rushed to the hospital in Sage Springs, but died before reaching the facility. At 2:37 a.m., two of the nurses on duty started to become ill. A check of the other eighteen people in the building revealed that all but three were experiencing similar symptoms. These included headaches, body aches, and a general sense of exhaustion. One of the nurses had been on duty when the dead man arrived in the ambulance. She was smart enough to put two and two together, and immediately made calls to her county health department and the Center for Disease Control.

"I received a copy of the alert the CDC put out thirty minutes ago. This is not a public alert, and no media has been notified as of yet. CDC officials are on their way to the scene. In the meantime, the hospital has put itself under quarantine."

The doctor frowned at the speakerphone. "What are you trying to suggest, sir? That this illness has something to do with us? That's not possible."

Silence again, then, "The gas station where your man Ellison was found and eliminated is only thirty miles from the campground at Mesquite Dunes."

That gave the doctor pause. "Still," Dr. Karp finally said. "Mr. Shell's team burned the body and the car he'd been in. There's no way he could have been the source." Then a terrible thought hit him. "Unless he talked to someone first. But I find it hard to believe he would have done that."

"There is another way," the DOP said.

"What?" Karp asked, not seeing what it could be.

"One of the victims at the campsite was a man named Len Craddock." The DOP let the name hang out there as if it should mean something to the doctor.

"I don't know who that is."

"I do," Mr. Shell said through the speaker, a hint of dread in his voice. "He's the person who discovered the body of the gas station attendant."

Dr. Karp could feel the skin tighten across his arms. The station attendant had been killed because he'd witnessed what was done to Ellison. His death had been made to look like a robbery and having someone find his body had been part of the plan.

"But it's my understanding that precautions were taken," the doctor said. "The car and the body were removed. There was nothing there to infect him."

"Records indicate that the call Craddock made to the police was placed through a pay phone outside the station," the DOP told them. "The only other call on that phone that day happened minutes before Mr. Shell's team arrived on scene."

"Oh, dear God," Karp said.

"Mr. Shell?" the DOP asked.

Shell took a moment before he spoke. "There was obviously an oversight, sir. I will deal with it."

"Yes, you will. You will also help ensure this does not spread. Dr. Karp, Major Ross, you, too, if necessary."

"Perhaps it would be best for an immediate quarantine zone to be set up," Major Ross suggested.

Dr. Karp frowned. "I'm not sure if that—"

"What?" the DOP asked. "Necessary? It's an excellent suggestion, Major. Our people are already on it. We cannot afford mistakes. The only way we will succeed is to control events, not have them control us."

"Sir, if I may ask," Shell said. "Has anyone tried to trace the number Ellison called?"

"Why?"

"It could help in locating Captain Ash. Given this new development, I think it's even more critical that we bring him in. He can link this outbreak to Barker Flats. And while a connection from that to Bluebird would be impossible, it could raise concerns and interfere with some of our future work, creating unnecessary delays."

"Yes, Mr. Shell. We have discussed that here. In addition to helping with the outbreak, you need to continue hunting for Ash. Any additional men you need, please request from your department head and they'll be immediately assigned to you. As for the phone number, it was to a disposable phone purchased in Milwaukee, and no longer seems to be in service."

The doctor was relieved. He'd dodged a bullet with the outbreak, since most of the blame seemed to be falling on Mr. Shell. He was still vulnerable on the Ash issue, but there was a way he might be able to improve that situation, too.

"Director? I have an idea about how we might be able to flush out Captain Ash."

17

Ash pushed himself out of his chair and moved over to the monitor, his eyes firmly affixed on the image of Dr. Karp.

In rapid succession, he asked, "Is he some kind of spy? Who does he work for? Does the Army know?"

"Dr. Karp is an American citizen," Matt explained. "Until three years ago, he worked for the U.S. Army Medical Research Institute of Infectious Diseases. He was then transferred to a classified assignment. That assignment eventually brought him to Barker Flats."

Ash looked at Matt, confused. "Are you trying to say that the U.S. Government did this to my family?"

"We're saying that Dr. Karp and the people he's involved with did this to your family."

"But you just said he works for the Army."

Matt paused, then said, "The Army pays him a salary, yes."

"So you *are* saying the Army did this to us. There's no way I'm going to believe that."

"The Army didn't do this to you."

Ash stared across the table. "You're not making any sense."

"Captain," Rachel said, her voice soft. "You have unfortunately found yourself in a situation that is much, much larger than you can imagine. We have been…following this for many years, and sometimes it's too much for even us to grasp."

"Oh," Ash said, taking a step back from the table. "Oh, I get it. You're one of those conspiracy groups, aren't you? What is this? Some kind of indoctrination? Trying to recruit me? Well, thanks for your help, but it's time for me to leave."

He turned for the door.

"If you'd stayed in your cell in California, you'd be dead now," Matt said. "That much you can't deny. We got you out. We saved your life. The least you could do is give us a few minutes to hear us out."

"I think I've already heard enough."

Matt started to speak again, but Rachel silenced him with a look as she stood up and moved between Ash and the door.

"Captain, I understand your doubts and concerns. You *are* free to go, of course. But we don't think that would be wise."

"And staying here would be? With a bunch of crazies?"

She studied him for a second. "Just give me one moment."

She walked over to a cabinet along the wall. From Ash's angle he could see the envelope he'd brought from the desert sitting on the shelf inside. But if that's what Rachel was retrieving, she didn't get a chance to pull it out.

As she bent down, the door suddenly thrust open, and a man Ash hadn't seen before rushed in.

"PCN," he said quickly.

Matt touched the controls, and the television switched from the image of Dr. Karp to the Prime Cable News network. A Breaking News banner was running across the bottom of the screen, while the rest was taken up by a female anchor at the network's New York studios.

"...confirm twenty-two deaths at this point. Roadblocks have been set up around the town, and no one is being allowed in or out." The image changed to a shot of a desert highway. Parked across the road about fifty feet from the camera's position were several military vehicles and a couple highway patrol cars. In the distance beyond them was what appeared to be the edge of a town.

"Residents of Sage Springs have been advised to remain in their homes until otherwise instructed. We're told that a first-response CDC team is on scene now, and that more medical personnel are en route. To repeat, there has been a report of a severe outbreak of what looks like a deadly version of the flu in the town of Sage Springs, California." The anchor put her hand to her ear. "All right. We have Tamara Costello now just outside the roadblock. Tamara, can you tell us what's going on there at this moment?"

The voice changed but the picture remained the same.

"Catherine, we have just been asked to tell anyone who has been in the vicinity of Sage Springs or the Mesquite Dunes Recreational Area in the past twenty-four hours to call a special hotline the California Department of Health has set up. I believe that number should be on the screen now."

As if she were running the control room, the Breaking News banner was replaced by a new graphic that read *Crisis in the Desert* on one side, and had a phone number on the other.

"Though there has been no official announcement," the reporter went on, "speculation, confirmed by unofficial sources, is that this is not some naturally occurring outbreak, but has been caused by the deliberate release of a virus. One source I talked to believes this is a terrorist attack."

"Tamara, if it *is* a terrorist attack, why was it done in such an underpopulated area?" the anchor asked.

"Our viewers might be surprised to learn, Catherine, that this part of California boasts a lot of military installations such as Fort Irwin, the China Lake Naval Air Weapons Station, and, closer to Los Angeles, Edwards Air Force Base. There was a report of an explosion two nights ago at a small military facility less than a hundred miles from here that we are checking out. I should stress, though, that event remains unconfirmed, and any connections to the outbreak are unknown at this point."

"Tamara, I understand officials are looking for someone in particular. Is that correct?"

The guy who'd come running into the conference room suddenly said, "Here it is."

"Yes, Catherine. That's correct."

Ash stared at the television, stunned, as the image of the desert was replaced by a photo of him.

"Daniel Ash is believed to be a carrier of the virus, though apparently immune himself. We're told that if anyone sees him they should call the hotline or their local authorities, but should not, under any circumstances, approach him."

"Is there any indication that Ash is one of the people responsible for releasing the virus in the first place?" the anchor asked.

"No one is saying that, at least not officially. They are only saying he is a person of interest and—"

Matt turned the TV off.

"Thanks, Jordan," he said to the man who'd come running in. "Record it."

"Already going."

Jordan left.

Ash gazed at the blank screen, numb. *A person of interest?*

Rachel put a hand on his shoulder. "Are you all right?"

He continued to look at the TV a moment longer, then turned to her. "I...I should turn myself in."

"That's the last thing you need to do."

Suddenly realizing her hand was still on his shoulder, he pulled back. "What if they're right, and I am contagious? What if I've infected all of you? Oh, God! And those people who helped me get out of there, drove me here, they could be sick already."

Billy leaned forward. "The incubation rate and course for this particular virus is extremely quick. From infection to death—anywhere from eight to twenty-four hours. The point is, Captain, if you were a latter-day Typhoid Mary, most of us would already be dead, and the rest dying." He looked around. "Everyone looks pretty healthy to me."

"How do you know that? How can you possibly know anything about this...this virus?"

"The only way we could have gotten you out of that facility was if we had someone on the inside," Matt said. "The truth is, the only reason we even knew about you was because of him. The same person was also able to feed us information about the virus."

The size of the rabbit hole Ash had fallen into was cavernous. If he were to believe they had a man on the inside, it would mean he had to accept the idea that what had been done to his family and his neighbors was perpetrated by this Dr. Karp, an *Army* employee, and that all the families had been moved to Barker Flats specifically for the purpose of testing this virus. It was ridiculous. Completely unbelievable. Yet, if he didn't believe there was a man on the inside, then how did they get him out?

Finally, he said, "If you did have someone there, how did he let this happen? How could he stand by and watch all those people die? My family? Our neighbors?"

"He wasn't aware there was going to be a live test until it was too late," Matt said. "But don't read too much into that. Even if he had known, he couldn't have done anything anyway. He would have been killed, and stopped nothing. At least this way he was able to get you out before he died."

"Died?" Ash said, surprised. Then he remembered. "The guy who stayed behind so we could get away. The one who got caught in the explosion—he was your inside man."

"Yes. But the explosion didn't get him. He fled before it was set off, so he could get us one last report. Only..." Matt paused. "He said he was sick, and that he didn't have long. The phone he called from was thirty miles from...from Sage Springs."

Ash's eyes widened. "The outbreak. He's responsible?"

"It would seem so."

"Then I *must* be contagious," Ash said. "How else could he have gotten infected?"

Billy shifted in his chair. "Your immunity was of great interest to those running the test. The entire time you were in that cell, they were bombarding you with the virus, trying to see if it could break through your system."

"Are you serious?"

"Absolutely. Our man reported that when the power came back on in the building, the system spraying the virus into your cell started up again, and the bug leaked into the main corridor."

Ash finally sat back down, the weight of everything too much.

"Under the circumstances," Matt said, "I think we're going to have to insist you stay."

"You mean you *will* stop me."

"No. But we won't help you either. And we're a long way from anywhere out here."

Rachel took her seat beside Ash, shifting her body so they were facing each other. "You're a fugitive now, Captain, and the whole country knows it. Within twenty-four hours, they will finger you as one of those responsible. I guarantee it. You won't be able to go anywhere without someone recognizing you. You won't be able to talk to anyone. Here, you're safe."

"I don't care about my safety. I only care about making those who did this to my family pay."

"That's a goal we would be more than happy to help you

achieve," she said. "But you can't just blunder off and think you'll be able to deal with this on your own. Information is power, and at the moment, there's a lot going on that you don't understand."

He was quiet for a moment. "You'll help me understand?"

"We'll give you what you need," she said.

He looked at the others, and they all nodded.

"Okay. I'll stay for now. But the minute you deny me anything I think I need to know, I'm gone."

"Fair enough," she said.

"Then let's get started," he said.

Rachel exchanged a look with Matt, then focused once more on Ash. "The first thing you need to know is about your children."

His eyes narrowed slightly. "What about them?"

"They're alive."

18

Tamara Costello was getting frustrated. The only new information she'd been able to find was that a food truck would be serving lunch about a mile back along the highway. Not very broadcast-worthy stuff.

Without anything new, her network, and all the other twenty-four-hour news channels, would just keep playing the same crap over and over, eventually venturing into areas of wild conjecture. It's what always happened, and even though she was a part of the system, she hated that. This was supposed to be the age of information, not recycled garbage.

That's why, after she completed her update with the brain-dead Catherine Minor at 11:10 a.m., she found a quiet spot and called her brother in San Francisco.

"Look at you getting all that air time," he said as soon as he answered.

She couldn't help but smile. "You've been watching?"

"Riveted. So, really, how bad is it?"

"No way to know for sure. They've got the whole town blocked off. I've tried to call people who live there, but all I get are busy signals. Even the cell towers are down. Thank God for my sat phone." The network gave all its field reporters satellite phones in case they found themselves in areas that weren't covered by mobile phone companies despite those fancy maps they were always bragging about.

"The whole town? Man, it must be bad. Gives me the creeps just thinking about it."

She snickered and shook her head. "What are you? Ten?"

"Seriously, Tam. Think about it. Something so small you can't even see can kill you just like that."

She thought she heard his fingers snap. "Look, Gavin," she said, trying to get back on track. "I was wondering if you could do a little research for me."

"Ha! I knew that's why you called. You want to know more about the flu? The town? Give me five minutes and I can pull together enough info to fill up an entire hour."

While Tamara had chosen a life in the spotlight, Gavin preferred one that was more private, and spent most of his time in his apartment doing freelance software programming.

"No. The network can find that stuff out on its own. I'm interested in this Daniel Ash guy."

"The man the CDC's looking for?"

"Yeah. Who is he? Why is he important? Where are some of the places he'd go? If you can actually find him, I'll owe you big for the rest of the year. An exclusive interview would be incredible."

"From a distance, though."

"What?"

"From a distance. I mean, if he's infected, you don't want to get anywhere near him."

"Right. From a distance." She paused. "Think you can dig up a phone number?"

"If he's got one, I'll find it," Gavin said.

"And anything else you can learn?"

"Sure, sis. I'm waiting to hear back from a client, so I've got some time."

"Thanks, Gavin. You're my secret weapon."

Gavin Costello hung up with his sister then sat back down at his desk. Most of his non-computer geek friends were surprised by his setup. They expected multiple monitors, couple of high-end tower computers, and peripheral hard drives and gadgets stacked to the ceiling. What he really had was a 13-inch PC laptop and a back-up hard drive that ran automatically in the background over his Wi-Fi network. This gave him mobility on those rare occasions he worked away from his apartment.

Deciding to go the easy route first, he pulled up his current favorite search engine and typed in the name Daniel Ash. Not surprisingly, there was more than one. From the picture he'd seen on TV, the Ash his sister was looking for couldn't have been more than thirty-four or thirty-five, so that helped eliminate several of the possibilities. Then he tried to see if any of the remaining had a California connection. Two did, but the picture on the Facebook page that one of the links led to was definitely not the guy. The other lived clear up in Eureka and appeared to own a plumbing business. What would he be doing in the middle of the desert involved in a flu outbreak?

Gavin heard his sister's voice from his TV. The screen was placed so that all he had to do was swivel his chair around to see it. It looked like she'd moved to the opposite side of the highway, but what she was saying was pretty much the same thing she'd been saying most of the morning. Still, it always gave him a kick to see her work.

He grabbed his cell phone and typed in a text:

> Maybe you should report from
> the middle of the road next
> time. HA!

He sent it to her, muted the TV, then returned to his computer.

Five minutes later, as he was still trying to narrow things down, his phone rang. Expecting his sister again, he answered the call without looking. "Hey."

Though the line sounded open, no one said anything.

"Tammy?"

Still nothing. He looked at the display. *Blocked.*

"Who is this?" he asked.

A click, and the line went dead.

"Whatever, man." He dropped his phone on the table and returned his attention to his laptop, all but forgetting about the call.

Forty minutes later, he hit pay dirt.

It was a picture of a group of Army officers in a Fayetteville, North Carolina, newspaper from a few years earlier. The officers were from nearby Fort Bragg and had given a presentation to the local high school. One of the men in the photo was identified as Lieutenant Daniel Ash, and the more Gavin looked at him, the more he was sure it was the same guy in the photo shown on PCN.

"Nice," he said, congratulating himself.

Several minutes later, he located information indicating that prior to being stationed at Fort Bragg, the lieutenant had spent a short time at Fort Irwin outside Barstow, California—less than sixty miles from Sage Springs. Where Ash had gone *after* Fort Bragg, Gavin wasn't able to discover yet. Still, he knew Tammy would want to hear what he'd learned so far.

He grabbed his phone to call her, but for some reason he didn't have a signal.

"What the hell?"

He *always* had a signal at home. It was one of the reasons he'd picked this apartment. In his business, he couldn't afford to live in a cellular dead zone.

He decided to copy the links into an email and send them to her. He wasn't sure if she could retrieve email on her sat phone, but she'd get it at some point. A split second after he hit SEND, he got an error message telling him his cable modem was not currently connected to the Internet.

"You've got to be kidding me."

Now he was really annoyed. He glanced at his TV. With the exception of a blue box across the center of the screen that read *Channel Currently Unavailable*, the screen had gone black. Apparently, the whole cable system, or at least the part that came into his building, was out of commission.

Just his luck that both it and his cell phone would go out at the same time. Maybe they were tied together somehow. A massive communications glitch. That should make the news. Well, if anyone was still getting a signal so they could watch it.

He set the email to send as soon as the connection returned, and got up to grab a soda out of his refrigerator. As he was deciding whether he wanted to make a sandwich to go with his Dr. Pepper, someone knocked on his door.

He was barely out of the kitchen when whoever it was pounded again, more urgent this time.

"Just a minute," he yelled.

He looked through the security peephole in his door, but the person outside seemed to be covering it up. Had to be Dustin. He was always doing asshole things like that.

"Hilarious," Gavin said loud enough so Dustin could hear him. Donning a reproachful smirk, he opened the door. "What the hell are you bothering me for at this—"

"Not a word."

It wasn't Dustin. It was a man holding a gun pointed at Gavin's face.

"Sure," Gavin said, then realized he'd broken the rule and added, "Sorry."

The man stepped toward him, backing Gavin into the room. There were two others behind him, both big like the first man, wearing similar dark suits, and also armed.

Once everyone was inside, the last man in shut the door.

"Anyone else here?" the first guy asked.

"No," Gavin said, shaking his head vigorously from side to side. "Just me."

"Don't lie."

"I'm not lying." Gavin's voice cracked a little, and he could feel his hands shaking at his side.

The two other men headed into the hallway that led back to the bedroom. They were only gone about thirty seconds before they reappeared.

"Clear," one of them said, then stepped carefully into the kitchen with his partner.

There was another "clear" and they both returned.

"Your name's Gavin Costello?" the first guy asked.

"Yes."

The man touched a Bluetooth headset mounted on his ear. "We're secure. You can release the building." He looked at Gavin, then nodded toward the desk. "That your only computer?"

"What? Uh, no. I have a Dell in my closet."

"Is the laptop the only computer you *use?*"

"Yes. Yes, it is. You want it? It's all yours."

Who the hell were these guys? If they were trying to rob him, they were the best-dressed home invaders in history. Whoever they were, though, if they just wanted his computer, great. They could take it and their guns and leave.

The main guy glanced at the other men. "Grab it."

The slightly smaller of the two took the laptop from the desk. "Phone," he said, then raised Gavin's cell into the air so the others could see it.

"Bring it," the main guy said. "That your only phone, Gavin?"

"Yeah. Yeah, only one. I don't even have a landline."

"All right. Let's go."

Gavin tried not to show his relief. They'd be gone in just a second. And he was going to be okay.

But then the man grabbed his arm and pushed him toward the door. "You, too."

"What? Why me? What do you need me for? You got my computer. You'll get good money for that."

"No more talking or I pull the trigger."

The man said this so matter-of-factly that Gavin bit his lip to keep from saying anything.

The main guy said, "We're secure. You can release the building."

Five seconds later, two doors down the hall, Mrs. McFadden's cable came back on.

Good thing, too. One of the local stations showed reruns of Perry Mason every day at noon, and she hadn't missed an episode in over a year. The moment the TV signal had gone out, she'd tried calling the cable company, but there'd been something wrong with her phone, too. Now all was right with the world again, and Perry would be on in just a few minutes to embarrass that stuck-up Hamilton Burger like he always did.

Of the eighteen other apartments in the building, there was only one additional person home, a man named Frank Bushnell. He worked graveyard dispatch for the police so he was sound asleep. The outage passed without him ever knowing anything was wrong.

In apartment 11, Gavin Costello's apartment, as soon as the cable kicked back in, the laptop's Wi-Fi reconnected with the Internet. While the main guy was telling one of his associates to grab the computer, the email program was going through its normal cycle. This time, after confirming that it was once more connected to the cyber world beyond Gavin's walls, it sent off the single message waiting in the queue, finishing its operation just seconds before the associate slammed the screen shut.

A few hundred miles southeast, Tamara Costello's sat phone pinged with an incoming email. At that moment, though, Tamara was on camera and didn't hear it arrive.

19

The moment Rachel said that Josie and Brandon were still alive, Ash's vision went gray.

In his mind, he could hear Josie's cry, and feel how cold she'd been as he tried to keep her warm. He could even sense Brandon's fear as they were being led out of the house at Barker Flats.

But most of all, he could remember the numbness, the horror, the disbelief, and the total devastation he'd felt when the voice in the ceiling had told him his children were dead.

When he finally regained his senses, he was on the ground, one leg tucked under him, with no idea how he'd gotten there. Rachel was kneeling on one side, while Pax was doing the same on the other.

"Are you telling me the truth?" he whispered.

"Let's get you back in your seat," Rachel said.

She and Pax lifted him to his feet and helped him into the chair.

While they were doing this, Matt walked over to the cabinet and pulled out the tape-covered envelope. From inside, he removed a folded legal-size envelope and a thumb drive. He handed the envelope to Rachel, and took the drive over to the control panel.

"We've already watched these," Matt said. "They might not be easy to look at, but you need to see them, too."

He stuck the drive into a port and hit several buttons.

The television screen was black for a moment, then gray, then...

A room, not too dissimilar from Ash's cell at Barker Flats. Only this room had a door that was open, and a window that Ash got the sense didn't look to the outside. The shot was from up high and angled down.

Lying on the bed was Brandon.

Ash couldn't help but lean forward. Here was his son. He hadn't seen Brandon's face since they had been separated. He remembered now what he told his son at that moment. "Go with them. It'll be okay. You'll see me in just a bit."

He'd believed it then, because that's what they had told him. But it wasn't true, so the last thing he had told his son was a lie.

"I made some time notations on the back of the envelope," Matt said to Rachel.

Ash could hear her flip the envelope over, but he didn't look. He couldn't tear his eyes from the screen.

"Oh-six twenty-seven," Rachel said.

The image started scrolling quickly forward, then slowed back to real time.

"This is six-thirty in the morning, just a few hours after you were both brought in," Matt explained.

Brandon looked like he was asleep. Suddenly the door pushed all the way open, and someone in a biosafe suit came in. The person knelt down next to the bed and put something on Brandon's forehead.

A few moments later, a voice said, "Temp, ninety-eight point five."

Ash thought back. Six-thirty meant he'd been in his cell for at least four hours. By that point, he'd already been told that Josie was dead. But Brandon? He didn't know for sure, but he didn't think so.

"Next," Matt said.

Rachel read off another time code. "Ten twelve."

That, Ash knew, was definitely after when he'd been told about his son. No way it was later than that.

Once more the picture raced forward before resuming normal speed. The time stamp in the lower left read 10:12. The boy in the bed was still Brandon. And he was very much alive.

"Stop," Ash said.

Matt hit pause.

"Skip ahead."

"How far?"

"Nowhere in particular. Just let it run."

Ash just wanted to see Brandon move, Brandon alive, Brandon definitely there longer than the voice had led him to believe. One hour, two hours, three, four. It was all the same, all revealing the lie he'd been told.

"Stop," he finally said. "Is there video of Josie?"

"There is."

"Show it to me."

Her footage was more painful to watch. She was still ill. But she wasn't dead. Ash made Matt speed through the footage like he had with Brandon's, this time not stopping until Josie sat up.

"Play it," Ash said quickly.

The image snapped to normal time. Josie had a hand on the wall, steadying herself.

"Hello? Hello?" she said. "Where am I?"

Dear God, he never thought he'd hear her voice again.

He could feel the tears gathering in his eyes, and the breath quivering in his lungs. But he sucked in deeply and forced himself to remain under control.

Matt turned the video off.

"What are you doing?" Ash said.

"I'll give you the drive and have a computer set up in your room. You can watch as much as you want there. But if I were you, I wouldn't. There's nothing else that will mean anything. The most important thing was for you to see that they're still alive."

Ash glanced at the envelope in front of Rachel. "You said you had different times marked. There must be something you thought I should see."

"Moments, only. Things I thought might help convince you. But you don't need convincing."

Ash hesitated, then asked, "Were they told anything about me?"

Matt looked at him for a moment. "Yes. At first they were told you were sick, then later that you had died." He paused. "I can show you that if you really want."

A spike of pain shot through Ash's heart. His children, how they must be suffering thinking both of their parents were dead.

He shook his head. He would have to watch at some point, but he wasn't sure he could take it right now. It was enough to know they were alive, that they had survived the mysterious illness that had apparently taken everyone else around them. That he would be able to—

His head whipped around, his eyes finding Matt. "They survived the disease, but…but the explosion!"

"No," Matt said quickly, shaking his head. "They weren't there. They were moved as soon as your daughter could travel, two days after they took you in."

"Moved where?"

"Some place where they…"

"Where they what?"

Matt glanced at Billy, so Ash did the same.

"What?" he asked. "What is it?"

Billy cleared his throat. "Captain, you have an immunity to this particular virus. They've been looking for someone like you. What happened at Barker Flats isn't the first time some variant of this virus has been tested. But we're pretty sure you and your children are the first to survive. It's obvious you've passed your immunity on to them. We think they are…running tests on your kids. Using them to pinpoint this immunity."

A mix of anger and horror flashed in Ash's eyes. "Tests?"

"Mostly with their blood, would be my guess," Billy said in his nonchalant way.

"The good news," Rachel said, jumping in, "is that it means they'll want to keep Josie and Brandon alive."

"I need to find them," Ash said, pushing himself up. "I need to go now. I have to get them back."

Rachel touched his arm. "If you go now, you won't get within a hundred miles of them. Your face is all over the television. You'll be caught, then all three of you will be lost."

Clenching his teeth, he said, "I can't just stay here and do nothing."

"We're not asking you to do nothing." Matt walked down the table until he was directly across from Ash. "We're asking you to let us help you get them back."

Ash was almost shaking now, his anger at those who had taken Josie and Brandon growing with each second. "How can you help me?"

Rachel smiled. "Let us show you."

20

Hector Mendez arrived home at ten a.m. He lived alone in an old house on the outskirts of Victorville, California. The place had belonged to his mother, but she'd been dead for three years so it had been his since then.

That had also been around the time he and Lucy finally went their separate ways. It was his fault, and he knew it. He'd been a long-distance trucker when they were together, away from home for weeks at a time. He'd made some big stink about this being who he was and how he wasn't going to change. But staying home by herself wasn't who Lucy was either.

The irony, of course, was that not long after she left him, he gave up the long-distance work, and took a local trucking job for a regional bakery that had him home every day just about the time everyone else was going to their jobs.

His daily route started at midnight and took him from Victorville through Barstow, up to Sage Springs, around to Trona, then Ridgecrest, Johannesburg, Adelanto and finally home. His employer supplied mostly hotels, a few restaurants, and a couple of hospitals.

As was his habit, he and a few of the other drivers had breakfast at the local diner and then he'd driven home. Once there, he had his usual pre-sleep beer, watched one of the shows he'd recorded the night before, and went to bed.

He woke at three p.m., two hours earlier than usual. The reason was simple. He'd coughed himself awake. He headed into the kitchen where he hocked up what was in his throat, spit it into the sink, then got a glass of water.

Great, he thought as he chugged the liquid down. He hated

being sick.

He decided to take a couple of cold tablets, the non-drowsy type since he'd have to be up and moving around in a few hours, and went back to bed.

When his boss called at 12:10 a.m. to find out why he was late, the ringing of his phone reached his ears but his mind barely registered it. Thirty minutes later, when Karl, a friend who also drove for the bakery, knocked on his door, he didn't hear anything at all.

Hector was dead.

Tamara Costello didn't see the email from her brother until after lunch. She wasn't used to checking for them on her sat phone. Ninety-nine percent of the time she relied on her smartphone for email. But finally she noticed the tiny icon glowing dully on her display, indicating she'd received something.

She'd actually become annoyed with Gavin. She'd been trying to call him, but kept going straight to his voice mail. The email, however, more than made up for his lack of communication.

Daniel Ash was in the Army. Could it be that this was some kind of military accident, and not an act of terrorism like officials were starting to characterize it? She couldn't help but make the connection to the still unconfirmed report of an explosion at a military installation two nights ago. Had that been an Army base? It was something to check.

She had another live spot coming up in one minute. She tried her brother one more time, wanting to see if he'd learned anything more. Voice mail.

"Dammit, Gavin. Where the hell are you?" she said.

"Tamara, thirty seconds," her producer, Joe, announced.

While she did consider trying to get independent confirmation on Gavin's information, the thought passed so quickly through her mind it was almost like she hadn't had it at all. The several times she'd relied on her brother in the past, his information had always proven to be accurate. And there was no question that the Ash in the picture from one of the links Gavin sent was the same man in the photo authorities had given to the media.

As she got into position, Joe checked the mic clipped to her shirt. The moment he stepped away, she looked at the camera.

"How's this?" she asked.

Bobby, the cameraman, kept his eye on the viewfinder and gave her the thumbs up.

"Okay, we're coming up," Joe told her.

As she put her earpiece back in, she could suddenly hear Greg Roberts in the studio. He'd taken over anchor duties from Catherine a half hour earlier. Tamara took a deep breath, put the appropriate concerned look on her face, then gave Joe and Bobby a nod.

She was ready.

"…that time until the CDC was notified," the PCN anchor said. The graphic at the bottom of the screen identified him as Greg Roberts. "The situation seems to have settled into a kind of wait-and-see. We should learn more at the next press conference scheduled for two hours from now." He paused. "Okay, we're going to go back out to our reporter on the scene, Tamara Costello. Tamara, how's the mood there?"

Dr. Karp frowned at his television. *Mood? Where do they get these people?*

The picture switched to the same desert shot beside the road-block the network had been using most of the morning. Centered in the frame was Tamara Costello, their on-scene reporter.

"The high level of tension we noticed when we first arrived at the western roadblock has become more of a simmer as we await word of what's actually happening in town," she said.

"I've talked to several members of the highway patrol who are manning this post with a squad of Army personnel, and I can truthfully say no one has any more information concerning the residents of Sage Springs than we do here."

The image on the screen split in two, with a shot of the in-studio anchor on the left, and Tamara in the desert on the right. "There's been a report that at least twenty-five people have died in town," Greg said, "and somewhere between seventy-five and one hundred are feared infected."

"We heard that, too, Greg. Unfortunately, we have not yet been able to confirm any numbers. I can say that twenty minutes ago, a convoy of vehicles, mostly Suburbans, passed through the road-block and headed into town at high speed." As she spoke, footage of the caravan replaced the two talking heads. There were five vehicles altogether, their windows blacked out. "Our producer, Tim, heard from someone on the roadblock that these were part of a CDC team here to help the situation."

The picture switched back to the double shot.

"Are there any concerns that the virus could reach where you are currently situated?"

Dr. Karp rolled his eyes. Ten miles away through a warm desert? His skills were excellent, but they weren't *that* excellent.

"Greg, we've been told that our position is completely safe. In fact, one of the officials who stopped here earlier made a point to say that even if the roadblock were just a mile out from the town, there would still be no problem. A source has told me that the extra distance gives the authorities enough room to spot anyone crazy enough to try and sneak into or out of Sage Springs. As we already know, two people have attempted this and have been arrested."

"Thanks, Tamara. We'll check back with you—"

"I do have one piece of new information that I can share with you, Greg. It concerns the man authorities have deemed a person of interest."

Dr. Karp leaned forward. Beside him, Major Ross did the same.

"Daniel Ash?"

"Yes. According to my information, Ash is either in or was in the U.S. Army. We know that three and a half years ago he was a lieutenant at Fort Bragg in North Carolina, and before that, he was stationed at Fort Irwin, which is less than eighty miles from Sage Springs."

"How the hell did she learn that?" Major Ross said.

Greg, the anchor, looked equally surprised by this new information. "That's certainly something we haven't heard yet. Is there more?"

"That's all I have at the moment, Greg, but as soon as I know anything else, I'll let you know."

"Thank you, Tamara. You and your crew be careful out there."

"We will, Greg. Thank you."

As the image switched to a one-shot of the anchor, Ross picked up the remote and hit MUTE. He then quickly punched a number into the conference-room phone, making sure the speaker was engaged.

One ring, then, "Yes?"

"Were you watching that?" Ross asked.

"If you're talking about the Costello woman, then yes, I saw it," Shell said.

"How the hell did she find that out?"

"Apparently her brother sent her the information in an email."

"Her brother? I thought you had her brother."

"We do. We only learned twenty minutes ago that the email had gone out before we were able to fully secure his equipment."

"Twenty minutes ago? You could have stopped her then!"

Shell was silent for a moment. "There was no reason to. The information was going to come out eventually. It's not going to do any harm."

Dr. Karp, who'd been content to let the other two fight it out, finally said, "I think we can use this to our advantage."

Major Ross glanced at him doubtfully. "You want to explain that?"

"We've already been putting the pressure on Captain Ash. A little more can only help. I say we identify him as a mole. People will already be thinking that's a possibility anyway."

"So change him from a person of interest into a suspect," Shell said, the hint of a smile in his voice.

"Not *a* suspect," the doctor said. "*The* suspect."

It would either flush Ash out or get him killed. Either way, he wouldn't be a problem anymore.

21

The one thing Ash was very good at was going all in when he decided on a course of action. The only goal he had in his life now was getting his children back. Rachel, Matt, and the others described a plan that, even a few hours earlier, he would have found crazy. But not only was his face plastered all over television, it was now being openly speculated that he was responsible for the virus outbreak, exactly as Rachel had predicted.

Give it another day and he would be branded a terrorist, something they were all convinced would occur. And when it did, not only would he be in danger of being arrested if anyone recognized him, there was a good chance some "concerned citizen" would try to kill him.

If he was going to save his kids, the Ash he saw every morning in the mirror had to go.

"Watch your step," Matt said as he opened a door that led down into the basement of the Lodge—the name that apparently everyone called the ranch's main building.

Matt went down first, with Ash following and Billy bringing up the rear. When they reached the bottom, Ash saw that the space was mainly being used for storage.

Matt headed straight to the south wall, stopping in front of a clear spot between two shelving units. For several seconds, he didn't move. Ash looked over at Billy, his eyebrow raised in question, but Billy was looking at the wall, too.

A sudden *thunk* caused Ash to look back around. Nothing had changed as far as he could see. Then Matt reached out and pushed on the wall. A door-shaped panel of stone moved inward, and a light in the space beyond came on.

Matt started to go through the opening, but Ash hesitated. "You're not going to lock me in down there, are you?" He'd had his fill of confinement.

Matt paused. "Absolutely not. Besides this, there are two other ways out—one that exits in the dormitory where your room is, and another in the ruins of an old barn in the trees. We'll show you both, and I promise no doors will be locked behind you."

The two men watched Ash until he nodded and said, "Okay."

Stepping through the door, Ash found himself in a five-foot-by-five-foot room. As soon as Billy closed the secret panel, Matt put his hand on the wall. A small square section surrounding his palm lit up for several seconds. As soon as it went dark, the wall to their right slid open, revealing a set of stairs.

These were at least double the length of the ones that led down from the first floor into the regular basement. When the trio reached the bottom, Matt palmed the wall again, and a door popped open.

The only thing about this new level that said basement to Ash was the lack of windows. Otherwise, he thought it was very much like a high-tech military facility. There was a long central corridor running down the middle, with rooms and other hallways leading off to the sides.

"How big is this place?" he asked.

"The footprint's about twice as large as the Lodge," Matt explained as they walked down the corridor. "We can comfortably house fifty people down here for several months, if necessary. There are actually two more levels below this, but both are smaller and used only for storage." He pointed to the left, down an intersecting hallway. "There's a firing range down there, and our armory. That room…" He pointed at a door just head. "That's the IT room, where all our servers and other computer equipment live." He nodded at another hallway. "We have a small cafeteria down there, and several dorm rooms just on the other side of it."

"I thought bomb shelters went out with the fifties."

Matt glanced at him. "There are a lot more things to be scared of than just bombs."

"Like what?"

"Like viruses that get out of control," Billy said.

"Or, more importantly, the people behind them," Matt added. "Here we are."

He opened a set of double doors, then ushered Ash in. Billy's examination room upstairs was nothing compared to the full-on operating room they'd just entered.

Billy pushed past both of them, heading straight for a sink against the wall. "There's a shower and some gowns back there," he said to Ash, pointing at a door in the far corner. "When you're done, come back here and I'll throw a couple ideas at you."

Ten minutes later, they were all standing in front of a computer screen on a counter not far from the surgery table.

"If we had time, I'd do a lot more, but for now we need to achieve the biggest change we can with the minimum amount of downtime for you. Now, this is what I was—"

"I don't care what you do," Ash said.

"Don't you want to have some say?"

"I just want my kids back."

No one said anything for a moment.

Matt gave Ash's shoulder a pat. "I'll choose for him."

Billy looked at Ash, silently asking if that was okay, but Ash said nothing.

The ranch's doctor shrugged. "All right, then. Let's mark you up."

Rachel was sitting next to Ash's bed when he woke, a book in her lap. "How are you feeling?" she asked.

His whole head throbbed. "I'm fine. What time is it?"

"Nine."

"Evening, or...or morning."

"Evening. You haven't been out *that* long."

It had been two p.m. when the surgery began, so he'd been unconscious for seven hours. He tried to touch his face, but it seemed to be covered in bandages.

"You're a mess right now," she said. "But in a couple of months it'll all look normal to you."

He tried to push himself up, but couldn't. "I can't...wait a couple of...months."

"Of course not. We talked about that, remember?"

Did we? Maybe.

"Two days only, and we'll use that time to get you as prepared as possible."

Two days also seemed like too long. But what choice did he have? Without the new face, there was no chance he would ever even get close to his kids.

"Do you want to go back to sleep? Or get started?"

"Get started," he said, his voice still weak.

"Excellent." She picked up a folder that was on the stand by his bed. "Who are you?"

He squinted at her. "What?"

"You can't be Captain Daniel Ash anymore, so who are you?"

Now he understood what she meant. A false name. "I don't care. Anything. John Smith."

"I think we can do better than that. Besides, you're not just choosing for yourself, you're choosing for your kids, too."

He started to shake his head, but it only made it pound harder. He gave it a few seconds, then said, "Once people know what happened...we can go...back. Be ourselves again."

She gave him a sad, knowing smile. "I tell you what. Why don't we just pretend it's important for right now? Better safe than sorry, right?"

"Sure. Whatever," he replied, thinking he'd just choose the first name that came to mind. "How about—"

She touched his hand, stopping him. "I have some choices for you." She opened the folder. "Tell me which one of these grabs you. Tyler Wright, Harold Boyce, Adam Cooper, William Keys, or Samuel Hunter. Anything stand out?"

He honestly didn't care at all. "The third one," he said.

"Adam Cooper?"

"Yes."

"Why?"

He was silent for a moment. "Because I like the number three."

She raised an eyebrow, then laughed softly to herself. "You're sure?"

"Yes."

She shrugged, rifled through the papers in the folder, and

pulled one out. "All right, Mr. Cooper. Let's see exactly who you are."

22

Karl Trainer could have just let it go, but he wasn't that kind of friend. Besides, his route took him near Hector Mendez's house anyway, so stopping for a quick check to see why his friend hadn't shown up for work wouldn't be that big of a deal.

When he got there, the first thing he noticed was Hector's car still parked out front. He'd been hoping that maybe they'd just missed each other on the highway, and Hector was already at the warehouse. Of course, it could have been that his friend was having car troubles and had gotten one of his neighbors to drive him in. That would definitely explain why he was late.

Sure, that had to be it.

Karl almost drove off, but, hell, he was here anyway. Might as well check. He went up to the door and knocked.

No answer.

"See? Not home," he said to himself.

As he took a step off the porch to head back to his rig, the nape of his neck began to tingle.

"Dammit," he said.

His wife called it his whodoo-voodoo. He'd get it every once in a while, a feeling that something wasn't right. The feeling *itself* wasn't always right, either. Still, there were enough times it was that he'd learned not to completely ignore it.

With an exasperated sigh, he decided to have a look around.

He'd been to Hector's enough times that he knew its layout. Contrary to most of the houses he'd lived in, the living room in Hector's place was in the back. Up front were the spare bedroom and the kitchen.

He skipped the window to the spare bedroom because he

knew Hector only used it to store his mom's old stuff, and glanced into the kitchen. There was nothing unusual there. An empty beer bottle on the counter, but what house didn't have one of those now and then?

Hector's place was far enough out of town that he didn't need a fence. So Karl simply moved around the house and looked through the sliding glass door into the living room.

Nobody there. Nothing out of the ordinary. But that damn tingle wouldn't go away.

He moved along the back to the window that looked in on Hector's bedroom. The shade was pulled down, but the window was open about four inches so air could get inside.

"Hector?" he called through the gap.

Silence.

"He's not here," he said, trying to convince the tingle this was one of those times it was wrong. But it just kept burning away back there, in no apparent hurry to leave.

The screen over the window was loose, so it was a simple matter to pull it out a few inches, slip his hand behind it, and move the shade out of the way so he could take a look.

The room was dark, full of shadows, but the glow from the clock radio on the nightstand was bright enough that Karl could see someone lying on the bed. By the guy's shape, Karl was all but positive it was his friend.

"Hector, is that you? Buddy, what are you doing? It's after midnight. Hector. Hector! Wake up."

Hector didn't even twitch.

Karl's first thought was that his friend had had a heart attack. Hector did love his greasy burgers so it wouldn't be a huge surprise.

"Goddammit. I swear if you're dead, I'm going to be pissed!"

Not knowing what else to do, Karl pulled the screen all the way off, pushed the window out of the way, and climbed through the opening. There was a dresser just on the other side, and as much as he tried to be careful, he ended up knocking a few things onto the floor before his feet reached the carpet.

"Sorry," he said automatically.

Hector was lying on his side, facing away from him, so Karl moved around the bed, flicking on the bedroom light as he passed the switch.

It was Hector all right.

Karl put a hand on his friend's shoulder, and was surprised at how cold Hector felt.

"You okay, man?" he said, shaking him.

He touched his friend's neck, searching for a pulse. But there was nothing.

"Oh, God."

He was too late. Hector had already passed. As he started to pull his hand back, he noticed a whole pile of tissues, half on the bed, half on the floor below it. Without even thinking about it, he leaned down to take a closer look, then suddenly stopped himself and took a step back.

The previous night had been his off night, which meant he'd gone to bed a lot earlier and gotten up around noon. While he'd been sitting around the living room, flipping through the channels on the TV, he couldn't help but get sucked into the news about the deadly flu outbreak in Sage Springs. Some of the reporters were saying that so far anyone who caught the disease had died. By the evening, after his wife had come home and they were watching the news together, the reports gave the impression that the situation was under control.

But here was Hector, dead from what looked like the flu to Karl. And didn't Hector's route take him through Sage Springs?

He stumbled back further, falling to the floor, his hand touching something moist. Quickly, he pushed himself back to his feet, not taking the time to see what it was.

"Oh, Jesus. Oh, Jesus. Oh, Jesus."

Facing the bed as if he expected Hector to rise out of it and attack him, he moved back to the window and scrambled outside.

There, he doubled over and rubbed his face as he tried to catch his breath. After several seconds, he stood up, knowing he had to get out of there. He raced to his truck and reached up to open the door. That's when he saw it. The damp spot on the side of his hand. Water or...

...mucus. *Hector's snot.*

Instantly he thought about the moist spot he'd touched when he fell.

Eyes wide in panic, he dropped to the ground and wiped his hand against the asphalt, but he knew it was already too late. He'd rubbed his hand across his face. It could have gotten in his eyes, his nose, his mouth. Hell, chances were he'd been infected the moment he stepped into the room.

"Unofficial sources have told me that, so far, no one who has caught this flu has survived."

I'm a dead man.

Karl's mother had been a saint, at least to him. She'd been the nicest, kindest person he'd ever known. "Just doing what's right," she'd say. "Don't know how to live any other way." Karl had learned from her example and tried to live that way, too. He was a good son, then later a good husband, and a good friend, as was evident by his trip to check on Hector.

Kneeling there beside his truck, he knew there was only one right thing he could do now.

He made three phone calls as he drove away. The first was to 911, reporting Hector's death and warning them that it appeared to be related to the Sage Springs flu. The second was to work, telling them that Hector was sick and would be staying home, in case they were thinking about sending someone else out to check on him. He didn't mention his own plans, that he wouldn't be finishing his route, or, in fact, wouldn't even be starting it.

The third call was to his wife's cell phone. At that time of night, she would have turned it off, knowing if he *were* going to call, he'd use their landline. But he didn't want to talk to her. He just wanted to tell her he loved her one last time, so he said it to her voice mail, then turned off his phone and shoved it under his seat.

After that, he drove into the desert, away from the highway, and down a side road he was pretty sure no one would be on for several days. After he parked, he found a couple scraps of paper in the glove compartment and wrote two identical notes:

DEATH FLU VICTIM INSIDE
DO NOT OPEN DOORS
CALL CDC

He then put them on the windows of both doors, and settled in.

If he were still feeling okay by noon the next day, he'd drive back into town and take whatever punishment the company decided to give him.

But punishment was unnecessary. Karl Trainer never did drive back into town.

Unlike Karl, the three guys who'd had breakfast with Hector—Luis Chavez, Diego Ortega, and Al Rangel—were not blessed with the foreknowledge of what happened to them. So the virus that was believed to be contained in the small town of Sage Springs gained more and more of a foothold in Victorville with every person the three men came into contact with. This included, but was not limited to: the waitress and hostess at Kerry's Diner where they'd eaten, the customers at Ralph's supermarket between 11:41 a.m. and 12:03 p.m., Al Rangel's neighbor Charlie Fisher, and their respective spouses.

The disease then spread further through the eastern part of the city, clinging onto new hosts wherever it could. It was only by pure chance that none of those touched were heading over the hill into San Bernardino or Riverside or Orange County or Los Angeles. If that had happened, things could have gotten a whole lot worse.

Once again, Karl proved to be a hero. His call to 911 about Hector led to the entire town being shut down before sunrise, and the quarantine zone being expanded to a roughly triangular area that went from Victorville in the West, to China Lake in the North, to Barstow in the East.

When the calls of more sick and dead started coming in, at least it didn't catch anyone by surprise. And by luck and the quick work of the National Guard, the Victorville branch of the outbreak ran its course without spreading further.

Unfortunately, health officials in Victorville weren't the only ones who started receiving calls.

23

When Ash woke the morning after his surgery, the pain in his head had become more of a throb—a huge, pounding throb. Pax was asleep in a chair in the corner. Apparently he'd been given the late shift.

Carefully, Ash swung his legs off the bed, then walked, painful step after painful step, to the bathroom. When he finally came back out, Pax was awake.

"I'd have helped you if you needed it," Pax said, getting out of his chair.

"I didn't need it. Where are my clothes?"

"You should lie down. Take it easy."

"Where...are they?"

Pax frowned and shook his head. "I'll get 'em." He opened the closet next to the bathroom, pulled out a set of clean clothes, and laid them on the bed. "I'll wait for you outside."

It took Ash fifteen minutes to get dressed. When he walked out of the room, he found Pax leaning against the wall in the hallway. "Looks like you'll live," Pax said, giving Ash the once-over. "Come on. Everyone's in the cafeteria."

Ash knew he wasn't a pretty sight. He'd taken a look at himself in the mirror, not because he was curious, but because he wanted to remember what the people who'd done this to his family had forced him to do. He wanted to remember the bandages, and the swollen face, and the bruises. He wanted to remember it all.

The cafeteria was more like a wide spot in the corridor than a room to itself. There were four long tables and, at the back, a counter that opened into a kitchen.

Matt, Rachel, and Billy were sitting together at one of the

tables, while a woman Ash hadn't met before was sitting at the next one over, alone. She had coffee-colored skin and long, black hair. After a moment, he realized she might very well be the woman he'd seen doing shoulder exercises outside the day before.

In front of the tables was a TV on a cart. As soon as Ash and Pax walked up, Matt muted the volume, and the others got up and walked over to greet them. Everyone, that was, except the unknown woman.

"You should still be lying down," Billy reprimanded Ash.

"I think he looks fine," Rachel said. "How do you feel?"

"Sore," Ash told them. "But I'm not going to spend the day in bed."

Billy moved in close, examining the bandages and touching Ash's face. Twice, Ash winced.

"I can give you something for the pain," Billy offered.

"No."

Matt smiled. "You look fine to me. Well, except for your face. Come. Sit down."

As Ash took a seat, he glanced at the TV. They'd been watching the news.

"What happened while I was out?"

Rachel said, "Daniel Ash is officially a suspected terrorist."

He took a breath, trying to keep his anger in check, then nodded. "Just like you said."

On the screen, there was a shot of the desert. It was flat and brown and looked very much like the desert he'd seen on TV the previous day, and the desert he'd lived in for a month or so before...*it* happened.

The only difference today, though, was that instead of a steady shot, the picture was wildly jumping around. In the upper corner was a small graphic that read *Earlier Today*.

"What's going on?" he asked, nodding at the screen.

Matt grabbed the remote and deactivated the mute.

Out of the speaker came the sounds of pounding feet, cloth rubbing against cloth, heavy breathing, and wind whipping across a microphone. Whoever was carrying the camera was running.

"Watch out! Bobby, Bobby. Watch out!" a female voice said.

The camera tilted quickly to the ground, revealing an offset crack in the asphalt. The cameraman seemed to take a hop step, then the image moved back up.

"This way," the woman said.

As the lens turned to the left, the back of a young woman came into view. She glanced over her shoulder at the camera. It was the reporter Ash had watched on TV the day before.

"Just carry it, Bobby. You're going to fall otherwise."

The picture swung wildly for a few seconds, catching sky, then ground, then feet, before stabilizing at a lower angle. The girl was still in the picture, running just a few feet ahead. Visible now beyond her was a military helicopter. As the image moved a bit to the right, Ash realized there wasn't just one helicopter, but several.

The woman looked back again, this time her gaze moving well beyond the camera. "Joe! Hurry up!"

There were uniformed soldiers standing outside the open doors of the helicopter. As soon as the reporter got there, one of the soldiers grabbed her arm and helped her up.

"All the way in, ma'am. All the way in," he ordered.

When the cameraman got there, the procedure was repeated. Once more the image became chaotic, then settled back down and angled out the door the cameraman had just come through.

There were several dozen people running through the desert toward the helicopters. In the distance, Ash could see cars and media vans parked along the highway, and the same large military trucks that had been blocking the road since the previous day.

Seven people seemed to be heading for the cameraman's helicopter. One of the soldiers took a few steps toward them.

"Only room for four more! Only four!" he yelled, holding up four fingers. He then pointed at the three people farthest away. "You, you, and you! Over there!" He directed them to a neighboring helicopter, but none of the three changed course. "No more room here! You're over there!"

The four who were okayed to get on reached the helicopter and climbed aboard.

"Glad you could join us," the reporter said to one of the men. Ash guessed he was probably the Joe she'd been yelling to earlier.

The other three were still coming, so the soldier who had been trying to redirect them got between them and the helicopter, then moved the rifle that had been slung over his shoulder into his hands. He wasn't exactly pointing it at them, but he was making it clear he could.

"No. Room. Here. That one!" He tilted his head at the other aircraft.

This time the three stragglers got the message.

The soldier and his buddy who'd been outside with him jumped through the door, then yelled up front, "We're good to go."

Almost immediately the helicopter lifted off. There was a final bird's-eye shot of the desert, with Sage Springs laid out in the distance, then the image on the screen switched to the anchor in the studio.

"Those startling images were taken by cameraman Bobby Lion. With him was PCN reporter Tamara Costello and their producer Joe Canavo. The video was shot earlier this morning as they were evacuated out of the expanded quarantine zone that now stretches over a large portion of the Mojave Desert in Eastern California. As a reminder, if you are watching us from within the quarantine zone, you are asked to stay in your homes until further advised and avoid contact with anyone other than those who are already in your home with you."

"It's spread?" Ash asked.

"Several cases reported in Victorville this morning," Billy said. "That's just northeast of L.A. They're also calling it the Sage Flu now."

"My God."

"You'll want to watch this," Rachel said, still looking at the TV.

"…alert for this man." The anchor had been replaced by the same picture of Ash the networks had already been showing. "Daniel Ash, a captain in the U.S. Army, is now thought to be behind this terrorist attack. His motives are unknown at this time, but sources do tell us he'd been showing signs of instability since returning from a tour of duty in Afghanistan. As we learned earlier this morning, this tragedy was made worse by the discovery that Ash apparently killed his own family prior to releasing the lethal virus."

The image changed to a picture of Ash with Ellen, Josie and Brandon.

All Ash could do was stare at the screen. Any doubts he may have had about what Matt and the others had told him—gone. Completely.

"That's enough," he finally said, then stood up. "I want to get to work."

"Sure," Matt said. "But why don't we get you some breakfast first?"

"I'm not hungry."

"You're going to need to eat something," Billy said.

"I said I'm not hungry. So what's next?"

Matt shared a look with Rachel, then glanced at Pax. "Weapons?"

"Sounds good to me," Pax said. He rose to his feet and smiled at Ash. "How about a little target practice?"

"Lead the way."

The door Pax stopped in front of not only had two deadbolts, but also a thumbprint-recognition screen that released steel rods holding the door in place from above and below. Inside was the armory. Weapons hung on all the walls, while more were stored on shelves.

"Most of these never get used," Pax explained. "They're here more for education, so we're familiar with anything we might come up against."

"Are you guys like some sort of militia? Is that what this is?"

Pax was silent for a moment. "That's really a hard question to answer. I guess in some people's minds we might be called that. But our purpose isn't to create our own little country, or take on the government, per se. But you should really talk to Matt about that. He's the explainer. Me, I'd just mess it up." He flashed a quick smile. "When was the last time you fired a handgun?"

"I don't know. Four or five months ago."

"How good are you?"

"Good enough. Better with a rifle."

"Probably gonna want to avoid rifles for a while," Pax said. "If that butt's in your shoulder and it kicks off and hits you in the face, you will not be happy. Of course, you could have the same problem with a pistol if you can't control the recoil." He smiled again.

"Break your nose all over again. That's not my idea of fun."

"Don't worry. I can control the recoil."

"Thought you could." Pax smiled. "How about a little pistol refresher? Sound good to you?"

"Sure."

Hanging on one wall were at least a hundred different handguns.

"The Army issue you an M9?" Pax asked.

"Yeah."

"I could pull down one of those, if you like, but I prefer one of these three here." Pax removed three pistols from the wall.

"I'm not married to the M9, so if you've got something better, great."

Near the door were two floor-to-ceiling cabinets.

"Here," Pax said, handing the guns to Ash.

With his hands free, Pax pulled a couple boxes of ammunition out of one of the cabinets. He then motioned Ash back into the hallway, and led him to the door on the opposite wall.

"Right in here," he said as he unlocked the door and pulled it open.

Ash could sense the depth of the room even before Pax flipped on the lights and revealed a space that moved out from the door for at least fifty yards. Not too far in was a row of narrow dividers, and tracks along the ceiling that ran the length of the room. A classic indoor firing range.

Pax set the boxes of bullets on the shelf of the middle divider, then took the guns back. "As you might have noticed, we've got three compacts here, all nine millimeter like your old M9." He set two of the guns down, then held up the third. "This one's a Smith & Wesson M&P Compact. Twelve rounds plus one in the chamber. Trigger pull at six and a half pounds." He put it down, and picked up the next one. "Glock 19. Fifteen rounds standard. Five and a half pounds on the trigger pull." He replaced it with the last. "And this one's the SIG SAUER P229. It holds thirteen rounds. Single-action trigger pull at four-point-four pounds. So, which would you like to try first?"

Ash decided to take them in order, starting with the Smith & Wesson. Although he had no problem controlling the kick, he could feel the first few shots all the way up his arms and into his head. Once he got going, though, the pain became more background noise than anything else.

Next he went to the Glock, then the SIG. After he took the last shot, Pax said, "So?"

Ash looked at the gun in his hand. "I like the feel of this one."

"Good choice. One of my favorites. Of course, I'm partial to all three of them, so you couldn't go wrong whichever way you went. You want to shoot some more?"

"Yes." Ash popped the mag out and handed it to Pax. "I'd like to tighten up my groupings."

With Pax's help, by the time Ash had polished off the last round in the second box of ammo, his groupings at fifty feet could be covered by a dollar bill.

"It's a good start," Pax said.

"Get another box."

Pax looked at him, surprised. "Don't want to take a break?"

Ash released the mag into his hand. "No."

As he plowed through the third box of bullets, he pictured the face of Dr. Karp on the target.

This time, his groupings were much better.

24

The members of the media who'd been covering the road-block at Sage Springs were flown to Fort Irwin Army base outside Barstow, California. Technically, they were still in the quarantine zone, but so far there had been no known cases in Barstow or on the base.

There, Tamara was able to learn that contingents of soldiers had been sent east on I-40 and northeast on I-15 to turn back motorists coming in from Arizona and Las Vegas. She'd also had an interesting, off-the-record conversation with one soldier who'd said the roadblocks had already dealt with several irate drivers insisting that they didn't have time to drive all the way to the I-10 to get to L.A. so they should be let through. Many promised to "keep their windows rolled up" and "not make any stops," while a couple of people had even gotten out of their cars and tried to physically intimidate the highway patrol officers who were handling most of the problems. Needless to say, those individuals had been arrested and taken east to a jail just on the other side of the Nevada border.

Even having learned all that, Tamara was frustrated. The Army was not allowing them to go anywhere. It was like the media were prisoners on the base, stuck with whatever news the Army decided to give them.

To add to her annoyance, her brother still hadn't gotten back to her. He'd given her that great lead then *poof*—disappeared. She'd just tried to call him again, but when she got his voice mail once more, she'd hung up and called her parents.

"Tammy, please tell me everything's fine," her mother said. The last time Tamara could call them had been the previous day right after the news broke. "We've been glued to the TV every second we've been awake. They keep showing that part where you and your friends are running to the helicopters. I wish they'd stop that. It nearly gives me a heart attack every time."

"Mom, just turn it off when it comes on," Tamara said. "Or just switch to another channel."

"I couldn't do that. Your ratings."

Tamara's mom had it in her mind that every single household was monitored and counted in a network's ratings. Even if that were true, PCN's ratings wouldn't have suffered from the temporary loss of one viewer. Especially not now, when Tamara was sure that if a TV was on somewhere, it was tuned to one of the news channels.

"Mom, have you heard from Gavin?"

"No, dear. But you know your brother. He gets tunnel vision. Probably working on a project."

Tamara frowned. He did get tunnel vision at times, but he'd never let her down like this before. "Okay. Thanks. That's all I wanted to know."

"Tammy?" her dad said. He'd obviously been listening in on the other line. "Have you talked to your boss? They need to get you out of there. You're right in the middle of everything."

"I'm a news correspondent, Dad. I'm *always* in the middle of things. Besides, everything's fine here. The closest outbreak is at least fifty miles away."

"But you never know, sweetie. The sooner you get out of there, the better your mother and I are going to feel."

"Don't worry so much. I'll be fine." She noticed Joe trying to wave her over to where the majority of the media was hanging out. "Look, I've got to go. I love you."

"We love you, too," her mother said.

"Very much," her dad added.

"Okay. Bye."

She hung up, then hurried over to her producer. "What's up?"

"Just got off the phone with Irene," he whispered. Irene was their boss in New York. "She says they've been negotiating with the Army to get us taken out to the I-15 roadblock."

"That's great!"

"What's great?" Peter Chavez, a reporter with one of the wire services, turned and asked.

"Uh, nothing, Peter," Joe said, then smiled. "Just...telling Tammy about what I'm getting my wife for her birthday."

Peter didn't look convinced. "Really?"

"Yeah," Tamara said, trying to cover her mistake. "He's taking her to Paris. Isn't that cool?"

Peter frowned. "Guess salaries are nicer over there at Generic Cable News."

"I guess they are," Joe replied. He then grabbed Tamara's arm and moved her away from the crowd. "What an ass."

"When will we know about going to the roadblock?" she whispered.

"I'm not sure. Soon, I hope."

Not too far away, a TV had been set up under a canopy so that people with nothing to do could watch. The screen suddenly filled with some jumpy, low-quality video, catching Tamara's eye.

"What's that?" she asked.

Joe looked over and shook his head. "I don't know."

Quickly they both made their way to the back of the group watching the television.

"Bobby," Tamara said, noticing her cameraman a couple people ahead of her.

When he turned, she motioned for him to join them in the back.

As soon as he moved in beside her, she asked, "What *is* that?"

"Somebody just uploaded it to the Internet," he said. "Some sort of skirmish at a roadblock just east of Tehachapi."

Tehachapi was west of the town of Mojave, which was in the quarantine zone, and east of Bakersfield, which was not.

The footage looked like it had been shot on a camera phone. There were several dozen people pushing and shoving. Most were civilians, but there were a few people in uniforms, too.

This went on for several seconds, then a face flashed across the screen that caused Tamara to jerk back, startled.

It was Gavin, or someone who sure looked a hell of a lot like him. She pushed her way through the crowd so she could get closer to the screen.

Whoever was holding the camera seemed to be moving slightly away from the crowd. She could see the whole mob now, pushing and shoving at each other. She tried to find the guy who looked like Gavin, but didn't see him.

A voice cut over the video, distorted by the poor quality of the camera's microphone.

"Most of these guys...I think have family...in the...zone." The speaker's voice was punctuated by deep breaths. "They want to get in...but...the soldiers are...trying to push them...back. It looks like some...people are getting through."

The shot zoomed in on a small group that was trying to go around the end of the roadblock while the soldiers were busy with the larger crowd. Suddenly several members of the big group saw what was happening and took off after the others, no doubt hoping that they, too, could get through. The trickle became a stream, then a river.

At the edge of the pack, two soldiers went down. As soon as their colleagues saw this, they opened fire.

"Oh, my God!" someone standing near Tamara yelled out as civilians started falling to the ground.

But Tamara couldn't even speak. She had seen Gavin again. He was wearing one of the shirts she'd given him for Christmas. And when the chaos was at its height, it looked very much like a bullet had hit him, too. Only unlike the others, he hadn't fallen away from the roadblock, but toward it, like he'd been shot from the other direction. And then there was the look on his face a moment before he went down, a look of disorientation and confusion.

Like he had no idea what he was doing there in the first place.

The pressure in her head built until she could almost take it no more. How she didn't scream, she had no idea.

There was another conference call at noon. Since this one had been arranged ahead of time, they were connected via video chat. Though both Dr. Karp and Major Ross were at the Marin County location, each was in his own office. Shell was in a hotel room somewhere near the quarantine zone, and the Director of Preparation was at Bluebird. Of course the DOP's feed was blacked out. The project's number one guideline was that the members of the Bluebird Directorate were to remain anonymous.

"Dr. Karp, do you have the latest statistics on the outbreak?" the DOP asked.

The doctor leaned forward a few inches. "I talked to our source at the CDC five minutes ago, so the numbers I'm about to give you are as up to date as possible. Dead—three hundred and twenty-one. Currently infected—five hundred and seventeen. This information, of course, has not been released to the public yet. But I doubt they will be getting any—"

"That's enough for the moment," the DOP said, cutting him off. "Mr. Shell, your update, please."

"Yes, sir," Shell said, adjusting himself in his chair. "On the quarantine front, state and military officials have a pretty good handle on containment for the majority of the population. Fortunately, the outbreak occurred in an open and underpopulated area."

"It was not *fortunate*, Mr. Shell," Dr. Karp broke in. "It was by design. Why do you think we chose Barker Flats in the first place?"

"Thank you, doctor," the DOP said. "Mr. Shell, please continue."

Shell took a loud, annoyed breath, then said, "As you know, our strategy is one of plugging the holes the official response can't handle. With your help, Director, I have my main team using Fort Irwin in Barstow as its base. Thank you for making that happen." He paused, but the DOP said nothing. "I, uh, also have a team set up at a private airfield north of Victorville. Using thermal satellite imagery, we have been able to track in real time individuals who've tried to get out of the zone over the open desert. So far there have been twenty-eight attempts, and my people have stopped all of them." There was no need for him to say what stopping meant. They all knew he was tasked with removing problems, not jailing them.

"Do you have any idea how many of those were actually infected?"

"Obviously, we wouldn't be able to know that without proper tests, but I can say with confidence that six showed outward signs of KV-27a infection. My teams continue to monitor the intel, and are ready to move on any new escape attempts at a moment's notice."

"It's critical that no one gets out," the DOP said.

"Yes, sir. Of course."

"Please continue."

"Yes, sir. There was the matter of the reporter's brother."

"Yes. Gavin Costello. A mistake to pick him up in the first place."

Shell looked uncomfortable. "Yes, sir. Things were a little fluid at that point, and there was no telling what he might dig up for his sister."

"Mr. Shell, I'm not fond of glossing over mistakes. There was nothing for him to dig up that would have harmed us. It was a mistake from the beginning."

"Yes, sir."

Dr. Karp kept his expression neutral, but inside he was laughing as Shell squirmed.

"Continue your report."

"Concerning Gavin Costello. Unfortunately, we couldn't just let him go, especially given his sister's high-profile job. Elimination was the only answer. We started spreading a rumor among people who were stranded in the Bakersfield area that the roadblock east of Tehachapi was going to be opened. When they arrived and found that it was still closed and would remain so, with the prodding of some of my men scattered within the group, they rioted. As soon as the military opened fire, one of my men eliminated Mr. Costello. When he is finally identified, his presence can easily be explained as concern for his sister."

"And Ash?" the DOP asked.

"As you know we traced the original car to a parking garage at a casino in Nevada. I then gave a team instructions to trace the paths of every car that left that garage in the following four hours."

Shell's face was replaced by a thermal satellite image. Along the left side was a busy freeway running basically from bottom to top. It was covered with dozens of bright, warm blobs indicating vehicles.

"Please notice the spot near the midpoint of the picture. This is the most likely candidate."

The spot in question was down an empty road that led off from the freeway. It was faint, but definitely warmer than the surrounding area.

"We were able to trace this car from the casino to this point. The heat signature you are looking at was generated by a person sitting inside a car. When it arrived here, there were two people, one up front, and one lying in the back. The driver got out, walked to the road, and was picked up three minutes later." He then explained how the person in back got out, and eventually took a seat up front. He showed another picture. In this one, a larger vehicle was parked next to the smaller one. "The man transferred to the new vehicle and they left."

"Were you able to follow it, too?" the DOP asked.

Shell hesitated. "We were able to follow them south for about twenty minutes. But we experienced a transmission problem that took us off line for an hour. In that gap, we lost them."

"So you're no closer to finding him now than you were earlier."

"We are very hopeful that Dr. Karp's suggestion of exposing Ash through the media will work," Shell said, surprising Karp with his implied praise. "At the very least, it will be a long time before he can ever show his face again. Which means he'll be unable to cause us any problems."

"We don't want that to be a reason for you to stop looking, though," the DOP said.

"Of course not. It's a top priority."

"Have we figured out yet who was behind his escape?"

"By the level of organization involved, I think we're dealing with the same people who aided Lauren Scott last year."

Lauren Scott? The doctor hadn't thought of her in a while.

"Thank you, Mr. Shell. You and Major Ross are excused."

"Yes, sir," Major Ross said.

"Thank you, sir," Mr. Shell replied.

A moment later, *Connection Terminated* appeared where both of their faces had been.

"Dr. Karp," the DOP said.

The doctor straightened in his chair. "Yes, sir?"

"First, progress on the vaccine?"

"As I've stated before, these things take time, but we feel like we're getting very close now."

"And the problem with the different reactions between the

sexes?"

"We're confident that we'll have that solved shortly."

"Good. See that it is," the DOP said. "Now, about the virus. I do not want Mr. Shell privy to any of the...safeguards. Is that understood?"

"Yes, sir," the doctor said, a bit unsure. "May I ask why, sir?"

There was no response for a moment, then, "Let's just say that your virus is not the only thing that's being tested."

Before Dr. Karp could say anything else, the black screen that represented the Director of Preparation was suddenly replaced by the words *Connection Terminated.*

25

The orderly was glad that they'd finally decided to room his two patients together. It had decidedly improved both their spirits, and made keeping an eye on them easier for him.

He watched them in the monitor, talking to each other.

The boy was sitting on his sister's bed. He usually did that. The girl, while markedly improved, was still taking her time fully recovering. She tired easily, and still wasn't eating enough to remove the IV from her arm.

The orderly turned up the volume so he could hear.

"…mise?" the boy asked.

"Of course."

"Then I promise, too."

She held out her arms and he fell into them, letting her hug him tight.

A few tears rolled down the boy's face, but the orderly could see that he was attempting to be strong, attempting to be an adult years before he should even think about it.

"If they try," the boy said, "I won't let them."

"I won't let them, either," his sister told him. "We only have each other now, so we have to stick together."

The boy nodded. Several moments passed, then he said, "Do you really think there's a heaven?"

She stroked his head. "Yes, of course."

"So Mom and Dad are there? Thinking about us?"

"I think they're thinking about us as much as we're thinking about them."

"I'm thinking about them all the time."

"Exact—"

The orderly turned the sound down, wishing he had done so sooner.

Paul Unger and Nick Regan were half-brothers and best friends. Paul was a year older than Nick, and though he had an on-again, off-again relationship with his birth father, he really considered Nick's dad his, too.

While they lived in Randsburg, California, Paul and Nick attended high school twenty-five miles away in Ridgecrest. That meant they had to get up earlier every morning than most people in town so they could catch the bus.

The morning of the quarantine, their mom, as she always did, flipped on the TV to catch the news while they ate breakfast. Even at that early hour, the quarantine had already been enlarged.

"Sarge!" their mom had yelled. "Sarge, quick! You have to see this."

Their dad—Nick's biological and Paul's chosen—rushed into the kitchen, pulling a robe over the gym shorts and T-shirt he usually slept in.

"What is it?"

She turned up the television, and the four of them watched with growing horror as the news reported the expanding outbreak and the new quarantine zone. When a map showing the actual boundary lines of the zone appeared on the screen, the true realization of their situation hit home.

"That's us, Dad," Nick said. "We're in the zone."

On the screen, the anchor said, "The CDC is asking all those in the Sage Flu quarantine zone to remain in their homes, and to avoid contact with anyone else. If you have questions, or are in need of medications, medical attention, or do not have enough food in your house, an 800 number has been set up to provide assistance." The promised number appeared on the screen.

Nick smiled. "I guess this means the bus isn't coming."

"Even if it does, you're not getting on it," his mother said, taking him more seriously than he meant.

Paul glanced at his stepdad. "The people who are sick are a long way away from here. Why are they making us stay inside?"

Sarge had come into marriage and family after spending twenty years in the Army, so he was a bit older father than most of the kids had. He was also a bit more experienced, having traveled the world and worked in, among other places, several base hospitals. So although Sarge didn't have a medical degree, Paul knew his stepdad might actually know the answer, or at least have an educated guess.

But if he did, he kept it to himself, because he only said, "They're probably just being cautious."

In a way, that answer scared Paul more than something concrete would have.

With little else to do, they, like most of the people in the zone, stayed indoors glued to the television. So they were all sitting in the living room in the early afternoon when the video of the Tehachapi roadblock riot was played. As soon as it ended, Sarge picked up the remote and turned the TV off.

The others looked at each other, confused, then Nick said, "Dad?"

Sarge stared at the television screen, saying nothing.

"Dad, what is it?"

After another moment, Sarge took a deep breath, then looked around at his family.

"Boys, can you give your mother and me a moment, please?"

"Why?" Paul asked. "What is it?"

"Please," Sarge said again.

"Sure," Nick said, standing. "Sure. No problem. Come on, Paul."

Paul hesitated a second, looking at Sarge, then rose and followed his brother into the hallway that led to their shared bedroom. Nick was going to head all the way back, but as soon as they were out of their parents' sight, Paul grabbed his brother's arm, put a finger to his own lips and said, "Shhhh." He pulled Nick down to the floor, and they crawled back to the open end of the hallway to listen.

"You can't know that," their mother said, sounding scared.

"Vonda, this is going to get worse before it gets better, maybe a lot worse. They want us to stay in our homes, but we're still sitting ducks here. The only way we can insure the boys don't get sick is to get them out of here, out of this zone."

"They're shooting people who were trying to get *in*. They

won't even think twice about doing the same to someone trying to get out."

"I've been thinking about that, and I think I might know a way."

"What *way* are you talking about?" she asked.

"Better if I tell them at the same time."

"I don't know. I'd rather they just stay here."

"Sweetheart, we can't argue about this. It's our boys' lives we're talking about. If they stay here, I think there's a good chance they're going to die."

There was silence for a moment, then, "Okay."

Sarge suddenly raised his voice. "Boys?"

Paul motioned for Nick to crawl back down the hallway with him.

"Boys! Come back out here!"

Once they reached the door to their room, Paul said, "What?"

"Come out here," Sarge said. "Your mother and I need to talk to you."

A few seconds later, they were all sitting around the living room.

"I think the news people aren't telling us everything," Sarge began. "My guess is they probably haven't even been told themselves. Here's the thing. I think this illness is a lot worse than they're making it out to be. The reason we're in the zone now is because someone who was sick must have passed through this area at some point. That means there's a chance someone right here in town is infected, maybe more than one." He looked down at his hands for a second, then back at the boys. "The bottom line is, you can't stay here. If you do, you might die. Part of our jobs as parents is doing everything we can to keep our kids alive. So I want you two to get out of the quarantine area."

"What about you and Mom?" Nick asked. "You're coming with us, right?"

"My hip would never make it," Sarge said. It was something that had bothered him for years. "And your mother…"

He seemed unable to finish, so their mom said, "I'd only slow you down."

"No, you wouldn't," Nick argued.

But they all knew she would. Their mom had put on some weight over the years. Not enough to be called fat, but enough to make her winded after a long walk.

"She's staying with me," Sarge said. "That's not open for discussion."

He pushed himself out of his recliner and went over to the desk in the corner. He searched through several of the drawers before he found what he was looking for and came back.

It turned out to be a map of Eastern California. He unfolded it and spread it out on the coffee table.

"You'll take your dirt bikes. We'll top off the gas from the tank in the car. Then you'll head out this way." He drew a path east across the map, toward Nevada.

"There's no road there," Nick said.

"I think that's the point," Paul told him.

"They'll be expecting people to head west or south," Sarge said. "That's where the cities are. And you can't go north because China Lake's right up there. The Navy will have that whole area blocked off. They'll never think anyone would go east." He tapped the map. "When you get past this point, you'll be out of the zone. Get on the first road you see, and keep going into Nevada. When you get there, keep a low profile, and don't let anyone know where you're from."

"I'll put some food together," their mom said, already heading toward the kitchen. "You can carry it in one of your backpacks."

"You'll need some money," Sarge said. "I got about five hundred dollars stashed away. I'll give that to you. But I don't know how long you're going to be out there on your own, so make it last."

"We will," Paul said.

Nick stared at his brother. "We're really going to do this? We're going to leave them?"

"Yes. You are," Sarge said before Paul could reply. "Now go get changed. You're going to need some warm clothes. The nights still get cold." As they headed toward the back, he added, "And bring your sleeping bags."

Sarge decided they should wait until just after sunset to leave. When the time finally came, the boys rolled their dirt bikes out of the garage. Paul's was an old Honda, while Nick's was an even older Yamaha, both 125s. Each boy was wearing two T-shirts, a sweater, a jacket, a pair of jeans, and long johns.

"Promise me you won't ride without your helmets," their mother said.

"We won't," Paul told her.

"And you'll call us once you're out."

"Yes. Yes."

Though they were carrying their cell phones, chances were they wouldn't have a signal out in the middle of the desert. But even if they did, Sarge told them not to use the phones until they were out of the zone, in case someone could track them.

Nick and Paul both hugged their mom.

"Remember, walk your bikes through town," Sarge said. "Don't start 'em up until you reach the other side of the highway. Better if nobody knows you've gone."

"Yes, sir," Paul said.

Sarge shook hands with his sons. "You guys take care of each other. Now, get a move on it."

Their house was on the western edge of town. The boys walked their bikes to the street, turned and gave their parents a long, final wave before heading east.

Randsburg was deathly quiet as they moved through town. It wasn't a big place to begin with, but there was usually someone outside at this time of the evening. But if not for the lights in several of the windows, it would have seemed like the place was deserted.

As they neared the western end, Paul said, "I need to make a stop first."

Nick looked at him for a moment, then his eyes widened in understanding. He shook his head. "Dad said no stops."

"I don't care. I'm not leaving without telling her goodbye."

"I don't think that's a good idea."

"Then keep going, and I'll catch up to you."

Nick stopped. "I'm not going without you."

"And I'm not going without talking to her," Paul said, halting beside him.

They stared at each other for several seconds, then Nick said, "Fine. But make it quick, okay?"

Paul smiled, and started pushing his bike again. "Sure. No problem."

As they walked up to Lisa Jennings's house, Paul sent her a text telling her to come outside, but not to tell anyone. Less than sixty seconds later, the kitchen door opened and she stepped out.

As soon as she saw Paul, she ran over and threw her arms around him.

"I'm so scared," she said.

"We all are," Paul told her.

They held each other for a few minutes, kissing a couple times, but mostly hugging. Finally, she noticed that Nick was there, too, then she saw the motorcycles and her face scrunched in confusion.

"What are you guys doing with your motorcycles? You heard everyone's supposed to stay home, right?"

"Uh, yeah," Paul said. "We know."

"Then what are you doing?"

"Come on. We got to go," Nick said.

"Go where?" Lisa asked.

Paul glanced at Nick.

Nick shook his head, then leaned toward his brother and whispered, "Dad doesn't want anyone to know we left, remember?"

"She won't tell," Paul said, not bothering to lower his voice.

"Tell what?" Lisa asked.

Paul hesitated only a moment before he spilled the whole plan to her. If he couldn't trust Lisa, whom could he trust?

As soon as he finished, she said, "I'm coming with you."

"I don't think that's a good idea. It's going to be dangerous."

"As dangerous as hanging around here waiting for the Sage Flu to get me?"

Nick stood silently by his bike, saying nothing, but the look on his face clearly showed he didn't think Lisa coming along was a good idea.

"What about your parents?" Paul asked.

"Dad's not even here. Got stuck in L.A. when this thing happened." She tilted her head toward the house. "Mom doesn't have to go to work at the motel tonight, so she's been drunk off her ass all day. Finally passed out thirty minutes ago. She won't notice." She looked over at Nick. "I don't want to stay here. I don't want to die."

Nick frowned, but then he nodded and said, "Okay."

Five minutes later, as the three of them were walking down the road toward the highway, Lisa's mother, still passed out on the couch, coughed.

26

Ash woke thirty minutes before dawn. In the bathroom, he peeled off most of the bandages that covered his head. His face was still swollen, though much less so than it had been the previous day. Bruises still encircled his eyes and covered his cheeks. Those, he knew, would be with him long after the swelling disappeared.

He studied himself in the mirror, trying to figure out what he would look like once trauma caused by the surgery had passed, but his imagination failed him. He'd have two eyes, two ears, a nose, and a mouth. Ultimately, that was all that was important.

After shooting practice the previous day, Pax had given him an extensive tour of the subterranean facility, and set him up with access to the computer room and the well-equipped gym.

The gym was where he headed as he exited his room at 5:45 a.m.

He was surprised to find someone else already there. It was the woman from the day before, the one he'd seen in the cafeteria but hadn't met yet.

She'd been doing stomach crunches as he walked in, but the second she heard him her head whipped around like he'd scared her.

"Sorry," he said. He took a few steps in her direction. "I'm Ash."

As she got off the bench, he thought she was going to walk over and shake his hand, but instead, she headed quickly to the wall, made her way around him in as wide an arc as she could, then exited the room without saying a word.

He stared after her, confused, but ultimately she wasn't important. There was work to do.

He had to be selective in what exercises he did so he wouldn't rupture the stitches that seemed to cover his head, but he was still able to get in a good workout.

After a shower, he went back to the firing range and spent two hours working with the SIG. His groupings had gotten to the point where they were consistent from set to set.

His next stop was the cafeteria for breakfast. Bobbi was in the kitchen, apparently on temporary assignment from upstairs. She made him an omelet with bacon and toast on the side. As he was finishing up, Pax arrived, holding a sweatshirt in his hand.

"Just took a look at your work on the range," Pax said. "We're going to have to offer you a place on our target shooting team."

Ash glanced at him, then returned his attention to his food.

"Bobbi, you got some more eggs back there?" Pax called out.

"You already had your breakfast upstairs," she told him.

"Doesn't mean I'm not still hungry."

"Doesn't mean I have to cook for you again, either."

Pax made a sour face toward the kitchen. "It's not like I have time to eat anymore anyway." He looked at Ash's plate. "You done?"

"Why? You want this?"

There was still half a piece of uneaten toast, but Pax shook his head.

"No. I need to take you up to see Matt."

As they walked toward the stairs, Pax handed the sweatshirt to Ash. "Put this on."

The sweatshirt was zip-up style with a hood. Ash figured it must be a little cold topside, so he did as Pax instructed.

"Hood, too," Pax told him.

"Why?"

"In case anyone's watching."

"Watching?"

"You'd be surprised how good surveillance is these days. Can see right through a window from miles away."

"That sounds a little paranoid."

"Welcome to our world."

At Matt's office, Pax opened the door for Ash, but didn't go inside with him.

Matt was the only one there, sitting at his desk and writing something in a hardbound notebook.

He looked up. "You're looking better today."

"Not as good as I'd like," Ash said.

"I can understand that. Have a seat."

Matt wrote something else in the notebook, then closed it and leaned back, considering Ash.

"What?" Ash asked. "Has something happened?"

Two quiet seconds passed. "The guy who helped you get out of Barker Flats wasn't our only inside source." He paused, then put his forearms on the desk and leaned forward. "We got a message this morning from another one of our people that appears to indicate time might be getting short for your kids."

"What was the message?" Ash asked quickly.

"The number four."

Ash furrowed his brow.

"It's simple code," Matt went on. "It means danger."

"Can you find out what kind of danger?"

"It doesn't work that way. This was all he was in a position to tell us."

"At the very least, can he give us their location?

Matt was silent for a moment. "We're pretty sure we already know where they are."

"What? You know?"

"You'll leave in three hours."

Pushing his chair back and standing, Ash said, "I need to leave *now!*"

"That's as soon as our plane can get back here. If you leave now, you'd still get there quicker if you wait. I know it's not easy, but we can use the time to finish prepping you as best we can."

Matt pressed a button on his desk phone.

There was a single ring, then Rachel's voice said, "Are you ready?"

"Yes. Bring her in." He hung up, then looked back at Ash. "Sit down. Please. I promise you we're doing everything we can."

It took all of Ash's effort to lower himself into the seat. Moments after he did, the door opened, and Rachel and the girl from the gym entered.

The girl's long black hair had been pulled into a ponytail when she'd been working out, but now, except for a strand she twisted nervously in her fingers, it hung free over her shoulders.

Rachel had a hand on the woman's back, urging her across the room. As they neared, Ash stood. Instantly, the woman took a quick step back.

"It's all right, Chloe," Rachel said. "We've already talked about this. He's not one of them."

One of what? Ash wanted to ask, but he held it in, not wanting to scare the woman again.

Finally, Chloe gave Rachel a nod.

"Good," Rachel said in a calm voice. "Chloe, this is…" She stopped and looked at Ash. "What do you want to be called? Adam? Cooper?"

"Ash, if it's all right by you," he said.

She smirked. "Your call." To Chloe, she said, "His name is Adam Cooper, but he apparently goes by Ash. Ash, this is Chloe White."

"Hello," he said, trying to keep his voice gentle.

Chloe cringed a bit, but didn't retreat. "Hi." There was a momentary lull, then she said, "You're *not* one of them, are you?"

"I don't know what you're talking about."

Chloe motioned at Rachel and Matt. "They say you're in the Army."

"Yes…well, I don't know now. Maybe."

"Some of them are in the Army. Not a lot, but some."

Ash looked her in the eyes. "I've only been in the Army. Nothing else."

"You're sure?"

"Absolutely."

She nodded to herself several times. "Okay, okay. I'm sorry. I just…I don't want to…go back, you know?"

"Go back where?" Ash asked.

"It doesn't matter. I don't want to think about it. Please don't make me think about it."

"Come on, Chloe," Rachel said quickly. "There are a few things we need to take care of before you leave."

Chloe allowed herself to be led back to the door. Once there, she turned to Ash and said, "Nice to meet you. I'm sorry. I'm not…I'm not always like this."

As soon as she and Rachel were gone, Ash looked at Matt. "What was that all about?"

"She'll be going with you."

"Her? Why?"

"She's your guide."

Ash stared at him. "Did you not just see her?"

"She's the only one familiar with the facility your children are in."

Ash glanced back at the door. "This girl can really help me?"

"Yes. She can." Matt paused. "You need to understand that these people did something to her while she was with them. She used to be strong, uncompromising, but they broke her before we could get to her. Piece by piece she's putting it back together, but it's slow. Most of her life…well, let's just say that it's like she's starting out again. Sometimes she slips. Maybe we shouldn't have told her you were in the Army, but it was better it came out now than later. She'll be okay."

"If she's taking me to where these people are, isn't there a danger she'll slip again?"

Matt hesitated. "Perhaps. But you were a surprise to her, an unknown. She already knows what to expect where you're both going."

"Are any of the rest of you coming?"

"I wish we could. This…outbreak has stretched our resources. We're already working with a skeleton crew here. If any of us leaves, it'll make it all that more difficult to support the rest of our organization, and many are in just as much danger as you will be."

Ash couldn't help but frown. "I'm having a hard time understanding just what your purpose is."

"Do you want to know? Because we'll tell you if you do. It's pretty heavy stuff, though." He paused, thoughtful for a moment. "Your children are your goal right now. Anything we tell you will only distract from that. It's your choice."

Several silent seconds went by.

Matt was right. Until Josie and Brandon were with him, Ash didn't need anything else clouding up his mind.

"Tell me about where they're keeping my kids."

27

The desert was tricky, even more so in the moonless night with their headlamps off. But Paul, with Lisa sitting behind him, and Nick didn't have much of a choice. The only thing they could do was keep their speed down, and hope they didn't hit any of the random holes and ruts too hard.

At midnight, they found a small canyon and stopped. About fifty feet in was a rock overhang, so they decided to use it as shelter and get a few hours of sleep.

Because none of them thought to set an alarm on their cell phone, those few hours turned into almost seven. By the time Paul opened his eyes, the sky was blue, and the warmth of the early spring day had already pushed back the cold of the night.

"Ah, crap!" he yelled, then nudged Lisa, who was sharing his sleeping bag with him. "Hey, baby, we got to get up."

She groaned, but didn't open her eyes.

"Come on, Lisa. It's already late."

"Just a little longer," she said, her voice low and raspy.

He gave her a kiss. "One minute. That's it."

"You're so generous."

He crawled out of the bag without unzipping it, then scrambled over to where Nick was sleeping and shook his shoulder.

"Time to get up."

Nick tried to turn away from him.

"Come on, Nick. We overslept."

His brother opened one eye halfway. "It's morning already?"

"We should have been gone four hours ago," Paul told him.

Nick grunted and rolled onto his back.

Now that Paul knew the other two were basically up, he went

over to his backpack, took out one of the sandwiches his mom had made, then all but inhaled it. Since their water was limited, he was careful to drink only a few ounces.

Nick and Lisa were both sitting up now, neither looking particularly eager to get going.

"Come on," Paul said. "We've got to move!"

"All right, all right," Nick said. "I'm up."

He unzipped his sleeping bag and rolled out.

"Me, too," Lisa said.

"I don't want to stop for a while," Paul told them, "so eat something. I'm going to go see if I can get above the rim and figure out where we are."

Nick gave him a halfhearted wave of acknowledgment, then held out a hand to help Lisa out of her bag.

Paul scanned the canyon. Near the back he saw that part of the wall had crumbled down, creating a difficult but not impossible ramp to the top. He jogged over and carefully climbed up the slope.

He was just nearing the top when a rhythmic noise began, echoing through the canyon. He looked around, trying to spot the source, but though it kept getting louder and louder, he couldn't see anything that might be causing it.

Nick stepped out from under the overhang, looked up at Paul, then lifted his shoulders and held out his hands, silently asking what was making the noise. Paul, having no answer, repeated the gesture back.

He was about ten feet from the top of the ramp, and thought maybe he could see whatever it was from up there. But the moment he started to climb again, two helicopters streaked low across the sky just beyond the edge of the canyon. As soon as they passed the open end, they turned and descended to the ground.

There was no question in Paul's mind why they were here.

"Hide!" he yelled down at Lisa and Nick.

There was no way they could hear him above the whirl of the helicopters, but they'd obviously had the same thought. They began running through the canyon toward the crumbled ramp.

Paul looked quickly around, then slipped into a crack between two large clumps of dirt, keeping his head elevated just enough so he could see over the top.

Six men piled out of the helicopters, three from each, and began running into the canyon. Paul wasn't sure what was scarier: their rifles, or the full bio-protective suits they were wearing.

He looked down the ramp for Lisa and his brother, but it was too uneven, so while he could hear them scrambling on the slope, he couldn't see them.

Two of the armed men stopped near the bikes by the overhang, while the other four continued toward the back of the canyon.

"Stop!" one of them yelled, his voice distorted by his suit.

Paul heard Lisa and Nick stop climbing, and knew they'd been caught.

Dammit! Sarge was not going to be happy.

He watched the men, expecting them to move in and herd Lisa and Nick away, but instead, two of them raised their rifles.

No! No! No! They've stopped! They've stopped!

Paul started to open his mouth to yell exactly that, but before the words could even reach his lips, the men fired. The double boom ricocheted off the canyon walls, but what Paul *didn't* hear was more upsetting. Neither Lisa nor his brother yelled out.

As the men lowered their guns, Paul felt as if the earth had just swallowed him up. He watched all four men walk over to the ramp, then pass out of his line of sight. He could hear them moving around and talking quietly amongst themselves. When they reappeared on the canyon floor, two had Nick slung between them, and two had Lisa.

His brother.

His girlfriend.

Both of them clearly dead.

Paul stared down at them, hardly able to process what he was seeing.

No one was going to believe this. No one would ever believe helicopters had found them in the middle of the desert and—

His hand snapped down to his pants pocket, and he pulled out his cell phone. He turned it on, and worried for a moment the people would disappear before it started up. But he was in luck, if you could call it that. They set the bodies down near the base of the ramp, while one of the two who'd stayed near the motorcycles ran back to the helicopters. The man returned a few moments later with a clump of black plastic.

As soon as Paul's phone was ready, he accessed the camera, flipped it to movie mode, and began recording.

The man with the plastic gave half to the guys standing near Lisa, and the other half to the ones next to Nick. As they unfolded their pieces, Paul realized they were bags—body bags—just like ones he'd seen in some of the Military Channel documentaries Sarge liked to watch.

He had zero doubt this had been a killing operation from the beginning. There had been absolutely no intention of simply bringing any of them in. Why else would they have the bags with them?

"That's my brother, and my girlfriend," he whispered next to the camera, hoping that the suits the people below were wearing would make it hard for them to hear anything. "Those...those men shot them. We weren't doing anything, but they shot them." He opened his mouth to say more, but decided he'd already pressed his luck enough.

Once the bodies were sealed up, the men started carrying them out of the canyon. They all stopped for a moment near the motorcycles and seemed to have a quick conference. When they were through, the two men not carrying the bodies picked up the backpacks and sleeping bags, and carried them to the helicopters.

As soon as everything was aboard, the helicopters rose into the air and flew off in the direction from which they'd come, the thumping of the blades fading until silence descended on the canyon.

Paul didn't move. There was a part of his mind that said if he stayed right there, none of this had really happened. That pretty soon Nick and Lisa would walk up the ramp looking for him. It would all be fine. They'd get on the bikes and get the hell out of there.

But there were no footsteps, no voices, no nothing, because the girl he loved and his brother were dead.

That's when Paul lost it.

It was ten minutes before he finally pulled himself together, his face streaked with tears, and climbed out of his hiding spot. The first thing he did was crawl the rest of the way up to the ridge of the canyon.

There, he looked everywhere to make sure the helicopters had really gone. There wasn't a speck anywhere, not even a cloud. Just blue, empty sky. The wrong sky for the kind of day it had turned out to be.

He hurried down the ramp, pausing for only a brief second as he passed the spot where Nick and Lisa had been killed. What blood he could see looked like dark stains against the dirt. It was…unreal.

When he reached the canyon floor, he ran to the overhang, wanting to get under the cover of the rock. It had occurred to him that the only way the men in the helicopters had known they were there was if he, Nick, and Lisa had been spotted from above. There must have been planes circling around that he and Nick hadn't noticed. He was going to have to expose himself eventually, but, for the moment, he wanted them to think no one else was there.

Thank God the bikes had been too bulky to put on the helicopters. He would never make it if he had to walk out, but the bikes gave him a chance.

Using a hose off of the engine on Nick's bike, he siphoned the remaining gas from Nick's tank into his to give himself the best chance for escape.

His first inclination was to wait until dark, hoping that would make it harder to spot him. But the problem with that was the same problem they'd had the previous night. He would have to keep his speed down so he didn't kill himself. If he left now, in broad daylight, he could race through the desert and that might be the difference between survival and a bullet in his head.

A bullet.

The rifles. The echo of the shots. The lack of any screams.

He shook himself. He couldn't think about that right now. He needed to go. He needed to get out. No one would know what happened to Nick and Lisa if he didn't.

He wheeled his bike to the edge of the overhang, then took a last look back at the earthen ramp where his girlfriend and his brother had died. Unconsciously, he touched the cell phone in his pocket, making sure it was secured. He couldn't lose that, no matter what.

He pulled on his helmet and hopped on the bike. There was no reason to stay any longer.

With a sudden roar, the motorcycle shot out of the canyon and into the desert.

Before the sun came up that morning, the Army finally caved to media pressure, and flew several people back to the roadblock outside Sage Springs. These were the people who had driven their particular network's vans to the location before the quarantine had gone wide. They were now allowed to drive the vans back to Fort Irwin under the escort of four Army Humvees and three helicopters flying above. Each had a soldier equipped with a radio riding inside with the driver. No one was to get out of their vehicle, and they were to stop only if the escorts stopped, too. If there were any problems, the soldier with them would radio it in.

Since the roads were empty, they made it back to Fort Irwin just after sunrise.

Tamara and Joe were both up and waiting when Bobby parked the PCN van in their newly assigned spot.

"Were you able to get any shots?" Joe asked as the cameraman climbed out.

Bobby gave him a quick shake of the head, then motioned to the other side of the van with his eyes. There, the soldier who had ridden with him was getting out. With an expression that conveyed tolerance at best, the soldier waved to Bobby and said, "Have a good day, Mr. Lion."

Bobby smiled broadly. "You, too." As soon as the soldier walked away, the smile disappeared. "I told him I just wanted to get a couple of shots from inside the van, but he made it very clear that we were only there to drive. Hell, he wouldn't even let me get in back to check the equipment before we left."

Tamara knew Joe had been hoping to get the shots, but, personally, she didn't care. Her mind was on something else.

"Can we check now?" she said.

Both men looked hesitant.

"Are you sure you want to do this?" Joe asked.

"Absolutely."

"Come on," Bobby said.

He led them around the van to the side door, then opened it up. Not only was the van used to haul equipment, but it was also a mobile editing facility, allowing them to put stories together, record voiceovers, and transmit everything back to the network. Via their uplink, they also had a speedy Internet connection.

Using this, Bobby accessed the website where the footage from the incident at the Tehachapi roadblock had been uploaded. He clicked around for a bit, then said, "Found it."

He downloaded the video and transferred it into the editing software.

Before hitting PLAY, he looked back at Tamara. "You're sure?"

"I'm sure," she said quickly. "Play it."

Together they watched the video all the way through. Tamara had told Bobby and Joe what she believed she saw, but had said nothing to anyone else. Every time the network replayed the video, she had watched it, pointing out to them the man she was sure was her brother.

Bobby and Joe tried to reassure her by saying things like "you can't tell for sure," and "the resolution isn't the best so you could have made a mistake," and "why would he even be there?"

As sure as she was, she wanted to believe them, so she had stared at the video every time it came on, but every time she came to the same conclusion. It was Gavin.

The reason she couldn't be absolutely positive, though, was that she had no control over what she was watching. She hadn't been able to stop it or start it or reverse it. She had to watch it all the way through, then wait until the network decided to show it again. But now that the truck was here, she had access to the equipment that would allow her to take a better look.

"Go back to the part right before he's shot, and hold it," she said.

Bobby scrolled back, then hit pause. The problem with video, especially lower resolution video, was that the clarity of the picture came from the motion. A single frame often looked blurry, with less detail. Such was the case here. The man she was sure was her brother wasn't much more than an indistinct human figure when paused on the screen.

"Can you go back a second or two," she said, "then scroll back and forth through this section until I tell you to stop?"

"Sure," Bobby replied.

He took it back to where the man in question turned in the direction of the camera, then he started moving forward through the footage at half speed. They had just passed the point where they'd originally paused when she said, "Stop."

The image on the screen froze again.

"You see that?" She pointed at the man's left arm.

"It's an arm," Joe said.

"On the arm. Those dots." There were three dark spots visible on the exposed underside.

"That could just be digital noise," Bobby said.

She pointed again. "Gavin has a tattoo on the inside of his left arm. One big dot, and two smaller. He was on the swim team in high school. It's the molecule model for water."

The two men looked at the screen again. Bobby then played that portion back and forth a couple of times. It was clear the dots were not digital artifacts, but were indeed on the man's arm.

"Jesus," Bobby said.

A tear began rolling down Tamara's cheek. There was no denying it now—Gavin was the one who'd been shot.

"Play it ahead some," she said. "Let's see if we can figure out who did this to him."

Bobby moved the video forward.

In all the times Tamara had watched it at normal speed, she had been unable to spot anyone who might have shot her brother. Her fear was that slowing the footage down wouldn't change that.

"Wait, wait," Joe said. "Play that last part back."

"What did you see?" Tamara asked. Whatever it was, she had missed it.

"It may have been nothing."

Bobby played the segment again, this time going super slow.

"There," Joe said. "That guy."

He was pointing at a man behind Gavin. The guy's eyes were clearly fixed on Tamara's brother. Something bright popped into view near the man's waist for just a couple of frames, then the man disappeared behind Gavin. Two seconds later in real time, Gavin would be shot.

"What was that?" Tamara asked, referring to the bright spot.

"Gun, I think," Bobby said.

"Then that's him."

Bobby froze the video. "This is right before your brother gets shot."

"The man's barely on screen," Joe said. "No wonder we didn't notice him before."

The video didn't actually show the man shooting Gavin, but it was clear to all three of them he had.

The question for Tamara now was, what was she going to do about it?

28

The plane arrived two and a half hours later, landing on a private airstrip on ranch land about a half-mile from the Lodge. It was a Gulfstream G250 business jet, outfitted for four passengers plus crew. After it was checked and refueled, Matt led Ash and Chloe aboard.

The main cabin was separated from the cockpit, so while Ash knew the flight crew was up front, he had no idea who they were. The cabin itself boasted four comfortable-looking leather chairs. The forward two had tables in front of them, while the back two did not. Chloe immediately went for one in the back, while Ash chose a seat up front, tucking the messenger bag that now served as his suitcase under it.

Ash was cleaned up as best as possible, but still looked like he'd been in a major accident. Rachel had cut his hair so it was now a uniform quarter-inch all the way around. She then did a quick bleach job making it and his eyebrows about three shades lighter than they'd been. The final touch had been contact lenses that changed the color of his eyes from blue to brown. He had two extra pairs in his bag as backups.

One thing was for sure: No one who used to know him would recognize him now.

"Pax will fly out with you, but this is as far as I go," Matt said, holding out his hand. "You're a good man, Ash. Get them back."

As Ash shook with him, he said, "Thanks for all the help you've given me."

"I've posted a message for our person on the inside, telling him you and Chloe are coming. He might get it, he might not. Even if he does, he might not be able to do anything to help, but…well,

I'm sure he'll try." He paused. "Pax will give you a number to memorize. Any time you get in trouble, you call that, now or in the future, and we'll do what we can to help." Matt smiled, then glanced toward the back of the plane. "Chloe, good to see you again. Stay safe."

"No such thing," she said.

She was calmer than any of the other times Ash had seen her, but he could still sense a cloud of nervous tension hovering around her.

"The window shades will be automatically lowered before takeoff," Matt told him. "It's not that we don't trust you, but we have certain procedures we need to stand by."

Ash shrugged. He didn't really care where Matt and Rachel's ranch was. He was focused on his destination. On his children.

Matt hung in the doorway as if he had something more he wanted to say, but he finally just gave Ash a nod and got out.

When Pax climbed in a few minutes later, he was carrying two cases—one a normal-sized briefcase, and the other a metal-sided container that could have easily fit a small microwave oven inside. He stored the metal container in a cabinet up front, then put the briefcase on the seat next to Ash. After securing the outer door, he gave the entrance to the cockpit a double tap and returned to his seat.

"Hold this," he said, handing the briefcase to Ash.

As he buckled himself in, a low hum filled the cabin, and hard plastic shades lowered over the windows. To compensate for the loss of sunlight, the interior lights brightened.

Pax leaned over to take the case back, but then stopped. "Might as well do this now."

Outside, the dull roar of the engines grew in intensity.

"Open it up," Pax said.

The plane started rolling down the runway. It was slow at first, but quickly picked up speed. There was no taxiing here, just get on and go.

Ash popped the latches on the briefcase and flipped it open. Inside was a padded envelope and two file folders.

As Ash removed the envelope, the vibration caused by the runway suddenly ceased, and like that, they were in the air. He leaned back for a moment as their angle of ascent increased.

A year earlier, he had taken his family to a small amusement park in Virginia. The park had one of those rides where you were basically in a box that went up and down and side to side, but didn't really go anywhere. The sense of travel was conveyed by the combination of the movement and a video that played on a front screen. While they'd been on the ride, something had gone wrong with the projection system, and for several seconds they only had the walls to look at while the box kept jumping around.

Taking off with the windows closed reminded him of that.

As soon as they were settled into a comfortable climb, Ash opened the envelope and emptied the contents into the briefcase. The thing that stood out first was a small stack of cash. He quickly thumbed through it. Three grand. With the money he already had, that made five thousand total. Not exactly a windfall these days, but it definitely could come in handy.

"Thanks," he said.

"You run out, you call us. We can get you more."

Not that Ash was looking for an answer, but he wondered for the umpteenth time who these people really were.

"I'll…I'll pay you back."

"No need."

Ash didn't argue, but he wasn't conceding the point, either.

He looked back into the briefcase. The other two items from the envelope were a piece of paper and a wallet. He picked up the wallet first. Inside were three credit cards, a membership card for AAA, and a Florida driver's license, all under the name Adam Cooper.

"The credit cards are all good," Pax said. "But use each only once. If I were you, I'd avoid using any of them at all. Cards leave trails."

Ash thumbed out the license and looked at the picture. It could have been him, or it could have been someone else entirely.

"We had to do a bit of fancy Photoshop work on that," Pax said. "But it'll pass for now. When that new face of yours settles in, you can get a real picture taken."

Ash put the license back, then picked up the piece of paper.

"Why is this here?" he asked. It was the pink slip for a 2009

Honda Accord.

"You don't want to walk everywhere, do you?" Pax asked. "It'll be waiting when we land. Registration will hold up even if you get pulled over."

Ash stared at the cash and the cards and pink slip. "What do you guys want from me? You can't be giving me all this for free."

Pax was silent for several seconds. "The hope is you'll come back and help us when your personal business is settled. But that'll be up to you. It's not an expectation. We'd do this for you no matter what."

"Come back and help you do what, exactly?"

Pax leaned back in his seat. "That's something you'll have to hear from Matt, when you're ready." He closed his eyes like he was going to take a nap.

Ash transferred the items into his bag, then pulled out the two files from the briefcase. The first folder contained a set of grainy, five-by-seven photos, eight in all. Five were of men, and three were of women. A note was attached to the front picture.

> If you see any of these people, or someone you think looks like any of them, I'd appreciate it if you would contact us.

> Matt

Ash looked at the pictures again. None of the faces were familiar to him. He put the photos back in the folder and set it aside. The second folder contained newspaper clippings. There was also a note with these.

> Some things to think about.

This one was not signed, but the handwriting was the same as the other.

Ash looked through the clippings, reading the headlines: *Earth Population Hits 7 Bil, Oil Spill Devastates Gulf Coast, Darfur Genocide Sees No End, Ethnic Cleansing a Worldwide Epidemic, Vanuatu Sees*

Territory Shrink As Oceans Rise.

Cheerful stuff.

"Those you can keep."

Pax's voice surprised him. Ash looked over, but Pax was still lying back with his eyes closed.

"The only things I need to take back are the pictures and the briefcase."

"Are these articles supposed to mean something to me?" Ash asked.

"Didn't cut them out. Don't know what they are. Was just told you could keep them."

Ash wasn't sure he wanted to keep them, but he slipped the folder into his bag. He could always throw them out later.

"How long are we going to be in the air?" he asked.

"A couple hours."

"Is there a bathroom on this thing?"

"In back."

As Ash passed Chloe, she eyed him warily but didn't pull back.

He had almost forgotten about her as he looked through the things Pax had brought him. Matt had said she would be valuable to him, but Ash was doubtful that whatever value she brought would outweigh the negatives he felt she had. It would probably be best to part ways once she pointed him in the right direction.

Because if she got in his way…

Rachel got out of the car and joined her brother at the edge of the runway. Together they watched the Gulfstream gain speed as it rushed away from them then lift off into the air. It wasn't until the plane was a little dot in the distance that either of them spoke.

"What do you think his chances are?" she asked.

"You know I'm not good at figuring out odds. But if you pushed me I'd probably say not a chance in hell."

"We've had people beat that before."

"Yes, we have."

She smiled. "You once said there was no way we would ever be able to defeat them."

He took a breath. "I'm still inclined to believe that."

"Yet we're still here. Still fighting."

"It's a war that should have started a lot earlier than it did. All we're doing is damage control and catch up."

They fell silent.

"Do you think he'll come back?" she asked.

"You mean after he beats no chance in hell? Maybe."

"We could certainly use him."

"We already are," Matt said.

Rachel knew he was talking about the vials of Ash's blood their off-site team was already working with. Their resources and facilities weren't as impressive as the organization they were up against, but they weren't working with kids' chemistry sets either, and their people were both dedicated and motivated.

"I think he *will* be back," she said.

Silently, they both looked west, in the direction the plane had finally disappeared. For the moment, there was nothing more to say.

29

Confirmation came at noon when Tamara's mother called, wailing, and told her that someone from the California Highway Patrol had just notified her that Gavin was dead. Thirty minutes later, a list of the Tehachapi casualties was handed out to the media at Fort Irwin.

Tamara knew Gavin's name would be there, but when she saw it, it was as if the breath had been ripped from her lungs.

Joe put an arm around her. "I'll call the network and let them know. You won't have to do any more reports."

"No," she said. "Don't call."

"You don't need to be a hero."

"I need to do this, okay? I need to have this right now. Understand?" What she didn't say was that while Joe had been off at a logistics briefing elsewhere on the base, she and Bobby had been working on a piece about her brother's death that she wanted to work into one of her upcoming reports.

"Seriously, Tammy. Your brother died. Don't push yourself."

"She'll be fine," Bobby said.

Joe frowned. "I don't know."

"What else is she going to do out here?" Bobby asked, looking around. "It'll give her something to take her mind of things until she can go home."

Joe thought for a moment, then looked at Tamara. "If that's what you really want."

She nodded. "It's what I want."

She allowed herself a quick glance at Bobby while Joe was distracted by a couple of helicopters landing nearby. "Done?" she mouthed.

He nodded.

Good. As soon as she could figure out how to work it in, the report would be ready to go.

"Who are *these* guys?" Joe asked.

Tamara turned around. The two arriving helicopters had settled down about fifty yards from where the press was camped out. The only other time helicopters had landed in that area was when they were all evacuated here. Though these were dark green, they had no markings on them, military or otherwise.

Three men jumped out of each helicopter, then gathered on the tarmac. After about half a minute, two of the men broke off and headed over to a waiting Jeep. The helicopters, though, had not powered down, giving the impression their stay was going to be short.

"I have no idea," Tamara said. "National Guard?"

"Could be, I guess."

They were just turning away when Bobby said, "Oh, crap."

Tamara looked over. Bobby, always looking for images they could use, had his camera on his shoulder, shooting the helicopters.

"What is it?" she asked.

He stepped back into the shade of the canopy and said, "Come here."

Tamara walked over, with Joe right on her heels. As soon as she got there, Bobby handed her the camera.

"The four men," he said.

She aimed the lens at the men on the tarmac.

"The guy on the left."

She centered the picture on the guy in question.

"Here," Bobby said. "Let me zoom it in for you."

He pushed a button on top of the camera, and the image of the man rushed at her.

"Whoa, whoa," she said. "Too much." The picture had pushed past the man, and into the passenger area of the helicopter. There was something yellow clumped on the seat, but she barely registered it. "Let me do it."

Bobby showed her where the button was, and she eased the zoom out a little, then adjusted the angle so she could see the man's face. He was in profile, and though he looked a bit familiar, she couldn't place him. Maybe one of the guys who'd flown them out during the evacuation?

She was about to ask Bobby what was so special about the guy when the man turned, suddenly bringing his whole face into view.

For several seconds she forgot to breathe. Finally, she pulled her eye from the viewfinder and allowed Bobby to take the camera from her.

"What is it?" Joe asked.

Bobby gave him the camera.

"Oh, my God," Joe exclaimed once he'd gotten a look at the man.

They had all made the same connection.

Standing a little over a hundred feet away from them was the man who'd killed Tamara's brother.

The orderly checked on the children one last time. Their vital signs were stable, and their breathing deep and even. He made sure the IV tubes would not get caught on anything when the beds were moved, then exited the room.

His colleague had finished packing up the pharmaceutical supplies and their workstation, so the orderly did a final walk-through to make sure they hadn't forgotten anything. They hadn't.

He picked up the radio from their desk and said, "Station K. Ready and awaiting removal."

"Roger, Station K. Removal team should be there in two minutes."

"Copy that, Control."

Together, he and his colleague double-checked all the latches on the containers to make sure everything was secure.

"I think we're good," his colleague said. The orderly was just starting to nod in agreement when the other man blurted out, "Wait."

"What's wrong?"

"Did you check the room at the end?"

The orderly shook his head. As far as he knew, there'd been no reason to go in there.

"I used the bathroom in there this morning," the other man said, already starting off down the hall. "I think I might have left a tissue on the sink."

"Jesus. Get it. We're not supposed to leave anything."

"I know. I know."

His colleague headed quickly down the hall and disappeared into the last room on the right. When he came back out several seconds later, he held up his hand. In it was a couple of unused tissues.

The orderly was about to read him the riot act for being sloppy, but right then the removal team arrived and he soon forgot.

"What should we do?" Bobby asked.

Though Tamara barely heard the cameraman speak, the only thought she had was that she was looking at the man who had put a bullet through her brother's back. Without even realizing it, she started walking toward him.

"Hey, where are you going?" Joe asked.

She didn't answer.

"Tammy. That's not a good idea," Bobby said.

Still, she didn't reply.

Footsteps ran up behind her, Bobby on one side and Joe on the other. Each grabbed one of her arms, stopping her.

"Snap out of it," Joe said. "Going over there isn't going to accomplish anything."

She struggled to pull free. "I want to know his name."

The four men on the tarmac seemed to realize something was going on. They glanced in the PCN team's direction, but then, as one, their gaze swung to the left. The two men who had separated from them earlier were jogging rapidly toward the helicopters. One of them was waving the other men toward the aircraft.

"No!" Tamara yelled as the man who'd killed her brother disappeared inside the helicopter.

Bobby grabbed her around the shoulders, holding her back.

The last man had barely gotten on board when both helicopters rose into the air and shot off toward the North.

"No!" she repeated.

"It's okay," Bobby said. "You wouldn't have been able to do anything."

"But he shot my brother. I...I don't even know his name."

"I got him on tape. If there's a name on his uniform, I probably got that, too."

"Hey, you guys all right?"

The three of them turned and saw Peter Chavez stepping out in their direction from under the canopy.

"We're fine, Peter," Joe said.

"You sure?" Peter asked.

"Yeah. Thanks."

As soon as the wire-service reporter returned to the shade, Tamara whisper, "I want to check the video."

Bobby nodded.

As they walked quickly back to where Bobby had set down the camera, she touched his arm, slowing him and putting a little distance between them and Joe.

"I want you to cut a shot of the guy into the story," she whispered.

He pulled back a little. "I don't know if that's a good idea."

"I don't care if it's a good idea. Will you do it?"

He grimaced, but then nodded. "I'll do it."

Paul was covered in dust. It had even gotten under his helmet and into his month. He tried spitting out what he could, but he was already parched. What he really would have loved at that moment was a nice long drink of water, but that would have to wait until he found civilization. His bottles had been in his backpack the men from the helicopters had taken.

So far he'd been able to make pretty good time. The roughest part had been right after he left the canyon. The gentle slope there had been deceiving. Decades of rainwater had carved out gullies that seemed to appear out of nowhere. If he had hit one of those too hard, he would have wrecked and broken his arm or worse.

But now he was on smooth, level ground so he was able to ramp up the speed. He figured the area was probably the bed of the ancient ocean that used to cover this part of the desert. Sarge would have known for sure.

He allowed himself a quick look around. Brown for as far as he could see. He glanced at his gas gauge. He had maybe another sixty or seventy miles left. Reluctantly he backed off on the accelerator. If he kept his speed down a bit, he might be able to squeeze out another ten or twenty miles. That could make all the difference in the world.

He let his eyes settle on the hills in front of him. Another fifteen minutes and he'd be there. If he figured it right, once he reached the top he'd be out of the quarantine zone. The thing he didn't know was how far he'd still have to go to reach anyone after that. The map his dad had given them was also in the backpack.

To this point, he'd focused all his thoughts on surviving—going as fast as he dared, keeping the bike upright, looking for holes in the ground. But the thought of the map brought everything back.

Mom and Sarge. Leaving home after the sun went down. Racing through the dark desert.

Nick.

Lisa.

The girl who meant everything to him and his best friend in the world—both dead.

The thing he kept coming back to was that he'd sat there and done nothing. He had watched the men raise their rifles. He had watched them fire.

And he had done *nothing*.

Maybe he could have created a distraction. Maybe it would have been enough for Nick and Lisa to get away. Would it have worked? Probably not, but, dammit, he should have given it a try. He should have—

He didn't see the rock.

One moment his eyes were tearing up with anger over his inaction, and the next he was flying over his handlebars, landing hard against the desert floor.

He lay on his back for a moment, groaning with the pain. The worse of it seemed to be coming from his left knee. He pulled off his helmet then felt his leg, checking if it was broken.

When his hand reached his knee, he nearly jerked back. It felt wrong. He tried to sit up, but that just made the pain worse, so he only raised his shoulder and tilted his head so he could see what was going on.

Immediately, he knew what had happened. He'd seen something similar before, during P.E. at school. They'd been playing soccer, and Ryan Young had tried to kick the ball but had stepped awkwardly and fallen to the ground.

Like Ryan's had been then, Paul's kneecap was sticking out like a shelf off the side of his bent leg, dislocated.

His eyes slammed shut as a new wave of pain washed over him. He took several deep breaths, trying to regain a little control. When it happened to Ryan, the school nurse had come down to the field and slipped it back into place while the rest of them stood around and watched.

Paul didn't have anyone to put it back in place for him. He was going to have to do it himself.

"It's okay. It's okay," he said out loud. "Two seconds and it's over."

He arranged his leg so that the back edge of his shoe's heel was on the ground. He then put his left hand on his kneecap, and his right on his thigh. Taking several quick, deep breaths, he tried to calm himself. Then, before he could talk himself out of it, he pushed down on his thigh and in on his kneecap. As the leg straightened, the cap moved back into place.

He yelled out, not so much in new pain, but in memory of the old. Because while his knee was indeed throbbing, the sheer intensity of the pain he'd been feeling had subsided.

He lay against the desert floor, panting.

It was several minutes before he finally pushed himself up. His bike was about ten feet away. At first glance, it didn't look like it had suffered much damage. He took a tentative step toward it, but immediately his left leg howled in pain. There was no way it was going to be able to hold his weight for any length of time, so he hopped as best he could to the bike.

As he pulled it off the ground, he smelled gas. There was a wet spot on the dirt under where the tank had been. He looked at the bike, checking for a hole, a loose hose, anything.

It was the cap. It had come loose somehow. He tried to think back to when he'd siphoned the gas from his brother's bike. Had he not made sure the cap was on tight? There was really no other explanation.

He took it off now and looked inside. There was still some gas sloshing around in there, but how much had he lost?

"Dammit!" he yelled. *I'm such an idiot.*

He put the top back on, making sure it was secure this time, then wheeled the bike over to where he'd left his helmet.

Once he was re-outfitted, he got on and started up the bike. His left leg was already starting to stiffen and was going to be a problem. With more than a little pain, he bent it enough to get his foot on the peg.

He coughed a couple times, and he couldn't wait until he could drink some water and get the dust out of his system.

Then he resumed his journey to freedom.

30

It wasn't until they landed that the window shades rose again.

Ash looked outside. They seemed to be at a small airport. He could see a few planes parked off to the side and a hangar in the distance.

"Where are we?" he asked.

Pax glanced out the window. "Well, unless we got lost on the way, this should be Sonoma County, California."

Though Ash had been stationed twice in California, he only had a vague idea that Sonoma County was somewhere in the North.

"This is where my children are?"

"As close as we can get." Pax tilted his head toward the back. "Chloe will take you the rest of the way."

Though they were still taxiing, Pax unbuckled himself and got up. He retrieved the metal case from the cabinet, then set it on the floor between his and Ash's seats. He undid the clasps and lifted off the top. Protective foam lined the box, while another thick sheet covered whatever was inside. Pax pulled this away, revealing a small arsenal.

"You liked the SIG so much, I got you three," Pax said as he touched the hilt of one of the three SIG SAUER P229 pistols inside. "You have four boxes of ammo, three extra mags...well, five if you only use one gun. I also packed a pair of binoculars, and something we call little bangs."

"Little bangs?"

Pax moved a few things around, then pulled out a hard plastic rectangular box about an inch thick, and opened the top. The inside was divided into two parts. On one side was a device that looked like a cell phone, complete with a touch-screen display. On the other side were a couple dozen half-inch squares lined up like crackers in a box, the majority of which were gray.

Pax pulled out one of the squares. In the center was a smaller black box that barely rose above the surface. Running out from it were tiny wires that spread over the gray square.

"See the number?" Pax asked.

Ash took a harder look. On the black box a number had been painted in gray. Hard to read, but not impossible. This square was numbered one.

"I see it."

Pax turned the gray square around. "This other side will stick pretty much anywhere. But you've gotta remove this first."

He flicked his finger across the edge, and Ash could see there was a clear plastic sheet covering the back.

"Put this wherever you need it. Then you use this thing here." He pointed at the black cell-phone-looking device. "This is your trigger device. Interface is easy. You input the unit number, then either set it off manually or set up a timer. These things don't create a lot of damage, but they're quite the noisemakers. Good for diversions if you need them."

"I'll bet."

"Careful, though. You see these four here?" He touched four tiles that were grouped together. Unlike the others, they were white. "These do more than just make a noise. They're what you use if you do need damage. They'll blow a hole in pretty much anything you'll come across. There's only the four, so don't confuse them with the others."

He closed the box and tucked it back in the case. He then gave Ash the emergency phone number Matt had mentioned, making him repeat it several times. It was an easy number. Ash knew he wouldn't forget it.

As soon as the plane stopped rolling, Pax said, "I believe this is your stop."

There was no one around as they stepped out of the jet. In fact, the whole airport seemed quiet and deserted. It was tucked between several green hills, and though Ash could see a few houses in the distance, there was no town visible.

Pax nodded toward the hangar. "Your ride's right over there."

Parked near the closed hangar door was a silver Honda Accord.

The metal case went in the trunk, while Ash put his messenger bag in the back seat. Chloe had a dark green backpack. She tossed that into the footwell up front before climbing into the passenger seat.

"You got GPS in there," Pax told Ash. "It's already preset to get you to the highway. Chloe will take over after that."

He held out his hand, and Ash took it.

"You've been put in a terrible position, Captain," Pax said. "Most people would have given up already. Think they crossed the wrong man when they found you."

"Yes," Ash said. "They did."

Pax stepped back. "Don't be a stranger."

By the time Ash got the car to the airport exit, the jet was already racing down the runway and taking off.

He let the voice of the GPS guide him through the countryside. In his other life, he would have appreciated the beauty of the area, mainly because Ellen would have loved it.

I should have brought her here.

I should have brought her a lot of places.

He gritted his teeth and continued to drive.

When they finally reached the highway, the GPS stopped giving directions. Ash looked over and saw that Chloe was staring out the window.

"Which way?" he asked. It was the first thing either of them had said since they'd gotten in the car.

She didn't move for a second, then she pulled up her head and looked over at him. "What?"

"Which way? Pax said once the GPS stopped, you'd know where to go."

"Oh." She leaned forward, looking out the window again, and seemed to notice their surroundings for the first time. "Where are we?"

"At the freeway. North or south?"

She started nodding. "South. Definitely south."

He headed for the on-ramp. "How far?"

She glanced at him again, then returned her gaze to the window. "Fifteen-point-seven miles."

"Serious?"

"Why wouldn't I be?"

He hesitated, then said, "Okay. Fifteen-point-seven miles."

"Almost point-six now."

Since Ash knew he'd be shedding Chloe as soon as he didn't need her any more, he was content to let the miles pass by in silence and avoid forming any kind of bond. For whatever reasons of her own, Chloe seemed fine with not talking, too.

The first thing either of them said came from Chloe at exactly fifteen-point-four miles from where they'd entered the freeway. "Next exit." Once they were on the off-ramp, she said, "To the right."

They were in a rural area, probably about fifty miles north of San Francisco. The area immediately surrounding them was hilly and green from recent rains. As they headed west the hills grew larger, and the trees started changing from scattered oaks and a few cottonwoods to a growing forest of evergreens.

"How far are we going?" Ash asked.

"At this speed, we'll turn in nine minutes."

Ash was tempted to go a little faster, but the road was only two lanes and had become winding with plenty of blind turns.

After a few minutes, Chloe said out of the blue, "They changed my face, too."

Ash glanced at her, then back at the road.

"I'd be dead now if they hadn't," she added.

Unable to stop himself, he said, "Is that why you're helping me?"

For several moments, she said nothing. Then, "I have to help. I have no choice."

Ash frowned. "Are you telling me that Matt forced you to be here?"

"No. Of course not. After you get your children, if someone else needs help, you'll have no choice, either. We have to fight them. We have to stop them."

"You mean this Dr. Karp? Don't worry. I'll deal with him."

"You don't understand. You just don't understand." She shook her head, then looked back at the road. "There," she said, pointing ahead. "Turn there."

The new road was narrower and obviously less used. The centerline looked like it hadn't been repainted in decades, and had become more of a faded suggestion than an actual demarcation. The road was dark, too, the sun hidden from view by a thick grove of conifers.

"Five miles," Chloe announced.

Ash glanced at the odometer and noted the mileage.

"I'm sorry they took your children," she said.

Ash didn't respond.

"They took someone from me, too. But I can never get her back."

Ash remained quiet for a moment longer, then said, "There's someone I can't get back, either."

Again, silence descended.

After a bit, Chloe said, "Slow down."

Ash checked the odometer, and saw that they had come almost four and a half miles. He reduced their speed.

The area was quiet. They hadn't seen a single car on this road, nor had there been any houses or buildings alongside it.

Chloe patted her hand against the air. "Slower."

Ash eased back on the gas some more.

Finally, she pointed at a spot just ahead and across the road. "There. Do you see it? Between those two trees."

Where she indicated he could see the ghosts of two tire ruts running into the woods. They were mostly filled with dry pine needles, and looked as if no one had driven on them for a long, long time.

Ash pulled across the road and stopped just short of the ruts. He stared into the woods. As far as he could see, there was nothing back there but more trees.

He grimaced skeptically, then looked at Chloe. "My kids are back there somewhere?"

She hesitated. "The building where I'm supposed to take you is back there."

"This isn't even a road. It's a path that no one's used for God knows how long."

She narrowed her eyes. "Would you rather I take you down the road they do use? Maybe right up to the front door so you can ring the bell? I can do that if you'd like. Except I'd probably just point the way and let you go on your own. I don't want to die today."

Of course she wouldn't do that. What was he thinking? And if this really was a way in, wasn't it a good thing it looked completely untouched?

"Right," he said, then added, "I'm sorry."

He turned the Accord onto the path.

Chloe guided him through a slalom course of trees, taking them deeper and deeper into the woods. Keeping their speed to a crawl, Ash still managed to scrape the sides a few times.

After they'd been going like that for about fifteen minutes, Chloe said, "You should turn the car around here. I'll get out and guide you. Then we'll walk the rest of the way."

It took a little effort, but with Chloe's help, Ash was able to get the sedan pointed back in the direction they'd come.

Once out of the car, he went around to the trunk and opened the weapons case Pax had given him. He grabbed one of the guns, then spent a few minutes filling its mag and the three spares. When he was done with that, he almost shut the case. Instead, he reached in and grabbed the box of little bangs before closing it up.

Chloe had been standing nearby the whole time, watching him. He wasn't sure if she'd been expecting him to give her a gun, but she didn't ask and he didn't offer.

"Let's go," he said.

They hiked for a quarter of an hour, then as they approached a ridge, Chloe motioned for him to get down on his hands and knees. When they reached the top, they dropped to their stomachs and looked down into the tree-filled valley.

At first, Ash thought it was as empty as the forest they'd just come through, but then Chloe pointed down and to the right. About a half-mile away he saw part of a roof jutting out from the side of the hill, like the structure was built right into the earth. If there was anything else around, he couldn't see it through the trees.

She then pointed at one of the evergreens about ten yards ahead of them, then at another about the same distance to the left, then at another and another.

"Twenty feet up," she said.

It took him a couple seconds to see what she was talking about. Attached to each tree at the height she'd indicated were some sort of electronic devices that had been colored to blend in. If Chloe hadn't pointed them out, he would have never noticed them.

"What are they?" he asked.

"Motion sensors. They circle the complex. You can't see it, but another fifty feet beyond that point is a fence."

Ash studied the area for a moment. "I take it there's a way through there."

Chloe shook her head. "Not that I know of."

"But Matt told me you could get me in."

"That's true."

He stared at her for a moment. "You want to stop being so cryptic?"

Several seconds passed, then she said, "This used to be an old mental hospital. It was closed sometime in the nineties and the land was turned over to the government, but don't expect to find it in any of their records. The...others took it over and fixed it up for their own needs. It's not one of their main facilities so they don't always use it. But according to Matt, this is where your kids were taken."

"You still haven't told me how I get in."

"There used to be a separate building where the mental hospital kept...problem patients. The building's gone, but the foundation is still there." She looked at Ash. "It's outside the motion detection zone."

"How does that help us?" Ash asked, still not following.

"They might have torn down the building, but they didn't remove the tunnel that connected it to the main hospital."

31

The throbbing in Paul's knee had become so constant he almost didn't notice it any more. He wished the same could be said for his growing thirst. His dry mouth and chapped lips were constantly nagging at him.

He'd reached the summit of the hill that marked the boundary of the quarantine zone thirty minutes earlier, but any elation he might have felt had been tempered by the miles of open desert that still stretched before him.

He coughed a couple times, then glanced down at his gas gauge. The needle was hovering just above E. He'd be walking soon, and in his condition, he wouldn't be walking far. If only he could find a road, hopefully someone would drive by and see him. Or perhaps it was his lot to die out here like his brother and his girlfriend. The only difference being that his fate would be delivered by the elements, not a slug of lead.

The ground was rising again in front of him like a gentle swell in the middle of a dirt ocean. As he did every time he neared a crest, he prayed that he'd finally see a road on the other side, anything that would give him a chance.

"This time," he began repeating. "This time. This time. This time."

Just before he actually reached the top, he steeled himself and prepared to see nothing. He was so sure that was exactly what would happen, that even as he stared at the distant highway, it took a moment before he realized what it was.

He stopped the bike, his good foot planting on the ground. Was the highway real? Maybe the pain and the dust and the lack of water were making him see things. He wanted to believe, but…could he?

His eyes followed the road, then his breath caught in his throat.

Not five miles away, he saw a handful of buildings grouped together. Parked around them appeared to be several cars and a couple of buses. He blinked. The buildings were still there. The cars and the buses were still there.

Finally allowing himself a smile, he started down the hill. He was tempted to open the bike up all the way, but he knew even five miles might be too far for the fumes left in his gas tank. So he eased all the way back on the accelerator and let the bike roll free down the hill.

He was laughing as he neared the bottom, his hand poised to feed the rest of the gas into the engine as soon as his speed started to slow. That's when he heard it. The thumping.

He didn't need to look back to know what was there, but he did anyway.

Two helicopters, like black blots against the western afternoon sky.

There was no doubt in his mind that these were the same two that had come to the canyon that morning, that had brought the men who had killed two of the people he loved most. And though he was out of the quarantine zone, he knew they were here to kill him, too.

He jammed on the gas and shot toward the buildings, already knowing they were too far away and that the helicopters would reach him first.

If only he hadn't stopped at the top of the ridge. If only he hadn't fallen off the bike and hurt his knee. If only he hadn't delayed himself a half dozen other times. But he couldn't change any of that now.

The only thing he could do was ride.

Martina Gable and the rest of the Burroughs High School softball team were doing what they'd been doing for the last day and a half. Nothing.

They'd been heading home in a school bus from a tournament in Reno, Nevada, when the quarantine had been imposed over much of the Mojave Desert, including their hometown of Ridgecrest. Unfortunately, one of the girls was pumping a steady mix of pop from her iPod through the bus's sound system, so no one had been listening to the radio at the time. But why would they have done that? They'd come in second in the tournament, much better than they'd hoped, so they had reason to enjoy themselves on the way home.

Ten miles past Cryer's Corner, they reached the roadblock and learned for the first time what was going on. Initially, there'd been panic and fear, of course. But when they went back to Cryer's Corner—not much more than a wide spot in the road with a café, a gas station, and a small convenience store—they were able to use the land phones there to contact their families and find out that everyone was fine.

They'd talked about driving back into Nevada to find someplace to stay, but when Coach Driscoll called around looking for a motel, everywhere she tried was full. Apparently the quarantine was stranding people all over the place.

The Cryer family owned all the businesses at Cryer's Corner. They offered to let the girls sleep on the floor of the café, so that's what the coach decided they'd do.

As the day progressed, a few other cars drove in—a couple of families and some solo drivers. They, too, were offered places to sleep.

The coaches tried to organize a practice out behind the café that first afternoon to distract the girls, but it didn't work out too well. So this second day they'd pretty much let everyone do what they pleased, as long as they didn't cause any trouble.

Martina had played catch with her friend Noreen for a while, then had thumbed through one of the gossip magazines another girl had brought along. After lunch, she'd found a spot on the side of the gas station, and was idly tossing rocks at a dumpster, wishing the damn quarantine would be lifted so they could go home. This put her at a good angle to see the helicopters the moment they popped over the hill.

Immediately, she got up and went around to the front of the station where several others were hanging out.

"Helicopters," she said, pointing.

Since everyone on the softball team lived next to the China Lake Navy base, they were used to the sight of jets and helicopters. But having already spent a day of monotony on the side of the road, seeing them now felt like something new.

"From the roadblock?" Cathy Thorwaldson asked.

"I didn't see any out there," Martina said. "Did you?"

"Maybe they flew in during the night while we were sleeping." This came from one of the drivers who'd arrived alone, a college-age guy. Cute, too.

"Hadn't thought of that," Martina said.

"Do you hear that?" their catcher, Jilly Parker, asked. She'd been standing near the pumps but had taken a few steps toward the desert.

Martina listened. There was a very faint whine in the distance. "The helicopters, probably."

Jilly shook her head. "Doesn't sound like helicopters."

A couple seconds later, they all heard a rhythmic *thump-thump-thump*.

"*That's* the helicopters," Jilly said.

She was right, Martina realized. The whine was still there, too. Its volume had increased a bit, and it seemed to be coming from ground level as opposed to the sky.

Sims was crouched just behind the two front seats of the helicopter, trying to spot the motorcycle below. The satellite images had gotten them this far, but now it was a matter of eyeballs.

"There, sir," the co-pilot said, with a quick nod out the window. "Running along that old wash."

Sims adjusted his position, then immediately saw movement about a mile ahead.

"Get us down there."

"Sir," the pilot said. "We're already twenty miles outside the containment zone."

"I don't care where we are. If the person on that bike is infected, we could have a new outbreak on our hands. Our job is to make sure that doesn't happen." *Yet*, he thought, but didn't add.

The other thing he didn't voice was his desire to clean up a situation that they had created themselves. The person on the motorcycle had come from the canyon they'd visited that morning. Apparently there hadn't been two riders, but three. This third person must have hidden from Sims and his men, and that annoyed him.

It should have never happened. They should have checked for additional people but they hadn't, and it had been his fault. Two bikes, two sleeping bags, two people. Logical, but wrong.

"Hang on, sir," the pilot said.

A second later, the helicopters dipped in unison toward the fleeing motorcycle.

Jilly and Martina used a stack of barrels to climb up on top of the gas station, then moved to the back edge so they could see what was going on.

"That whine's a motorcycle. I'd know that anywhere," Jilly said.

Martina had recognized it, too. It was a common enough noise in the desert around Ridgecrest. But though she was looking toward where she thought the noise was coming from, she couldn't see anything.

Jilly suddenly pointed repeatedly at the desert. "There, there, there!"

Martina put a hand on her forehead, shading her eyes. "I don't see it."

"It's there! Along that wash."

Something glinted in the distance, sunlight on a helmet, Martina realized as she finally spotted the motorcycle rider. For a few moments, she watched him—she assumed it was a him—heading in their direction.

"Is that one of the people who lives here?" she wondered out loud.

"I didn't hear anyone leave earlier, but I guess it could be," Jilly said.

Until that moment, Martina had thought the helicopters and the motorcycle had had nothing to do with each other. But suddenly both helicopters dove down toward the bike.

"What are they doing?" she asked.

Under Sims's directions, the helicopters bracketed the motorcycle, his aircraft coming up on its left, the other on its right.

"We'll take the shot," Sims said into the radio. "If he doesn't go down, you're up."

Paul felt the thumping of the helicopters in his chest. He allowed himself a quick glance back, and was surprised to see they were approaching him from either side.

There was movement at the open door of the helicopter to his left. He turned forward, checking the terrain ahead, then chanced another glance back. A man stood in the doorway now, held in place by what looked like a strap. In his arm was a rifle.

Without even thinking about it, Paul released the accelerator and pulled on the brakes.

Just then he heard something whiz by him through the air. Involuntarily, he jerked the handlebars to the side. The front tire of the bike turned with it, catching the edge of a sagebrush. Before Paul knew it, he was once more tumbling through the air.

"Is that a hit?" Sims asked. "Is that a hit?"

There was a brief delay. "I'm not sure, sir. But he *is* down."

"Get us back there."

Martina actually screamed when the driver of the motorcycle flew off his bike.

"Did they...*shoot* at him?" Jilly asked.

"I'm not sure," Martina replied.

"I thought I saw a flash."

Below them, one of the cars in the lot started up. Almost immediately, they could hear tires spinning for a moment on the dirty asphalt, then catching hold. Martina glanced over the other side, just in time to see the cute college boy race away from the gas station in his Jeep and head into the desert toward the downed driver.

The helicopters had both swung around and were now hovering above the motorcyclist. Sims was pretty sure it was a man.

"Does anyone see any movement?" he asked.

"No, sir."

"No, sir."

"All right, then everyone suit up, and let's bag him—"

The radio crackled. "Sir, civilian approaching."

Out of reflex, Sims looked over at the other helicopter. "What?"

"Just ahead, sir," the man in the other aircraft said. "A Jeep. There are also a couple people standing on one of the buildings at the roadside stop along the highway, looking this way, and several more doing the same from ground level."

"You've got to be kidding me."

"No, sir."

Sims looked out the open doorway and spotted the Jeep. He quickly realized it would get to the motorcycle rider only seconds after they landed. What would they do then? Kill the Jeep driver, too? What about the people in town watching? He was pretty sure Mr. Shell did not want that kind of bloodbath.

Dammit!

He looked down at the motorcyclist again, then tapped the pilot on the shoulder. "Head back to base."

Even before they made the turn for home, he had his satellite phone out. The quarantine zone would have to be expanded to include that little bit of nowhere in case the motorcyclist was infected. But even if he wasn't, and those in the town didn't actually die from the disease, the quarantine would make it easier for Sims and his men to go in and deal with the witnesses.

It was an aggravating problem but fixable.

It didn't even dawn on him that he should have also requested a communications blackout of the area. He thought that was already a part of the quarantine. Why wouldn't it be?

It was another lesson they'd learn for next time.

Paul remembered flying off his bike, but didn't remember landing. That was because the impact had knocked him unconscious. So the next thing he was aware of was a man lifting him off the ground.

"What…what's going on?"

"Just relax," the guy said. "You're going to be fine."

Where had the guy come from? The helicopter? But they were going to shoot him, weren't they?

Then he saw the vehicle he was being carried to, a dark red, old-model Jeep, not a helicopter.

Someone passing by on the road, maybe? Did it really matter?

As the man helped him into the front seat, Paul knocked his injured knee against the dash, which caused him to wince in pain, which in turn caused him to cough a couple of times.

"Sorry," the guy said.

"I'm...okay."

The man got behind the wheel and started up the Jeep. As they turned around, Paul caught sight of his motorcycle. It was lying half in a creosote bush, its handlebars skewed. He could see a hole in his gas tank, but nothing was dripping out.

Just enough, he thought with a smile. *Just enough*.

32

Martina and Jilly climbed down off the roof as the Jeep returned. By then, many of the rest of the people stranded in Cryer's Corner had come outside to see what all the noise was about. Word of what had happened spread quickly.

When the Jeep pulled to a stop, several people crowded around. The guy who'd been on the motorcycle was a mess. He looked like he'd been rolling in dirt for weeks, then had the side of his head dipped in blood.

There was something familiar about him, but Martina couldn't place it. This thought, though, was soon forgotten as the cute college boy came around and helped the motorcycle rider out of the Jeep.

"I don't suppose anyone here's a doctor?" College Boy asked.

"My dad is," Amy Rhodes said.

"Yeah, but he's not here, is he?" Jilly asked.

"Isn't Coach Delger a nurse?" someone asked.

"Yeah, I think she is," Martina said. "Where is she?"

"Last I saw her, she was in the café," Amy told them, no doubt trying to redeem herself.

When no one moved right away, Martina said, "I'll get her."

She raced over to the café and rushed inside. There were only three people there—an old woman behind the counter, and Coach Driscoll and Coach Delger in one of the booths. The coaches both had their backs against the window, with their legs stretched out, and seemed to be asleep.

"Coach Delger?" Martina called out as she ran over.

Both coaches cracked open their eyes.

"What is it, Martina?" Coach Driscoll asked. She was the head coach. Coach Delger was a volunteer from town.

"Someone's hurt. And we thought…well, Coach Delger, you're a nurse, right?"

Both of the women sprang to life and pushed themselves out of the booth.

"Where?" Coach Delger asked.

"Outside. Some guy on a motorcycle got thrown to the ground."

Coach Delger raced ahead and shot out the door.

"Medical student," Coach Driscoll whispered to Martina as they followed. "Her residency starts after the end of the season."

"A student? Oh, uh, maybe we should ask around and see if anyone else is a nurse."

"She'll do just fine," Coach Driscoll told her.

As soon as Martina stepped back outside, she saw that the college boy had an arm around the motorcyclist and they were both walking toward the café. Coach Delger ran up beside them and took a quick look at the injured rider. She then glanced over at Martina.

"Open the door," she called out.

Once they were inside, the college boy helped the rider to a corner booth. It was one of those circular kinds that could fit a lot of people and had a correspondingly large table. Coach Delger had the injured kid sit on the table, then told Martina to get everyone else outside.

"You heard her," Martina announced to the group who'd followed them in. "Everyone out."

Soon she had the place cleared, but since the coach hadn't specifically told *her* to leave, she returned to the table.

She'd barely walked up when Coach Delger said, "Martina, I need you to look for a first-aid kit. There's got to be one here somewhere." Before Martina could leave, she added, "And I'll need some warm water and towels to clean him up, too."

Martina found the old woman in the kitchen already filling up a large bowl with water.

"I heard her," the woman said, then nodded toward the back of the room. "First-aid kit's hanging on the wall by the bathroom. Just lift it and it'll come right off."

The kit was a large metal box. Martina got it off the wall and carried it back into the dining area. When she got back to the table, the coach was examining the rider's head where all the blood was.

"Not too bad," Coach Delger said. "A cut and a little bump. I'm guessing you were wearing a helmet, right?"

"Yeah," the boy said.

"Some of the cushion missing on the inside?"

"A little."

Smirking, she said, "Get a new helmet and that won't happen next time."

The old woman came out of the kitchen with the water and some towels.

"Susan," Coach Delger said to Coach Driscoll. "Can you clean up his head? I'm going to check if there's anything else wrong."

"Sure," Coach Driscoll said. She grabbed a towel and got it wet.

"My knee," the boy said.

"Which one?"

"Left. From before."

"Before?"

He gave a little shrug. "Not my first crash today. Dislocated it."

While Coach Delger used a pair of scissors from the first-aid kit to cut away his pants leg, the boy looked at Martina.

"What are you guys doing here?" he asked.

"We were at a softball tournament. Got stuck outside the quarantine zone on our way home."

"Did you win?"

She figured he was just trying to distract himself from his pain. "Second place out of sixteen teams. Not too bad."

"Go Burros," he said.

She smiled for a second, then looked down. She wasn't wearing one of her school shirts. Maybe someone outside was. That must have been it.

"Yeah, go Burros."

"Who did most of the pitching? You or Sandra?"

Martina wasn't the only one who was suddenly staring at the rider. Both coaches had stopped what they were doing and were looking at him, too.

"Do I know you?" Martina asked.

"Do I look that bad?"

She squinted her eyes, studying him. "You look familiar, but…"

"Spanish class," he said.

"Paul?"

"Hey, Martina."

"I'm sorry, who are you?" Coach Driscoll asked.

"This is Paul Unger," Martina said, surprised. "He goes to Burroughs, too."

"What were you doing out there on a motorcycle?" Coach Driscoll asked.

Paul got a faraway look in his eyes, and the small smile that had been on his lips disappeared. "Trying not to die."

They got the whole story out of him.

As soon as Coach Delger realized he'd come from the quarantine zone, she immediately segregated everyone into two groups: those who had come in contact with Paul, and those who hadn't.

The hardest part of the story to believe was the deaths of Nick and Lisa. That was until he showed them the video.

It was Martina's idea, however, to post it on the Internet.

33

Chloe guided Ash through the woods, circling around to the top of the rise behind the building, just beyond the line of motion sensors. After crossing a small clearing, she walked on for another dozen feet, then stopped under the cover of the trees.

Without a word, she got on her knees and started digging. At first Ash couldn't figure out what she could possibly be doing, but after she removed a thick layer of needles and branches, she exposed a manhole cover.

"Where does it go?" he asked.

"I have no idea. Just thought I'd randomly show it to you." She stared at him for a second as if he were an idiot. "Where do you think it goes?"

She was right. It was a dumb question.

"How do we get it open?"

"That's a better question than the last one, at least," she said.

She got off her knees and walked over to a tree a dozen feet away. Jumping up, she grabbed one of the low branches and pulled herself onto it. She reached to the branch above her and moved her hands around for a moment. When she dropped back to the ground, she was holding a long metal rod that had an L hook at the bottom.

With a smirk, she stuck the hooked end through a hole in the cover and yanked the disk off, surprising Ash with her strength.

He took a step closer and looked down through the opening. The filtered afternoon light was only able to penetrate a few feet into the dark hole, illuminating just the concrete sides of the tube and the first rung of a built-in iron ladder.

He thought for a moment. Perhaps it was now time to part

ways with his guide. "Is it just down and follow a tunnel?"

She scoffed. "No, it's *not* just down and follow a tunnel."

"Okay," he said, revising his plan. "I was just asking."

Chloe went first, pulling a flashlight out of her pocket he hadn't known she'd brought along, and he followed. At the bottom was a large, damp tunnel running perpendicular to the entrance tube.

"This leads back to the main building?" he asked.

Chloe grimaced, annoyed. "Do you not listen to me? I already told you it doesn't." She huffed out a breath, then said, "Come on."

She headed to the left, the glow of her flashlight leading the way, then stopped after forty feet and said, "Here."

She turned her flashlight toward the wall and revealed a big V-shaped break. Ash examined it for a moment. There was an opening through the dirt on the other side of the concrete, not really a tunnel, more of a rift through the earth. Just at the furthest reach of the light he thought he caught a glimpse of more cement.

"This happened during the Loma Prieta earthquake in 1989," she said. "You know, the one that took down that freeway in San Francisco?"

He vaguely remembered that from when he'd been a kid. "What's on the other side?"

Instead of answering, she climbed into the rift and started working her way through the cramped space. Ash knew it was going to be even tighter for him, so instead of crawling as she had, he got on his stomach and pulled himself forward.

The distant cement turned out to be a wall, the break in it not a giant V, but a lopsided oval. As he slipped through the opening and got to his feet, he found himself in a wide space that fell quickly off into darkness beyond the spill of the flashlight.

"Welcome to the Palmer Psychiatric Hospital's special patient facility. Or what's left of it," Chloe said.

She moved the flashlight through the room. There were piles of wood and old office furniture and what appeared to be mattresses. Trash was strewn throughout.

"When they tore down the building, they left the basement," Chloe explained. "They threw some dirt over the top and let the earth reclaim it. Above us is that clearing we walked through."

"Why leave the basement?" he asked.

"You ask me like I was there. I wasn't. I do know, though, that they tore the building down not long after the earthquake." She paused. "You want my guess?"

He shrugged. "Okay."

"The hospital was still open then. The people who were running it would have known about the tunnel, and probably thought they could still use this place. It's nice and hidden from the view of anyone. I wouldn't have put it past them."

That was a bit on the conspiracy side of things for him, but then again, hadn't his whole life slipped firmly to the conspiracy side? God, what was happening to him?

"Show me the tunnel into the hospital."

"Follow me."

She led him to a door in the far corner. Inside was a staircase leading down.

"There's two underground levels?" he asked.

She shook her head. "Just the stairs," she said as she started down. "And the tunnel."

Directly left of the stairs at the bottom was a wide opening. Chloe shined the light into it, but it revealed nothing more than walls on each side before the darkness took over again.

As she started to walk into it, Ash said, "Wait."

She turned back.

"This isn't your fight," he said. "I appreciate you getting me here, but I think I should go on alone from this point."

She stared at him, then said, "Really? Do you know how to get out of the other end of this tunnel?"

"Is it that hard?"

"It depends on your definition, I guess."

He shrugged. "If you tell me how to do it, I'll manage."

"And what are you going to use for light? You're not taking my flashlight."

"Actually, I am," he said. "You can wait here until I get back."

She took a step away from him, toward the tunnel. "You want to leave me here in the dark? Are you kidding me?"

"It'll be safer."

"Yeah, until I go crazy because I keep hearing things, then I run straight into a wall and knock myself out. I'm sorry, Mr. Not-

In-The-Army-Anymore, but no way in hell I'm staying here in the dark." With that she turned and started down the tunnel.

Once more he found himself in the position of following her.

The tunnel between the buildings was a good six feet wide and at least eight tall, with a gentle downward slope. Ash realized that explained why the stairs from the annex basement had been built. If the tunnel had been dug directly from the main building up to the annex, it would have had a considerably steeper incline.

After they'd gone nearly fifty yards, Chloe whispered, "We're getting close, so best to stay quiet."

Ten yards further on, they came to a stop in front of a cinder-block wall that closed off the tunnel.

"I thought you said this went all the way through," Ash said, feeling suddenly panicky.

"You're such a downer."

She knelt by the wall and worked her fingers into the gaps on either side of a block on the bottom row. Within seconds, she slid it out. Peeking through, she shined her light into the opening then sat back up. Four more blocks came out. When she was done, she'd created a hole big enough for them to snake through.

"This was apparently put up when the hospital finally closed. They were supposed to fill in everything on this side of it." She shrugged. "I guess they didn't have the money."

"How did you find out about it?" he asked.

She was silent for a moment. "Matt's people, when they got me out. They showed me."

Before he could ask another question, she disappeared through the wall. Ash, left in the dark, had to feel his way down to the opening then slip through and join her. On the other side, the tunnel went on for another twenty feet, then T-boned into a wide corridor.

"Where exactly are we?" he asked.

"This is the main hospital. The part that was built into the side of the hill," she said. "We're on the top floor, but still under-ground."

Ash tensed. "Where will my kids be?"

"Two floors down," she said without hesitation.

Once more he thought about leaving her behind, but she'd

proved more useful than he'd expected. So instead, he said, "Show me."

"There are five stairwells," she told him. "One at each corner, and a fifth along the south wall." She pointed off to their left. "We're actually on the fourth floor. Your kids'll be on the second, in the northeast corner." As she said this, her jaw clenched a little. She was quiet for a moment. "The quickest way is by either of the north-side stairwells, but there's an excellent chance the others will hear us before we can even get close."

"So we use one on the south side," he said, eager to move.

"Yes, but not one in the corners," she told him. "The one in the middle. This floor used to be where the doctors' offices were. The middle stairway is attached to the old hospital director's office. It was his private way of getting in and out."

"Fine," he said impatiently. "Can we just go?"

She glanced at him without moving. "You might want to get your gun ready."

The middle stairway creaked a bit as they went down, but not enough, Ash hoped, to draw attention. When they reached the closed door at the second floor landing, Chloe stopped and listened.

"I don't hear anything," she whispered.

"What's on the other side?"

"An examination room. Or at least I think that's what it used to be."

"Do they use it?"

"No," she said, shaking her head. "There was a stack of old wheelchairs there when I came through. That was about it. They only use a small area in the back of the building. "

As she reached for the door handle, Ash grabbed her arm, stopping her.

"I'll go first."

Holding the SIG in one hand, he grabbed the knob with his other and eased the door open.

Indirect sunlight filtered into the examining room from a window on the south wall, providing more than enough illumination to see the stack of wheelchairs Chloe had mentioned. From the dust on the floor it was clear no one had been through here in a long time. Ash stepped inside, and moved quickly across the room to the main door. There was only silence on the other side.

He hesitated for a moment, then turned to Chloe. "There's light here. If you want, you can wait until I come back."

She raised an eyebrow. "If I want? You're not *telling* me to stay?"

Shaking his head, he said, "It's up to you."

"Let's go, then. You're going to need me."

He nodded reluctantly, then opened the door. The hallway on the other side was dark, but not pitch-black like the tunnel or the basement. The scant bit of illumination was courtesy of sunlight spilling out of a couple open doors to the left.

"I assume we go right?" he asked.

She nodded.

"Mind if I carry the flashlight now?"

She hesitated for a moment, then handed it to him.

The hallway got darker and darker as they headed back into the section that was embedded in the mountain. There were doors along both sides. The few that were open led into rooms that Ash sensed hadn't been used in decades.

They'd been going for just over a minute when Chloe touched his back and pointed ahead at an opening to another hallway. He stopped at the corner, listened, then peered around it. There was a very dim light at the far end, but that was it.

"If they're here, that's the part of the building where they'll be."

If…

He was beginning to wonder. So far there had been no sign of anyone else in the building. Surely by now, they would have heard at least one of these mysterious people who were supposed to have his children. It was just too damn quiet. The condition of the building didn't help his mind, either. It was a dump. Why would they have brought his kids here in the first place?

He turned down the hall, knowing the only way to find out for sure was to keep going.

Silence continued to reign as they got closer and closer to the other end. With each new step, Ash couldn't help but think that

Matt's information must have been wrong. There was no way anyone was here. He moved all the way to the end of the hall, then stopped for another check.

Stone. Dead. Silence.

Even in places with just a few people around, there was always a sense of others. Ash didn't have that sense now.

He stepped out into the intersecting hallway without checking first, knowing no one would be there. And he was right.

"We're alone," he said, not bothering to whisper. "Matt was wrong. They're not here."

Chloe was more tentative as she stepped out to join him. She looked one way down the hallway, then the other, her face full of confusion. "He was sure of it. I know he was."

"Maybe he was just—" He stopped himself and shook his head.

"Just what?"

"Nothing."

"What did you mean? Just what?"

"I didn't mean anything, okay?"

She stared at him, obviously waiting for more. When he remained quiet, she said, "I'd be dead if it wasn't for Matt and Rachel. There's no question about it. And you'd be dead, too, if they hadn't changed how you look and given you a new name. So if you're questioning whether Matt was lying to you or not, don't. He wasn't. He never would."

Without another word, she turned and walked down the hallway to the right, fading into the black.

"Are you coming?" she called out. "I can't see anything without the flashlight."

"What's down there?" he asked.

"If your kids were here, they would have been kept down this way. We should check."

Doubting they'd find anything, he walked down the hall and joined her.

34

Within fifteen minutes of being posted online, video of what appeared to be two teenagers murdered by soldiers somewhere within the quarantine zone had been picked up by several blogs, and spread through the Internet via Twitter, Facebook and a half dozen other social networking sites.

Its first television appearance was on a German network, thirty-five minutes later. Another hour passed before the American networks finally started showing the footage. While some immediately dismissed it as phony, others pointed not only to the effort that would have been needed to intentionally create something like it, but also to the footage's incredible realism.

Network researchers worked feverishly to find out who had posted the video. The account had an ID made up of numbers and letters that, on the surface, meant nothing to anyone. When the video-hosting site was contacted, they denied requests for the user's true identity, citing privacy guidelines. The only information that had been uploaded with the video was the line: *Shot by my friend this morning in the Mojave quarantine zone, so sad!*

While the search for the poster was going on, the Army vehemently denied any connection to the events in the video. They, too, pushed the idea that the footage was staged.

The breakthrough came in the form of a phone call from a teenage girl named Frances Newcombe of Ridgecrest, inside the quarantine zone, to her cousin John working at Glitz, an entertainment-focused cable channel based in Los Angeles. John was a producer on the long-running show *Tinseltown Tales*, which, in his case, meant he spent most of his time in edit bays making sure the shows were fast-paced, exciting, and made at least a little sense.

"I don't know what you're talking about," he told her when she said she knew who had uploaded the video. He'd been tied up most of the day on an episode about a recently failed celebrity marriage, and was unaware of the latest developments concerning the Sage Flu.

"How can you not know?" Frances said. "It's been on the news, like, nonstop for the last hour."

"What has?"

"The video of the soldiers carrying away the bodies of two people they'd killed in the quarantine zone!"

The producer frowned. Sure, there was the unfortunate incident in Tehachapi, but soldiers openly firing on civilians? Not likely. Besides, his cousin was sixteen, an age when kids easily jumped to conclusions and felt everything was the end of the world.

"Hold on," he said, then put his hand over the phone. "Tony, you know anything about some footage on TV of soldiers and dead bodies in the quarantine zone?"

Tony, the editor, spun around in his chair. "Yeah. It's wild, isn't it?"

"You saw it?"

Tony nodded. "When I went to get more coffee a few minutes ago. It was on the TV in the break room."

"Who shot it?"

"They don't know. They're trying to figure that out. Someone uploaded it to the Internet but didn't give their name."

John took his hand off the phone. "You know who shot this video?"

"That's what I've been trying to tell you," Frances said. "Okay, I don't know who *actually* shot it, but I do know who put it up. It's my friend Martina's account."

"You're sure."

"One hundred percent positive."

"Have you asked her about it?"

"I tried calling her cell, but I couldn't get through."

"Give me a second," John said. If his cousin was right, and this video *was* generating a lot of buzz, then this could be a very, *very* big moment for him. "Okay. Give me her name and her number." She did. "What about her home? If we can't get through to her cell, maybe we can find her there." His cousin gave him that, too.

"Don't forget I'm the one who gave it to you," she said.

"Don't worry. I'll pass this on, and maybe someone will call you to find out more."

"You mean like one of the reporters? Will I be on the air?"

"You never know. I'm glad you called me, Frances. I'll talk to you later."

He hung up before she could ask anything else.

"What was that all about?" Tony asked.

John just smiled, then ran out of the room. He didn't stop running until he reached the door of the network president, who, it turned out, was watching the desert canyon footage on their sister network PCN at that very moment.

When the video of the desert shooting first aired on PCN, Tamara and Joe had been arguing about the story she and Bobby had put together about the riot at Tehachapi, and, specifically, what they thought had really happened to Gavin.

"I'm telling you," Joe said. "The minute that goes on the air, we are all fired."

"You saw what I saw," she argued. "I could tell. It was in your eyes. You know it was the same guy."

"We all *think* it was the same guy. We don't know one hundred percent. But that's not even my point."

"Oh, come on, Joe. How can you say that? That man *killed* my brother."

"See, *that's* what I'm talking about. You aren't objective on this. Even if it is the same man, and he did kill your brother, you are too emotionally involved to be the one reporting it."

"Of course I'm emotionally involved, but I've kept myself in check and you know it! That's a damn fine report and we need to air it."

"Oh, we do, do we? And when whoever's anchoring comes back to you, that is, if they haven't fired us already for airing something we haven't warned them about, when he comes back and asks you questions about the report, you're going to keep your cool? You won't show any emotion? What if he questions the connection? What if he just hints that maybe there's another explanation? You going to be able to hold it together then?"

She clenched her teeth together. "It's the truth, and you know it."

"No. I *don't* know it. Not for sure."

She gawked at him. "What? You saw the same thing I—"

"Hey, guys!" Bobby called from inside the van.

"—did. You *know* it's the same guy. You *know* he—"

"Guys, seriously! Get in here!" Bobby yelled.

Tamara glanced over at the van, then back at Joe. "We're not done," she told him, then headed over to see what the other member of their team wanted.

Bobby was sitting in the chair in front of the mobile editing station. On one screen was footage he'd been shooting around the base. He was supposed to be putting together a report about the conditions the media had to work under since being moved to the base. On the other screen was a live feed from the network of some amateur footage shot in what looked like a desert canyon. Tamara could see several people in biohazard suits, and, during a brief second when the camera tilted up just a bit, at least one helicopter outside the canyon.

The suited people were standing next to a couple of bodies.

"What is this?" she asked.

"More Internet video," Bobby told her. "Network's played this one a couple times already."

As she watched it, Tamara couldn't help but feel the sense of something familiar.

Whoever was doing the filming seemed to be above the action. As the bio-suited people began bagging up the two bodies, a voice said in a haunting whisper, "That's my brother, and my girlfriend. Those...those men shot them. We weren't doing anything, but they shot them."

"My God," Tamara said.

The image zoomed in, intending, it seemed, to identify the people in the suits. But the angle was making it difficult, and the suit masks weren't helping. Still, the camera operator was able to hold on two of them just long enough to get an idea of what they looked like.

Tamara tensed. "You're recording this, right?"

Bobby nodded. "Every second."

She said nothing for a moment, willing herself to remain as calm as possible. "Bobby, can you bring up that video of the soldiers from the helicopters that landed here?"

He gave her an odd look but said, "Sure."

He punched a few buttons, and the report he'd been working on earlier disappeared from its monitor, replaced by the requested shots.

"Scroll ahead to that part where you were trying to zoom in for me," she said.

He sped up the footage.

"There," she told him a few seconds later. "Back it up a little bit, then let it play."

He did. On the screen they watched the soldiers talk together, then the picture zoomed in quickly, rushing past Gavin's killer and focusing for a few moments on the interior of the helicopter. Just like she remembered, there was a clump of something yellow on the seat.

"Freeze there," she said. Once the shot stopped moving, she looked at the other two. "Am I seeing things?"

Both men stared at the screen, then looked back at the network feed.

"Son of a bitch," Bobby said under his breath.

The yellow clump looked very much like one of the bio-suits worn by the people in the desert canyon.

"Hold on," Joe said, shaking his head. "I'm sure all crews have been outfitted with these kinds of suits. They probably all look alike."

"I'm sure you're right," Tamara said. "But then that means you're also conceding those people in the video are part of the military."

Joe didn't have a response to that.

"There's something else," she said.

Once the network finished playing the desert clip, Tamara had Bobby go back to where the kid whose friends had been shot zoomed in on the biohazard face masks. Bobby paused on the image she requested, then went back to the footage he'd shot of the men outside the helicopter there at Fort Irwin. Once more, she had him pause on an image.

She didn't have to say anything.

The features and expression of the man on the left screen were exactly the same as the features and expression of the man on the right.

"I want to talk to whoever shot that footage," she said.

Without looking away from the screen, Joe said, "Let me see what I can do."

35

The door Chloe opened led into a dark section of the building that was obviously built into the side of the hill. Ash moved past her into the room, swinging the light around to get a quick take on the space. But he barely registered anything before the overhead lights came on.

He whirled around. Chloe was standing by the door, her hand next to a switch.

Power in this decrepit building?

It seemed odd, but then, as he looked around, he realized the room he was in wasn't decrepit at all. It was clean, almost sterile—white walls, black-tiled floors, no dust, no mud. Even the air smelled pure. It was as if they'd been transported out of the abandoned building they'd been in, and into a brand new hospital a million miles away.

The room wasn't particularly large. There were benches against two sides and a row of empty bins along the wall.

Chloe pulled open the only other door in the room and passed through. As Ash followed, she switched on a light in the new space. They were in a corridor, with a dozen doors leading off it in either direction.

"They're gone. Definitely," she said.

"If they were here at all."

She looked at him. "Let's check."

She began opening doors. Behind each were shorter hallways with what appeared to be a nurse's station near the front, and anywhere from three to five doors on either side. These spaces were as immaculate as the first room had been.

Starting at the far end, Chloe and Ash entered each hall and went door to door, checking inside. Each door opened onto an empty room. It wasn't hard to imagine the rooms were designed to hold a bed, and that each of these small hallways was like a hospital ward.

"What do they use this for?" he asked.

Chloe said, "Whatever they want."

That seemed to be all the answer she was willing to give. Ash noticed that with each new ward they entered, she seemed to draw more and more into herself.

So far, they had found nothing. As Ash approached the door for the next ward, Chloe said, "Not that one."

"Why not?"

She walked past him to the next door down. "We'll try this one."

But it was as empty as the others, and so were the final two after that.

"We haven't checked that one yet," he said, nodding at the door they'd skipped.

She stared across the hall at it for several seconds, then finally said, "Okay."

When he opened the door, the new ward looked exactly like all the others. He walked in and checked the first room. Empty. As he stepped back out, he noticed that Chloe was standing in the ward doorway, her feet not having crossed the threshold.

"You okay?" he asked.

She gave him a quick nod, but didn't say anything.

He knew this must have been where she'd been imprisoned. He wondered what they'd done to her, what had affected her so deeply.

He walked over to the room directly across the hall and looked inside. It was a mirror image of the first room. He moved to the room next door—same again—then crossed over to its opposite.

When he flicked on the light this time, he got a surprise. The room was furnished. There were two hospital beds, two tables that could be rolled into position so a patient could use them, a padded chair by the door, and a cabinet between the beds.

He walked all the way in.

"What is it?" Chloe called out.

"This one's not empty."

There were no sheets on the beds, but the mattresses themselves looked new. He leaned down to take a cautious sniff. Neither smelled of age or decay.

He checked the cabinet, then searched the rest of the room to see if anything had been left behind. The only thing he came up with was a hair, thin and brown and long, that had fallen between the mattress and the headboard of one of the beds. It could have belonged to a million different people, a billion even, but it could have also belonged to Josie. Had his children really been here? Was it possible?

He carefully rolled up the hair, put it in the change pocket of his jeans, then continued searching the room but found nothing else. When he turned to leave he was surprised to see Chloe standing at the door.

"I…I had the same kind of bed," she said, her eyes flicking to the left down the hall, unconsciously looking in the direction of the room Ash assumed had been hers. "But it was…it was only me. Your kids are lucky they have each other."

"There's no way to know if they have each other," Ash said. "I don't even know if they were really here." He looked back toward the beds, trying to hold himself together. "The only thing we know for sure is that they *aren't* here now."

When he looked back, Chloe wasn't in the doorway any more. He exited the room, assuming she'd be back at the ward door, but instead she was standing in the middle of the hall, staring at the last room on the right.

"Let's go," he said. "There's no reason to stay here."

But as he took a step toward the exit, she didn't move.

"Chloe?"

Without looking at him, she said, "Matt's…Matt's inside person…is the same one who helped me." The words were obviously causing her a great deal of distress, but Ash couldn't understand why. "He would…leave me…messages. You know…so I'd know I wasn't…alone. That helped me to survive."

"You don't need to torture yourself like this," Ash said. "Come on."

"Matt told him I was coming with you," she went on as if she hadn't heard him. "If something…changed, he…might have left me…a note."

Ash took a step toward her, suddenly hopeful. "A note?"

She continued to stare at the door. "We don't even know if…he got Matt's initial message…but if…if…if he did…"

"If he did, what, Chloe?"

She took a couple of deep breaths. "He would probably leave it somewhere only I would know."

"Where?"

The silence stretched out for a dozen seconds, then she said in a barely audible voice, "In my room."

"It's okay," Ash said, trying to calm her down. "Just tell me where it is, and I'll check."

Her head began shaking left and right. "No. I have to do it. It's my spot. My place only."

Her breath shuttered in and out one more time, then she took a step toward the door, then another step and another, each coming quicker than the last. When she reached the room, she went inside without hesitating.

Ash wasn't sure what to do. Should he let her look on her own or should he help? When half a minute passed and she hadn't reappeared, he decided he needed to see what was going on.

As he opened the door, he could hear her sobbing.

"Chloe?" he said, rushing in.

She wasn't there.

"Chloe?"

Another sob, this one from his left through the doorway to the bathroom. He found her inside on her knees in the middle of the tiled floor.

He dropped down beside her. "Are you hurt?"

She jumped when he touched her, surprised that he was there. "I can do this. I'll be okay."

"Just let me help."

"I can do this," she repeated, but didn't move.

Her put his arm around her shoulders. She tried to pull away again, but then she took another breath, this one longer and slower, and she let him leave his arm where it was.

"What did they do to you?"

She said nothing for several seconds, then finally turned and looked up at him. "I don't remember."

"Well...that's probably...good, right?" he said, realizing he shouldn't have asked in the first place. "Maybe it's best that way."

"No," she said quickly. "You don't understand. I *don't* remember. *Anything.*"

"What do you mean, anything? From when you were here?"

Again, her head shook. "From before. I remember waking up here. I remember being strapped to the bed. I remember the needles and the pills and the tests. I remember all that. But anything that came before in my life? I don't remember." She looked around the room. "This place took my past from me."

Good God, Ash thought. "You don't...know anything about your past?"

"I *know* about it. My name used to be Lauren Scott. Matt and Rachel showed me family pictures, articles in the local paper where I apparently grew up, my college diploma. I even sat in a car down the street from my...my parents' house, and watched them walk along the sidewalk. If I hadn't been shown a photo of them, I would have never recognized them. They were just two people I didn't know. I had no feelings for them whatsoever." Her eyes narrowed. "These people took that from me. They took *me* from me. That's who I can't get back."

Ash wasn't sure what to say. Was it better to remember that his wife was dead, and that he had two children who were in need of his help, or to be conscious of the fact you could remember nothing at all?

She wiped a hand across her cheeks. "I'm sorry. This isn't helping. We're here to find your kids, not watch me break down."

"Don't worry about it. You have every right to be upset."

She tried to smile, but failed, then said, "Help me up."

Once they were back on their feet, Ash asked, "Was there a note?"

"I...I haven't checked yet." She stepped toward the shower. "It's over here."

"I can get it."

"No. I'm okay now."

Whether she was or not, she was at least more in control of

herself as she stepped into the shower stall. Water for the shower was controlled by a handle that could be moved left or right. Behind the handle was a concave metal plate that curved into the wall. Chloe pressed her fingertips around the edge of the plate, then twisted it to the left. It moved about two inches, then slipped out of whatever clamp was holding it in place. She moved it as far out as the still-attached handle would allow, then reached into the gap behind it. When she pulled her hand back, there was a piece of paper between her fingers.

Ash tried to temper his anticipation. The paper could still be nothing. A note from when she'd been here before, perhaps, or...or...

She unfolded it, read what was there, then showed it to him.

There was a date at the top, that day's date, and a time, ten a.m., with the word "gone" after it. That meant as few as six hours before, Josie and Brandon had still been there. The next part read:

Kids still alive. Taking to NB7.

Alive. They're alive. But what did he mean by "still"? Did that mean their time was almost up?

"What does NB7 mean?" Ash asked.

"It's the way the others refer to their different facilities. They each have alpha-numeric designations."

"Do you know where this place is?"

She shook her head. "I've never heard of it."

Ash felt his world start to crumble. He'd been so close. He put a hand over his eyes, and could feel the pressure in his head building. He had to do something, but he didn't know what.

Chloe touched his back. "Hey. We're not done yet. There's someone who might know."

He looked at her. "There is?"

She hesitated. "Yes. A woman named Olivia."

"Can we call her?"

Chloe shook her head. "We can't call. We need to go see her."

"Where is she?"

"Not too far, I think. Maybe an hour, hour and a half away. Matt's the one who knows exactly where she is."

Without even hesitating, Ash pulled out his phone and called the emergency number Pax had given him.

36

Rachel entered Matt's office as he was finishing up his call with Ash.

"Did they find the children?" she asked when her brother hung up.

"The place had already been cleared out."

"Oh, no."

"It's not as bad as it could have been. Winger was able to leave a message. They've taken the kids to someplace called NB7."

"Is that on our list?"

"No. I checked while we were talking." He paused for a moment, then looked at his sister. "Chloe suggested Olivia might know where it is."

"Olivia?" Rachel frowned. "Even if she does, she might not tell them."

"You don't think it's worth trying?"

Rachel looked out the window. Her history with Olivia was not a particularly pleasant one. "Does it matter? You've already sent them to the Bluff, haven't you?"

He adjusted himself uncomfortably in his chair. "If you can think of any other way to find out in a hurry, I'm more than open to it. But, yes, I've already sent them there."

Rachel stared at the distant hills, knowing her brother had done the right thing, but also not sure if she would have done the same if it had been up to her. Of course, truth be told, if it *had* been up to her, Olivia would have been dead a long time ago.

Finally, she turned back to him and set the paper she'd been carrying on the desk. "We have another situation."

Matt read the message. "Damn."

"I think there's a better than fifty-percent chance we're going to have to perform an extraction," she said.

He glanced through the message again, then nodded. "Keep a close eye on it, and get everything in place."

"I have a truck already on its way."

He eyed her suspiciously.

"It's going in with a CDC pass," she said. "There won't be any problems."

"Still, an extraction's going to be tricky, given the location."

"But not impossible."

"No. Not impossible."

At Bluebird, a similar high-level conference was being held. The Director of Preparation—who, among other things, oversaw Dr. Karp's work and the operation Mr. Shell was heading up to keep a lid on things—and two of his counterparts were meeting in a small room specifically designed for these kinds of quick, private meetings.

"It's getting out of hand," the Director of Recovery said. "We are dangerously close to exposure."

"I don't think we're even near that point yet," the DOP said.

"Don't you? What about that video that the networks are blasting all over the place today? Those weren't military troops doing the shooting. Those were *our* people."

"Yes, they were. And even if they weren't covered in bio-suits, there would be no possible way for the connection to be made back to us."

"What were they doing out there anyway?"

"Their job."

The DOR didn't look as if he liked the answer.

"Is there a problem?" The DOP asked.

"Given the safeguards of KV-27a, it just seemed…unnecessary."

The DOP looked at his colleague for a moment. "Are you worried about the deaths of two people?"

"Of course not," the other man said quickly. "There just seems to be a lot of…glitches with this particular operation."

"You're right. There have been several *glitches*."

"Starting with KV-27a reaching the public in the first place!"

"True, but I think that has actually been a benefit to us. As have these glitches. They've exposed areas of concern that are much better for us to know about now than later, don't you think? If we had to do it all over again, I think I would have pushed for something like this to occur by design as opposed to by accident."

"You've got to be…" The DOR fell silent.

"What? Kidding? Is that what you were going to say?" The DOP's eyes cooled to hard steel, his voice cutting the air as he spoke. "The stakes we're playing with are enormous. I can't worry about two kids being killed in the desert. They're not even a drop in the bucket of what's to come if we're to achieve what we've set out to do. The future of humanity is in our hands alone. That's the oath we've all taken, or have you forgotten? Perhaps you think we need to change the parameters of the entire project. Perhaps you think we need to go easy." He paused. "Tell me, how are you going to react when implementation day comes? Are you going to raise your concerns then, too?"

The DOR tensed. "Of course not." He stood up. "Perhaps I was…hasty."

The DOP immediately became calm and conciliatory. It was one of the abilities that made him an excellent leader within Project Eden. "We're all under a lot of pressure. Don't worry about it." He offered his hand.

The DOR shook it, nodded at the silent third man in the room, then left.

As soon as the door closed, the DOP said, "He needs to be replaced."

The third man, the Director of Survival, rose to his feet. He was smaller than the others by a foot, and one of the most dedicated members of the project. "Yes, he does. But he also has a point about the mistakes."

"I know." The mistakes *were* good learning tools, but the ones who had made them would need to be dealt with.

"What about the KV-27a safeguards? Any word?" the DOS asked.

"I'm told everything is on schedule."

"Excellent." Changing the subject, the DOS said, "Where are

we on the vaccine?"

"Almost there. We should have a working batch within a few weeks."

"Then we're on to the next phase."

The Director of Preparation smiled. "Yes, we are."

By late afternoon it was clear to Martina and the others in the segregated group at Cryer's Corner that Paul Unger was not just suffering from his wounds, but was also ill.

Coach Delger had said that if he only had the increased fever, then it could have been explained by his injuries. But there was the cough, too, and the growing congestion, all symptoms that had been previously reported in connection with the Sage Flu.

Martina was a smart girl. She knew if things played out the way they had everywhere else, she and the others in the segregated group would all be dead within a day or so. It scared her more than she wanted to admit, but she tried to stay calm because a few of the others were totally freaking out already, and someone had to keep their head.

It didn't help that the news reported the virus had spread throughout the entire quarantine zone, including their hometown of Ridgecrest. And even though the correspondent had said the new outbreaks seemed to have been contained to a handful of people here and there, the sense of doom that hung over the café was stifling.

There was no report, though, on the fact that the quarantine roadblock had been moved from ten miles west of Cryer's Corner to ten miles east. Perhaps they were the only ones who knew about that. And given the fact that the phones, and therefore the Internet, had stopped working not long after Martina uploaded Paul's video, there was no way they could share that information.

The only good news as far as she was concerned was Ben. That was the name of the cute college boy. He was from San Mateo in the Bay Area and had been driving home from a skiing trip in Colorado. Luckily for Martina, he wasn't one of the people flipping out so, naturally, they had gravitated toward each other.

At that moment, they were sitting in a booth at the far corner of the café, absently watching the TV. The reporter was a woman who'd been caught inside the zone, and was now at Fort Irwin near Barstow with several other members of the media. Martina wasn't paying her much attention, though. The woman had pretty much been saying the same thing over and over all day.

"This sucks," Martina blurted out.

"The news?" Ben asked.

She glanced at the screen. "Well, yeah. That, too. But all of this. It completely sucks. We can't even call our families to see how they're doing. It's like we're in prison."

"At least this prison has cushioned seats," he said, smiling.

"Ha ha." She turned her attention back to the TV, but could only take it for another minute before she said, "I wish I'd just start coughing and get it over with, you know?"

Ben didn't say anything.

"Did you hear me?"

She looked at him. He was staring out the window at something in the distance. Finally, as if on delay, he said, "Sorry." Then, with a sudden burst of energy, he scooted out of the booth. "I'll be right back."

"Where are you going?" she asked, but he was already halfway toward the front of the café, so she got up and followed him.

He stopped at the counter near the register and looked around.

"What are you doing?" she asked, walking up.

"Have you seen Molly?"

Molly Cryer was the older woman who, it turned out, owned the café.

"Maybe in back?" Martina suggested.

With a nod, Ben passed through the opening in the counter and back into the kitchen. More curious than ever, Martina continued to follow him.

Molly was sitting on a little stool in back, watching a DVD of some old black and white movie on a small TV set on a desk. She had a soda in one hand, and an unlit cigarette in the other.

"The gas station across the street," Ben said. "There's a big rig behind it."

"Yeah," Molly said without taking her eyes off the screen.

"Whose is it?"

"The rig? That'd be Eddie Jackson's truck."

"Is he around?"

"Nah. He's in…" She paused for a moment. "Reno, I think."

"Who has the keys?"

"I assume Lance does over at the station."

"Great. Thanks."

As Ben headed back out, Martina said, "Tell me what's going on."

"I don't want to get your hopes up."

"About what?"

He said nothing.

"Whoa! Where are you two going?" Coach Driscoll asked as Ben and Martina reached the front door.

"I need to check something," Ben said.

"Well, just stick around right out front. Don't want to expose anyone else."

Most of the unexposed group had been hanging out at the mini-market just down from the café. No one had really laid claim to the gas station on the other side of the road yet, because there really wasn't much to claim other than a couple of pumps and a greasy garage.

Once he was outside, Ben started jogging straight for the station.

Before he reached the road, Martina said, "I don't think we're supposed to go across."

"Then you don't have to come."

Though she'd bent one or two rules in her life, she wasn't a big one for breaking them, but given the fact that by this time tomorrow she'd probably be dead, what did it matter? She picked up her speed and caught up to him midway across the asphalt of the empty highway.

"Still not going to tell me what you're doing?" she asked.

"Still not."

No one seemed to be around as he led her into the gas station's small office. He then started pulling desk drawers open, and slamming them closed when he didn't find whatever it was he was looking for.

After a few minutes, he moved into the garage and took a quick scan around. His gaze locked onto a black cabinet on the wall.

He pulled the door open, then let out a yelp of triumph.

Martina moved around so she could look inside. There were several rows of hooks. Most were empty, but a few had keys hanging from them. Ben moved his finger along the sets that were there, pulling off several.

"Come on," he said. "Let's see if I'm right."

As they stepped out of the garage, a voice yelled out, "What are you doing in there?"

Lance Cryer, the guy who ran the gas station, was standing near the highway looking at them. He'd been in the group deemed unexposed.

"Just borrowing some keys," Ben said.

"Dammit. You shouldn't have gone in there. That's my place. Now I can't use it until someone washes it all down."

Ben grimaced. "I'm sorry. I wasn't thinking about that."

"Too late now, isn't it?" Lance said. "What are you going to do with those keys?"

Ben looked down at the sets in his hand. After a second, he seemed to come to some decision. "Tell Eddie Jackson I'm sorry, too."

"What?" Lance asked, confused.

Ben touched Martina on the arm. "Come on."

They circled around the gas station to the semi truck parked in back. The first set of keys didn't work, but the second opened the door.

"Go around to the other side," he told her. "I'll open it up for you."

By the time she got there, the passenger door was unlocked.

"Okay, so are we going to make a run for it?" she asked, smirking, as soon as she was inside.

"Not a bad idea. But I kind of think I'd rather die of a cold than a bullet."

That wiped the smile off her face.

"Sorry," he said. "I was trying to be funny. But..."

Shaking her head, she said, "It's okay. Don't worry about it." She glanced at him expectantly. "So why are we here?"

Ben put the key in the ignition and turned it enough to get the electricity inside working.

"That," he said, pointing at a device mounted in the dash-board.

"What is it?"

"CB radio. If we can get it to work, we might be able to get you in touch with your mom."

Martina looked at him. "You...you think so?"

"That's the hope."

It took him a few minutes to get the hang of it, but soon he got it working.

"Hello, hello. Is anyone out there?" he said into the mic. Static. "Hello. I'm calling from Cryer's Corner inside the quarantine zone. Can anyone hear me?"

Static again, then, "...hear you."

Martina hit Ben's arm excitedly.

"This is Ben. Ben Bowerman. Who's this?"

"...ame's Marty Zimmerman. Everyone calls me...ee."

"Sorry, you faded out. Calls you what?"

"Zee. Everyone calls me Zee."

"I can't tell you how great it is to hear your voice, Zee."

"Where'd you say you are?"

"Cryer's Corner."

"Kinda near Death Valley?"

"Yes, sir."

"Hell, I know where that is. Tiny speck of a place. Did you say you're in the quarantine zone?"

"Uh, yeah. Where are you?"

"Sitting in the parking lot of a casino just east of the Cal bor-der along I-15. Stuck here with a load of potato chips I was sup-posed to be taking to Barstow, while I wait to hear where I'm being rerouted. But better stuck here than inside the zone, I guess. What're you hauling?"

"I'm...not a trucker. There's a whole group of us stuck here at Cryer's Corner."

It took a few minutes to explain everything, then another as Zee made the requested call on his cell phone before Martina heard the voice she thought she would never hear again.

"Hello?" her mother said, her voice distorted by the fact it was coming out of a speakerphone on a cell that was then being transmitted over the CB.

"Mom?"

A slight delay. "Martina? Is that you?"

"Yes, it's me," she said, her eyes welling with water.

"This connection is horrible, sweetie. Can you try calling back?"

"No, no!" Martina yelled. "We don't have any service here. I'm on a radio."

"You're on a what?"

Martina loved her mom dearly, but there were some things she didn't get right away. "Just don't hang up, okay?"

A moment later, her dad joined in on another extension. They talked about missing her and wishing she were home. She tried to sound upbeat, and was careful not to say anything about being exposed to the virus. *Let them have one more night of peace,* she thought.

"I want to know about this video you apparently put on the Internet," her father said.

"It's so horrible," her mother cut in. "Please tell me it's not true."

"How did you know I put it up?" Martina asked, confused. Her video account name was a completely random series of numbers and letters.

"We've had several calls from people at PCN, including that reporter out in Barstow. They apparently learned about it from your friend Frances."

Frances, of course.

"Did you really put that up?" her dad asked.

"Yes, Dad. I did."

"But it's fake, right?" her mom said. "That didn't really happen."

"It's not fake, Mom."

Her dad said something, but the static on the line covered most of it up.

"Dad, can you say that again? I couldn't understand you."

"…wants to talk to you, sweetie."

"Who wants to talk to me?" she asked.

"The reporter. From PCN? She gave us her number and wants you to call. I'm not sure you should or not, though."

Martina looked at Ben. "They want to talk to me?"

He shrugged. "It makes sense. That video must be a big thing right now."

Over the radio, her dad said, "Sweetie, are you there?"

She moved the CB mic back to her mouth. "I'm here, Dad."

"Do you want us to give you the number?"

"I'd talk to her, but I can't call from here."

Zee cut in. "I could do it for you, if you want."

"Who's that?" Martina's dad asked.

"That's Zee, Dad. He's helping us with the radio connection." She looked at Ben. "Should I talk to her?"

He shrugged. "I don't see why not. Someone needs to get the word out about what happened to Paul and his friends."

She thought for a moment, then keyed the mic again. "Dad, go ahead and give Zee the number. I'll talk her."

37

Matt had called the place where Ash and Chloe were going the Bluff. It turned out to be two and a half hours away from the old Palmer Psychiatric Hospital, not one.

The directions took them into the Sierra Nevada Mountains, east of Sacramento. Ash was surprised by how light the traffic was until he realized it was probably due to the outbreak down south. Though there had been no reports of cases up here, that didn't mean the fear didn't stretch well beyond the quarantine zone. Better to play it overly cautious and keep your family at home than to risk infection.

They left the interstate behind as they entered the mountains and proceeded up a narrower, windier road into the thickening forest. From there it was down a series of smaller roads. Ash carefully followed Matt's instructions, but even then he almost missed the gate in the darkening twilight.

It wasn't anything special, and in fact looked like a half dozen others they'd passed on the way up. Metal-pipe frame, three twelve-inch-wide planks running from side to side, and that was it. The fence it was connected to was made of wood posts with barbed wire strung between, the majority of it covered by vegetation.

Though Ash was tempted to climb out and push the gate open, Matt's instructions had been clear. "When you reach the gate, stay in your car and wait."

Two full minutes passed before the gate swung open on its own. Once it was completely out of the way, Ash drove through.

The road on the other side was narrow, the feeling reinforced by the pine trees that grew right up to the edge and the overarching canopy created by their branches. This went on for nearly a hundred yards, then suddenly the trees fell away, and they entered a grass-covered clearing at the top of a hill.

Chloe drew in a surprised breath. "It's so beautiful."

At the far edge of the clearing was a house, and beyond it an amazing view of the Sierra Nevada Mountains.

In many ways, the house looked like a smaller version of Matt and Rachel's lodge. Wood-stained sides and large windows and warm outside lighting. This Olivia person obviously lived pretty well.

There were two cars parked out front—a pickup truck and a decade-old Cadillac. Ash pulled in behind them then cut the engine.

"Are you staying here or coming with me?" he asked Chloe.

"I'm certainly not staying here."

They both got out and headed over to the house. As they stepped up onto the porch, the front door opened and Ash got his first shock. The smiling couple who came out to greet them was the same couple who had picked him up in the Winnebago out in the middle of nowhere when he'd been fleeing Barker Flats.

He glanced quickly side to side, thinking he must have missed the RV, but it was nowhere to be seen.

The man, Mike—if that hadn't been a fake name—thrust his hand out at Ash. "Great to see you again," he said. As Ash shook his hand, Mike pulled him into a quick hug. "Simply great." He turned to Ash's companion. "And Chloe, it's been far too long."

"Hi, Mike," she said.

They hugged with genuine affection.

Janice came over next and gave Ash a coy, contrite smile. "I'm sorry about the coffee. I hope you'll forgive me, and know I was only trying to help you."

A day or two earlier, he might have still been mad at her, but now it didn't seem important. "It's fine. I know you were doing what you were supposed to."

Her smile widened in relief, then she gave him a hug. When she stepped back, she said, "Your face looks horrible."

"Janice!" Mike said.

"Are you going to try to tell me it doesn't?" she asked.

Ash touched the bandage that covered his nose. He'd almost forgotten about the surgery. "She's right," he said. "I wouldn't even want to look at me."

"Oh, I didn't mean that," Janice said, then turned away. "Chloe, you are as beautiful as ever."

The women hugged.

"Come, come," Mike said. "We've got a fire inside."

Mike ushered them indoors and led them into a living room.

"Would anyone like coffee?" Janice asked. She looked at Ash. "I can guarantee you this pot is completely harmless."

"Are *you* Olivia?" he asked.

"Me? God, no. I'm Janice."

"Sit," Mike said. "She'll bring us coffee."

Ash remained on his feet. "I don't mean to be rude, but I'm not here for coffee or small talk. I'm here for someone named Olivia. Matt said she'd be here."

Mike and Janice shared a look, then Mike said, "She is."

"Then I'd like to talk to her now."

Mike's smile disappeared. He nodded. "Of course. This way."

He crossed the living room and entered a small hallway near the back corner. As Ash followed, he realized Chloe was behind him.

"Just me," he told her.

"I'm coming, too."

"This isn't your business. It's mine."

"I'm coming, too," she repeated.

He stared at her for a moment, then said, "The second you get in my way, you're out."

They found Mike standing halfway down the hallway, in front of an open door.

"Inside," he said.

They crossed the threshold into what turned out to be a large bathroom.

Ash looked at Mike, confused. "We're in here because…?"

"You've been allowed to come to the Bluff only because Matt trusts you. He thinks you might be able to help us someday. If that trust is misplaced, and you try to betray us, you won't last very long. I'm not threatening you, I'm just telling you. So before we go any further, I need to know if he's wrong about you."

Ash took a moment, then said, "Matt and the rest of you saved my life. And you've all been very generous in helping me try to find my children. I have no intention of ever telling anyone about him or his ranch or even your little house here. But if you do try to block me from getting my kids, all bets are off."

"Good. Then there's no misunderstanding between us," Mike said.

He stepped over to a closet with accordion-style doors and opened them. Inside, there was nothing earth-shattering or unusual, just a washer and dryer and a stack of towels. Mike reached behind the washer and touched something. There was a subtle *click*. Then, with a simple, one-handed push, the dryer moved to the side, and a section of the wall behind it slid open. Mike motioned for Ash and Chloe to pass through.

The space beyond was dark and not particularly large. As soon as Mike joined them, the wall slid shut. The moment it was fully closed, a light came on, and the small room they were in began moving downward.

An elevator.

There might have been more than a little bit of crazy in these people, but they were certainly well funded, Ash thought.

The car continued downward for much longer than he'd expected. When it finally came to a stop, the door opened onto a brightly lit room. There were two men standing just inside, both armed.

"Please step out of the elevator and raise your arms to shoulder height," one of the men said, demonstrating what he wanted them to do.

Ash was surprised to see that he and Chloe weren't the only ones who needed to follow the instructions. Mike, too, had his arms out, as he let one of the men first use a metal detecting wand on him, then pat him down.

When they were all through, the man who'd spoken originally said, "Follow me."

The door on the other side of the room buzzed and he pushed it open. They then entered a long, wide corridor that was as brightly lit as the space they'd just left. About twenty feet from the door was a see-through wall of either glass or Plexi, dividing the area in two. There was a very elaborate-looking security door inset on the right-hand side of the wall.

Prior to this divider, there was a room off to the side that also had a clear wall along the front. Inside, Ash could see at least five more men. Two were standing right at the wall, looking out. Like the guys who'd been waiting outside the elevator, they were armed. The other three were sitting at desks looking at screens, their faces lit by their computers.

The guide led Ash, Chloe, and Mike over to this wall, then said, "Adam Cooper and Chloe White cleared for entrance."

"Cleared for entrance," one of the men inside repeated, his voice coming out of a speaker somewhere nearby.

The elaborate security door on the large divider began to hum as locks disengaged. Finally, there was a slight sucking sound before it swung open toward them.

"Through here," the guide said, leading them to the other side.

There were twenty doors in the back half of the corridor, ten on each side, paired in twos. Down the center of the space were three more armed men, walking back and forth as if they were protecting something.

"What is this place?" Ash asked Mike.

"I'm sorry," the guide said. "No talking here, please."

Frustrated, Ash fell silent as they continued down the hallway.

The pair of doors their guide finally stopped in front of was the second to last on the left side. He opened an eye-level panel on the left door, looked through it, then closed it again. He gave Mike a nod, then opened the door on the right.

This time it was Mike who took the lead, with their guide staying outside.

As if the whole facility wasn't odd already, this new room was even stranger. The first part was a narrow passageway that took a jog to the right, then turned back to the left before opening into a wide space with five comfortable chairs sitting side by side. The chairs were facing the wall on the left, which seemed to be made of opaque, black glass.

"Take a seat," Mike said.

"Where is she?" Ash asked.

"You'll see her in a moment." He gestured at the chairs. "You should take the one in the center."

Once they were seated, Chloe to his right, and Mike to his left, Ash said, "So what now?"

"Now we talk to Olivia. But I want to warn you first, don't buy everything she tells you. Are you ready?"

"I'm ready." Though ready was probably not the right word. He had no idea from which direction she was going to enter. And where would she sit? Down at one of the ends? How could he talk to her there?

Mike pushed a button on his armrest.

A voice came out of a speaker. "Station one."

"This is Mike. We're ready."

"Copy that, Mike."

Suddenly, it was as if the wall in front of them melted away. The opaque black was gone, replaced by clear glass, a window into another room.

Not just a room, Ash realized. *A cell.*

There was a bed in the back and a sink on the wall next to a toilet. Hanging from the ceiling in the corner, enclosed by a wire cage, was a television that was currently off. But the most striking thing in the room was the woman sitting on a plastic stool just a few feet on the other side of the wall, facing them.

Her blonde hair was short, maybe no longer than half an inch. She had an angular face with high cheekbones and eyes that seemed to smirk. She'd barely moved since the wall became transparent, staring at it, a smile resting on her lips.

"Can she see us?" Ash whispered.

The woman suddenly laughed. "Yes. I can see you. Hear you, too."

"This is Olivia," Mike said. "Olivia, we have some guests who need to ask you a few questions."

"So I've been told." Her gaze shifted to Chloe. "You look kind of familiar. We've met before, haven't we?"

Chloe said nothing.

The woman shrugged, then turned her attention to Ash. "You're one ugly son of a bitch, aren't you? Someone throw you in front of a train?"

Ash ignored her comment. "I'm looking for a location, and I'm told you might know where it is."

"Hold on. You know my name. I don't know yours."

He paused for a second, then said, "Ash."

"As in cigarette?"

"Do you know the location of something called NB7?"

Her eyes widened a fraction of an inch, as if he'd actually surprised her. "What are you? One of their hunters?" she asked, nodding toward Mike. "Out to bag you a big-name baddie, is that it?" She smiled, then leaned forward, her elbows resting on her knees. "Have you ever considered for a moment that maybe you guys are the black hats?"

"I don't care about sides," Ash said. "I'm just trying to find…some people who are important to me. I've been told they've been taken to NB7. I just need to know where it is."

"Look, honey. You might as well stop what you're doing right now. If they've been taken to NB7, then they're probably already dead. Time to move on."

Ash tried to maintain his composure. "Just tell me where it is."

"Out of the goodness of my heart? I don't think so."

Ash couldn't hold back. He jumped up and slammed his fist against the wall. "Tell me where it is!"

"Oh, touchy. Who'd they take? Your girlfriend? Wife, maybe? Your mom?"

"Dr. Karp took my kids!"

Olivia stared at him, once more looking a bit surprised.

"Please," he said. "Where is this place?"

"Even if I told you, do you think they'd just let you walk out with them?"

"I'll do whatever it takes."

She leaned back. "Really? Because that actually makes it interesting. Whatever it takes?"

"Yes."

"Hold on," Mike said. He pressed the button on the armrest. "Cut audio."

"Audio off," the voice from earlier said through the speaker.

Ash twisted around. "What?"

"She's tried to make deals before," Mike explained. "The one time someone actually took her up on it, it was a trap."

"I don't care. If it gets me close to my kids, that's all I'll need.

I can take it from there."

"If you're dead, that's not going to help your kids at all."

"And if they're dead, there's no reason for me to live. Switch the sound back on."

Reluctantly, Mike did.

"Can you tell me where my kids are or not?" Ash asked.

"Oh, you're back. Mikey there telling you not to trust me?" Olivia said.

"Answer my question."

She held up her hand and wagged a finger at him. "You know very well how this works. Trade-off."

"There's nothing I can do for you."

"Isn't there?"

He stared at her for a second. "You obviously have something in mind. What is it?"

Her upper lip curled in a faux pout. "I get so little entertainment in here, and you deny me even a little negotiation. Fine. Here's all I want you to do. When you find the fabulous Dr. Karp, just before you put the bullet in his head, because I know that's exactly what you want to do, I want you to tell him hi from me, and ask him why he gave up on me. One more thing. If he says anything after that, tell him he'll be heading to the afterlife before me."

"That's it? That's all you want?"

Her smile was back. "It would mean the world to me."

"That, I can do."

"I thought you probably could."

38

The only thing that kept Ash from speeding down the mountain was the fear of skidding off the side and plunging down the slope. Not only would he and Chloe die, but he'd be effectively killing his children, too. Still, it was hard to keep from pressing the pedal to the floor.

"I'd wish you good luck," Olivia had said after she gave them the location of NB7, "but I'm guessing you're already too late." She stood up and walked right up to the glass, directly in front of Ash.

"Stand away from the wall," the voice from the speaker ordered. "Stand away from the wall."

She locked eyes with Ash, her feet firmly planted where she was.

"Stand away from the wall."

"But just because they're dead," she said, "doesn't mean you can't deliver my message to Dr. Karp."

She obviously hoped that whether his children were dead or alive, Ash would want Dr. Karp to pay for what had been done to his family. And though he wasn't about to accept the possibility that Brandon and Josie were gone, she'd been right.

The biggest problem now was that NB7 was in Eastern Oregon, 370 miles away from the Bluff.

The jet Matt had sent them west on wasn't an option. Mike had checked. The plane was apparently somewhere in Texas, and wouldn't be able to get to an airport close to them for nearly four hours. Add on the flight time, and the fact that the closest place they could land would still be an hour away from NB7, and the balance decidedly tipped in favor of driving.

Mike had suggested they get at least a few hours' sleep at the

Bluff before they left, but that was out of the question. Every minute saved could be the difference between Ash's kids living or dying.

According to the car's GPS, the trip should take them six and a half hours. Ash planned on slicing at least an hour to an hour and a half off that once they hit level ground.

"You going to hold the steering wheel like that the whole time?" Chloe asked.

He shot her a quick look. "What?"

"You're gripping it like you want to tear it out of the dash. You're wasting energy."

He glanced at his hands. His fingers were wrapped around the wheel so tightly his knuckles had turned white. Now that he was aware of it, he could feel the stress running up his arms and into his shoulders. He forced himself to relax, then looked back at the road.

"I can drive, if you want," she said. "I'm pretty good." She paused. "I didn't forget how, if you're worried about that."

"I'm fine," he said.

"Sure, whatever you want. I'm here though, okay? 'Cause, you know, I think you'd want to be at your max when we get there. But that's your choice."

He didn't respond, but he knew she was right. It would be after midnight when they arrived and he'd need to be sharp. Maybe after they got out of the hills, he'd let her drive for a couple of hours while he slept.

"What did you think of Olivia?" Chloe asked.

Ash shrugged. "I just wanted the location from her. I didn't think about her otherwise."

"Last time I saw her she was mad as hell because we'd just caught her, like a cornered wild animal." She paused. "She used to work with Dr. Karp on the experiments. Yours wasn't the first, you know. Not even close. But probably their most successful, huh? Not only did they find something that worked, they found you and your kids, too."

Without looking at her, he said, "What do you mean?"

"The experiments. You know about that, right? Matt told you?"

"He just said we were part of a test."

"Oh. Well, then…maybe…I shouldn't…I mean it's not my place. Oh, dammit. Just forget it."

The silence lasted for nearly a minute.

"He was going to tell me," Ash said. "Back at the ranch, but I just wanted to focus on getting my kids. That first day, he started talking about things that were bigger than I could imagine, like I'd been caught up in some sort of…of…"

"Conspiracy?" she asked.

"Conspiracy," he said, nodding. "That's exactly what it sound like to me. Some nut-job theory like NASA faking the moon landings or the U.S. Government being behind 9/11."

"NASA landed on the moon?" she asked.

He looked at her, his eyes narrowing in concern.

"I'm kidding," she said. "I forgot about who I was, but things that I learned, things that weren't about me, I remember most of those."

"How is that possible?"

She shook her head and shrugged. "Maybe we can ask Dr. Karp when we see him."

"He did this to you?"

"Not him directly. One of his colleagues."

"Now we're back to the conspiracy theory," he said.

"Yeah, except this one isn't a theory. It's conspiracy reality."

Once Ash had realized his kids were still alive, the only thing he'd concentrated on at the ranch was them. He hadn't cared one way or the other what Matt and his friends were really involved in, but he was beginning to think maybe that was a mistake. Maybe he should care, maybe there was something to whatever it was they seemed to think was happening.

"Who are they?" he asked.

"Who are who?"

"These people you all seem to be fighting, who are they?"

"I…I don't know. It's not my place."

"Maybe it's not, but Matt's not here."

"You're going to think I'm crazy."

"I already think you're crazy."

They glanced at each other, then she laughed.

"All right," she finally said. "Are you buckled in?"

He rolled his eyes, then smiled. "Yeah. I'm buckled in."

"I'm serious."

He held up a defensive hand. "Okay, sorry."

She was quiet so long that he looked over to see what was wrong. She had twisted in her seat and was studying him.

"What?" he asked.

"I've never been the one to tell anyone before. I've only listened as others have done it, so I want to get it right."

"Okay," he said, drawing the word out. "Just let me know when you're ready."

He heard her take a breath, then she said, "I'm ready now."

Outside, the mountains had finally started to fall behind them, and the road started to straighten out.

"The end of our world is coming. And it's happening on purpose."

39

"Can you hear me?" Tamara said into her phone. She was sitting in the front seat of the van, with the door closed so that no competing reporter might overhear the conversation, trying to figure out who she was talking to.

"Yes, I can hear you," the female voice replied.

Tamara glanced into the back of the van where Bobby was sitting at the editing console. "Is it okay?" she mouthed.

He gave her the thumbs up, nodding. Often phone conversations needed to be recorded, so they had a device that hooked Tamara's phone into the van's equipment, only this time the setup was a little stranger than other times, as the voice of the person on the other end was coming via another phone being held up to a CB radio.

"Can you please give me your name?" Tamara asked.

"It's Martina Gable."

Tamara gave it a beat so that Bobby would have a place to cut out the first part of the audio, then said, "Martina, can you tell us where you are, please?"

"Yes. We're in Cryer's Corner, California."

"Who's we?"

"Well, I'm here with the Burroughs High School softball team. We were headed home from a tournament when we got stuck here."

"Because of the quarantine?"

"Yes."

"And there are others there, too?"

"Yeah, there's the people who live here, and a few others who showed up in cars and got stuck, too. And Ben, of course. Ben Bowerman. He's the one who figured out the CB."

"And that's how you're talking to us?"

"Yeah. All the phones and the Internet stopped working. And there hasn't been any cell service here since we arrived."

Now that Tamara had gotten the basics out of the way, she started in on the more important questions. "It's our understanding that Cryer's Corner is in the quarantine zone. How did you get there?"

"Well," Martina said. "It wasn't *in* the zone when we arrived. Until this morning, the roadblock was west of us."

Interesting. "And then they moved it east?"

"Yes."

"Any idea why?"

Martina didn't respond right away.

"Are you still there?" Tamara asked.

"Yes, I'm here. We think they moved it because of Paul."

"Who is Paul?"

"Paul Unger. He's the one who took the video your channel's been playing."

Tamara smiled. This was exactly what she wanted. "And you're the one who uploaded it?"

"Yes."

"How long after this did the Internet go out at Cryer's Corner?"

"Maybe an hour or two."

"So, after it started playing on television."

"Yeah."

"I'd like to talk to Paul about the video. Is that possible?"

A pause. "He was…injured just as he got here. He's in the café across the street."

"How bad is he hurt?"

"Messed up his knee and hit his head when the guys in the helicopters took a shot at him."

Tamara froze for half a second, stunned. "Can you repeat that?"

Martina did.

"Can you tell me exactly what happened?"

"Sure. I saw most of it from the roof of the gas station."

The girl then proceeded to tell Tamara about Paul's escape.

After that she relayed the story Paul had told her about his brother and his girlfriend, and their murders in the desert canyon. Through it all, Tamara and Bobby kept sharing shocked looks.

"There's…there's something else, too," Martina said as she finished Paul's story.

"Yes?"

"Coach Delger thinks Paul might be sick. You know, with the Sage Flu. We've split into two groups. One that was exposed to Paul and one that wasn't. No one else has shown signs of anything, though, so maybe he just has a cold."

Tamara had already been feeling a strong connection to the girl, but now she felt her stomach sinking. "Which group are you in, Martina?" she asked, afraid she knew the answer.

"I…I was exposed. That's how I found out about the video. Bu please don't put that part in your story. I don't want my mom to know yet."

"Sure. We'll keep that part out," Tamara said, meaning it. "Can we talk again in the morning?"

"We'll have to come back to the truck where the radio is. What time?"

"Eight?"

"Zee?" Martina asked. "Is eight okay for you?"

"As long as I'm still sitting here, which looks pretty likely," the trucker who'd connected them said.

"Great," Tamara replied. "We'll talk to you then."

As soon as she hung up, she turned to Bobby. "Oh, my God."

"Oh, my God is right," he said.

"I'll bet you that the helicopters that shot at this Paul guy are the same ones we saw. The same ones who killed his brother and his girlfriend."

Bobby didn't reply, but the look on his face said he was thinking the same thing.

There was a knock on the passenger window beside her. Joe was standing right outside. He'd been on lookout to make sure nobody got near the van while she was on the phone. She motioned for him to climb into the back.

"So?" he asked, once he'd joined them.

"You're not going to believe it," she said.

"Tell me."

While Bobby worked on cutting the important parts of the interview into their already prepared piece, Tamara filled Joe in.

"I think we should go up with it on my next spot," she said once she was done.

She could see the hesitation in Joe's eyes.

"Come on. It's great stuff," she told him.

"It is," he said. "I would just feel a bit more comfortable if we sent it to the network first, so they know what we have."

"I think we should just go for it," Tamara argued. "I don't want them messing this up."

"You know that's not the way we're supposed to do things. Network has the right to see all this first."

"Oh, I see. You're Mr. Corporate-Rule-Follower now?"

"No," he said, his face hardening. "But I am a man with a family who would like to keep his job. We do this on our own, there's a very good chance we get fired. You'll have no problem finding something else. Me, it won't be so easy."

She looked out the window, annoyed, but knowing Joe was right.

"Fine," she said. "But if the network tries to change any of this, our version gets posted to the Internet."

Mr. Shell had been right to keep his eye on the reporter. Perhaps taking her brother had been a mistake, but it had revealed that she was a problem.

If people would just let things go, they had a much better chance of living.

He had watched the report the woman and her editor had just sent to their bosses in New York, and knew it was time to do something about it. But given the slapdown he'd gotten over the death of the girl's brother, he decided to cover his ass first.

The Director of Preparation called five minutes after Shell sent him an email with a link to the video.

"Tamara Costello appears to be very good at her job," the DOP said as soon as Shell answered.

"Unfortunately for her, sir."

"Yes."

Shell hesitated a moment. "I assume you'd like her removed."

"Mr. Shell, I believe part of your job is making those decisions yourself. I don't have time for you to run every little aspect of your operation by me first."

Shell gritted his teeth, but pushed his frustration down and said, "I'm just bringing this particular case up in light of what happened concerning the subject's brother."

"Well, he *was* a mistake. You should have seen that from the beginning."

"Yes, sir. You're right, of course."

"I'm sure you'll make the right decision this time, Mr. Shell."

The line went dead.

The Director of Survival was sitting across the table from the DOP. They had both been eating their dinner when the email from Shell came in. Together they had watched the video, then the DOS listened as his counterpart talked to Shell.

"So he was looking for guidance, then?" the DOS asked once the other director had hung up.

"Yes, he was."

"Disappointing."

"It is, but given recent history, not necessarily surprising."

The DOS cut his asparagus into three parts. "Better to know now."

"Very true."

"Is his replacement ready?"

"Of course."

With nothing more to say on the subject, they both began eating again.

40

"On purpose?" Ash asked.

Chloe was still watching him. "I know it's hard to believe, but yes."

"I'm not really sure I know what you mean by that."

"What I mean is that this group of people we're up against, the group you've unintentionally become entangled with, is working toward bringing about the end of civilization as we know it."

He tried hard not to laugh as he shook his head. "You're starting to make the idea of a fake moon landing sound reasonable."

"I warned you," she said.

"You did." He should have known better than to ask questions. Whatever delusions these people were operating under were their business, and obviously had little to do with his kids. But as he watched the road his curiosity got the best of him. "Just exactly how are they supposed to be bringing about the end of mankind?"

"I didn't say the end of mankind. I said the end of civilization as we know it."

"What's the difference?"

She was silent for a moment, then said, "How many people are on Earth right now, at this minute?"

With a smirk, he said, "Well, I'm not sure I have the *exact* number."

She frowned at him. "Roughly."

"I don't know. Four or five billion?"

"Over seven."

"Okay, seven."

"When do you think we reached one billion?"

"I have no idea. Why is it—"

"The early eighteen hundreds. Just a little over two hundred years ago. That means it took over a hundred thousand years for us to reach that number. Do you know how long it took to reach two billion? Just over one hundred and twenty years. Three billion, *thir-ty-three* years. Four, fifteen. You see the pattern?"

"So are you saying we're growing so much it's going to bring about the end of civilization?"

"These people, the ones that Dr. Karp works for, they believe exactly that. They believe the end of civilization is impossible to avoid. But they also believe that if they can control how things end, they can create a new beginning without sacrificing the resources the planet still has."

"Okay, so how are they planning to do that?"

"You ready? This is the good part, relatively speaking. They're going to eliminate over 99% of the current population."

Ash snorted a laugh. "Right. Sure. They're going to kill off 99% of the planet."

"More than ninety-nine. We don't know the exact target number, but we think they want to end up with around ten million people. They start again, only without losing any of the knowledge the human race has already obtained."

Ash shook his head. This was ridiculous. Chloe, Matt, Rachel, and the others had been more than helpful, but they were clearly operating on the fringe of reality. Check that, beyond the fringe.

"What do you think was going on at that base where you and your family lived? You said Matt told you, right? It was a test, Ash. They're trying to find the best method to get rid of everyone else. And when they do finally unleash whatever it is they come up with, you better believe that those they've chosen to remain behind will have been immunized against the disease by a vaccine developed from someone who had true immunity." She paused. "Someone like you and your children."

The sneer that had been on his face disappeared.

"No one ever believes it the first time," she went on. "I didn't. So I don't expect you to, either. But you've heard it now. It's there in your mind. In time, you'll see that everything I've told you is true."

See that everything you've told me is crazy, more like it. But even as he thought that, there was a small kernel of doubt tapping at the back of his mind.

He took the next exit, then switched places with her and tried to get some sleep. But each time he started to drift off he would see the same emergency vehicles that had been parked on his street the night Ellen died. Only they weren't parked just on his street now.

They were everywhere.

41

Night had descended over Fort Irwin, the sky filling with the arcing band of the Milky Way. But Tamara wasn't looking at the sky as she paced impatiently near the lights Bobby had set up for her next report. Joe had disappeared fifteen minutes earlier. She had been under the impression he was taking a call from the network, but how long did it take for them to say, "Yes, play the video"?

The three of them had already been waiting for over an hour for a response. An *hour!* It was enough to make her want to punch the side of the van over and over. Couldn't the network see how important this was? Couldn't they understand she *needed* to do this for her brother? The reporting was good, and the evidence was there. She just needed the damn go-ahead.

Maybe she should have just ignored Joe, and had Bobby send it up live during her spot. Maybe they should still do that.

Not maybe.

With a renewed sense of determination, she headed around the van to tell Bobby to get the report ready, but before she reached the door, the sound of multiple helicopters cut out any ability to have a conversation.

She moved to the end of the van. The area near the media area had seen a drastic increase in the amount of helicopters using it for a landing area. Every time they arrived, Tamara would check, hoping they'd be the two helicopters from earlier, the ones with the man who'd killed Gavin. But they hadn't returned.

Until now.

"Bobby!" she yelled.

Realizing he couldn't hear her over the noise, she ran back and grabbed his arm, then pointed at the camera. As soon as he picked it up, she pulled him to the end of the van. When he saw the helicopters, he raised the camera and turned it on.

Like earlier, several men climbed out of each helicopter, then gathered together. When they finished talking, they started heading as a group in the general direction of the media area.

"What are they doing?" Bobby asked.

"I don't know," Tamara replied. "But try to get a shot of each of their faces."

"It's a little dark." While the landing area was flooded with bright light, the media area had to make do with a few scattered floodlights on poles.

"Do what you can."

As the men got closer, she could see the two in front scanning around, looking for something. Then one of them seemed to settle on the PCN van. He said something to the other man, then the whole group veered slightly to the left and headed straight for Tamara and Bobby.

"What the hell?" Bobby said.

The men were still a good hundred feet away when someone grabbed Tamara and Bobby's arms from behind. They both turned quickly. It was Peter Chavez.

"Come on," he said. "We've got to get you out of here."

"What are you talking about?" Tamara asked.

"I'm talking about saving your lives."

"Saving our lives?" She tried to pull her arm out of his grasp, but he didn't let go.

Moving his face close to hers, he said, "Those soldiers? They're here to kill you. Just like they killed those two kids out in the desert. Like they killed your brother."

"What? How did you—"

"Come on!"

He pulled at her until she was running along with him. Bobby, who'd heard it all, fell in beside her. Chavez led them on an angle that kept the van between them and the approaching soldiers until they were able to duck around the back of a transmission truck belonging to a Los Angeles network affiliate.

"How do you know that's what they're here to do?" Tamara asked, shaken.

"They know about your report. They've killed it in New York, and they've already got Joe, but you're still a loose end."

"Joe? But how—"

"It doesn't matter," he said, cutting her off. "We have to keep moving."

He pushed off the truck, and ran toward the building the media had used to sleep in. Tamara shared a quick look with Bobby, then they both took off after Chavez.

"All the way through," Chavez whispered once they were inside.

The large room in front still had cots set up all over the place, so they had to weave around them to get to the door on the far wall. Passing through it, Tamara glanced back at the building's entrance, sure that soldiers would rush through and pursue them. But, so far, they hadn't shown up.

Perhaps Chavez was wrong. How did he even know the soldiers were after them in the first place?

"Are you sure—"

"Come on, come on!" he yelled.

They were in a corridor now that seemed to run the rest of the length of the building.

"Peter, please," she said, desperately trying to convince herself that everything was all right. "How do you know they're really after us?"

Peter kept looking toward the door that led back into the main room, obviously anxious to keep moving. "I have a friend at your network. Dean Gaboury. Do you know him?"

"Dean? Yes, sure." Dean was one of the suits in charge of afternoon news coverage.

"He told me your story's been killed, and that Joe's already been detained. He said they were coming after you, too, and asked if I could hide you someplace safe, until they can get this worked out. Your network doesn't like the idea of its reporters being arrested."

"Arrested for what?"

"Does it matter?"

"Jesus," Bobby said.

"No kidding. Now, let's go," Chavez said.

Just as they passed through the door at the end of the hall that led back outside, a voice called out from behind them. "Stop right there!"

Tamara's fear level skyrocketed.

"Over there," Chavez said.

He moved across a short expanse of concrete, and pulled open the door of a building that looked very much like the one they'd just exited. Tamara was the last one to pass inside, but Chavez was still able to get the door closed before the soldiers exited the other building.

Halfway through, Tamara stopped. "Hold on, hold on. We can't keep running like this. What's really going to happen if they find us? They'll put us in a room and ask us some questions?"

"You know what they did to those kids in the desert, to your brother."

Her eyes widened. "But...but we're on a base. People have seen us, right? They can't do anything like that to us."

Chavez stepped over to her and grabbed her shoulders, looking her in the eyes. "All right. The truth. Those men are *not* in the U.S. Army. They are something else entirely. They operate on a whole different set of rules. Their only goal is to get rid of loose ends. Joe is dead, and if you don't come with me, you'll both be next." He dropped his hands to his side.

"Joe's dead?"' Bobby asked, shocked.

Tamara stared at him, unable to speak.

"Blue pill or red pill," Chavez said. "Blue pill, you stay in your ignorant world, go out there and talk to your soldier friends, and stay happy for maybe another hour until they put a bullet in your brain. Red pill, I save your lives."

"I'm taking the red pill," Bobby said quickly.

Tamara's lower lip trembled slightly as she licked it. "Okay."

Chavez nodded once, then continued down the hallway.

When they exited the building, they found themselves in a small parking lot. There were half a dozen cars, a couple pickups, and a medium-sized, white cargo truck. Chavez led them over to the truck. The back was already open so he jumped inside, then held a hand down to help them up.

"This is too obvious," Tamara said. "They find us in here for sure."

"Trust me. They won't."

Bobby climbed up on his own, then Tamara reluctantly took Chavez's hand. Once she was on board, he went to the front of the cargo area and touched two of the screws holding the panels in place. A small section of the wall popped open about a quarter inch. He put his fingers into the gap, then pulled it all the way open like a door.

Inside was a three-foot-wide space that ran the width of the truck.

"It's not a ton of room, but you'll be safe. The walls are insulated. Still, I wouldn't talk very much. There's food and water, and a pot in case you need to relieve yourself."

"How long do you think we'll be in there?" Bobby asked, surprised.

"I don't know."

"Whose truck is this?" Tamara asked. "I don't remember it from the roadblock."

"Don't worry about it. It's safe. Once you're inside, there's a latch. Close that and no one can open it from out here. Don't undo it until you hear someone knock three times like this." He tapped lightly against the metal, knock-knock, then paused a second before adding the final knock. He looked out the open end of the truck as if he'd heard something. "I know you have questions, but now's not the time. Just get in."

Bobby immediately went inside.

Tamara looked Peter in the eyes. "You're not lying to us, right?" she asked, already knowing he wasn't.

"I'm not."

"And Joe is dead?"

He nodded. "Yes. I'm sorry. Now get in quickly. *Please.*"

She took a breath and passed through the opening, then watched with a nightmarish sense of the unreal as Peter closed the door behind her.

42

In the dead of night, the landscape of Eastern Oregon didn't look much different than that of the Mojave Desert surrounding Barker Flats. Perhaps it had a bit more scrub covering the ground, but like the Mojave, neither the flatlands nor the nearby mountains had any trees.

Chloe had done well, and had already saved them an hour by the time Ash took over driving again. Their destination was approximately fifty miles north of the Nevada border, in the southeast corner of the state. That was, of course, if Olivia had told them the truth.

What buildings they'd seen so far had been few and far between. There were stretches where it seemed as if this part of the country had either been abandoned or never claimed in the first place. None of it served to boost Ash's confidence.

"Should be five-point-two more miles," Chloe said, her gaze never leaving the road.

Ash glanced at the odometer. She was right. "How do you do that?"

She shrugged. "It's just the way my mind works, I guess."

They drove another tenth of a mile before he asked, "Do you think you could do that before? When you still had your memories?"

"I have no idea."

More silence. "Do you think they did that to you?"

"Can we not talk about this?" she asked, obviously uncomfortable.

"Sorry."

He looked over at her, but she had her back partially turned to him, her eyes staring out the side window. He started to say something else, but decided it was best to leave it alone. Besides, they were closing in on NB7, and he needed to focus so that he didn't miss anything.

According to Olivia, just ahead they would find a road that led to the West.

"It's more asphalt than dirt," she had said. "But not by much."

At the forty-nine-mile mark, Ash started scanning the left side of the road in case Chloe's mileage estimate had been wrong, but it hadn't been. The road was right where she said it would be. It had the forgotten look of having been abandoned to the elements long ago, as if its construction had been well intended, but its promise never fulfilled. Given the fact that it was literally in the middle of nowhere, Ash wondered why it had been built at all.

Even if Olivia had not cautioned them that the road would be watched, Ash would have still kept driving by just like he was doing. She had told them their only chance was if they hiked in. He didn't like the idea of following her instructions precisely, but there didn't seem to be much of a choice.

He drove on for another half mile, then pulled the car to the side of the road. In the wide open landscape, there was really no place to hide the vehicle.

As he turned off the engine, he looked at Chloe. "Stay with the car."

"No way."

"I want to make sure it's still here when I get back with my kids."

She looked outside, scanning both ways down the road. There were no other headlights in sight. "Where would it go?"

"Just stay here."

He got out and circled around to the trunk. From the weapons case, he removed another gun, filled its mag, then set it on the floor of the trunk. He grabbed his spare mags and the container of little bangs, and distributed them between his jeans and his jacket. Picking up the spare pistol, he shut the trunk, then walked around and knocked on the passenger window.

Chloe stared at him for a moment, then lowered it.

"Here," he said, handing the SIG to her. "Just in case."

She pulled back as if it might bite her, but then reluctantly took it.

"You know how to fire that?" he asked.

"I'll figure it out."

He nodded, then said, "I'll be back as soon as I can."

Her only response was to roll the window back up.

He checked both ways before he crossed the empty highway, then angled into the desert on the other side, paralleling the access road that was supposedly being watched. Olivia said NB7 was about a mile and a half in, on the side of the road Ash was currently on.

His eyes quickly adjusted to the moonless night as he made his way through the scrub-covered land. At one point he thought he heard something in the brush. He paused, listening, but the sound didn't return. He decided it was rabbit, perhaps, or whatever other types of animals might choose to live in this nothingness.

As he passed the mile mark, his jaw tensed. Mike had warned him to be careful about believing anything Olivia said. Maybe this was just a lie. Maybe he was the only thing out here. Maybe Josie and Brandon were hundreds of miles away, and would die because he had chosen to follow the directions of an obviously deranged woman locked up in a secret prison.

If that turned out to be the case, he would go back to the Bluff and kill her.

He slowed his pace. If NB7 was here, he had to be close. Better to sneak up on it than to stumble.

Again, he heard something in the brush. It came from behind him, maybe thirty yards. He crouched down, then looked back the way he'd come, letting his eyes focus on nothing in particular.

There. Just off to the right of the line he'd been following, a shadow hovering above the brush and moving in his direction.

A lookout, he thought. *If he's already seen me, I'm done.*

If that was the case, half a dozen others were probably closing in on him from different directions, and he was going to get taken down before he even got to NB7.

Should he run? Stay where he was? Or what?

He looked at the shadow again. It had moved to about forty feet away, then stopped. Carefully, he turned, scanning around, looking for others, but the only thing he could see was more brush.

If there was anyone else out there, they had to be lying on the ground.

If he'd had time to play games, he would have kept moving to see if the shadow was really following him. But time was something he didn't have.

He pulled out his gun, and made a beeline straight for the shadow. Before he'd even gone halfway, it disappeared. Not moved to the right or the left, or any other direction, just disappeared. But he didn't slow until he was within a few feet of where it had been.

He was sure whoever it was had dropped to the ground, blending in with the brush, but there was no one there. He swung his gun around, angling it toward the ground, knowing the person had to be close.

"I could have killed you if I wanted to."

He whipped around. Standing directly behind him, her gun at her side, was Chloe.

"I told you to stay with the car," he whispered.

"And I never said I would. You need me," she whispered back.

"I don't need you. I can do this myself. Now just go back."

He turned and started walking in the direction he'd been headed. After only a couple of seconds, he could hear her following him.

"Chloe, it's not safe," he said, turning back.

"And going into the psych hospital earlier was?"

"That was different. You were the one who knew the layout. I had no choice. But you don't know this place. I'm not going to put you in a position where you might get hurt."

"Not your decision," she said. "I'm here, and I'm coming with you. Now let's go, unless you want to stand here all night arguing."

Short of carrying her back to the car and locking her in the trunk, he saw there was nothing he could do to stop her.

"Okay," he said. "But you do everything I say."

He took her silence for assent, though deep down, he knew it wasn't.

For the next five minutes, his concerns that Olivia had been lying continued to grow. There was nothing but dirt and brush. No buildings at all.

"What's that?" Chloe whispered a couple minutes later.

She was still behind him, so he had to look back to see what she was talking about. She pointed twenty degrees to their right. It took him a moment, but then he saw it, too.

Just ahead, the terrain dipped into a shallow wash, then rose on the other side, perhaps not high enough to be called a hill, but definitely higher than this side of the wash. At the very top was a post or, maybe, the trunk of a small tree. It appeared to be less than a half-foot in diameter, and stood two feet above the brush.

"There's another one," Chloe said. "About twenty feet to the left."

She was right. After that, it was easy to pick out others. They spotted seven in all, stretching in what looked like a line blocking their path.

"A fence?" she suggested.

"Seems kind of low."

They walked through the wash, then up the embankment, finally stopping ten feet short of the first post Chloe had seen. Though it was hard to judge color in the darkness, Ash got the sense the pole had been painted to blend in with its surroundings. Why? There didn't appear to be anything attached to it, or anything sitting on the flat top. It was just...a post.

Chloe pulled out her flashlight and flicked it on.

"Turn that off. Someone will see it," he whispered.

"Anyone who can see this probably watched us walk up the hill," she told him, then pointed the light at the post.

Instead of wood, it appeared to be fabricated out of a plastic-like material. Near the top, a thin slot ran all the way around the post with what looked like curved, tinted glass covering it.

"Any idea what this is?" he asked.

"Motion sensor?"

"Could be," he said. "Let's see how far it goes."

They went approximately seventy-five feet to the right before the row of posts took a sharp left turn. As they followed the new section, the hill fell away and they were on level ground again. Three hundred feet this time, then another turn to the left.

They'd gone twenty feet down this third part when Chloe touched Ash's arm.

"There it is," she said.

Ash had seen it, too.

Land had been carved out of the hill across from them and leveled off. Built exactly in the center of this area was a one-story, commercial-style building with no visible windows. On a large concrete slab next to it were several satellite dishes.

Exactly how Olivia had described NB7.

From their current angle, they could only see the back and west side of the building. There were no cars visible, but given the helicopter that sat on another concrete pad closer to the front of the building, maybe cars weren't necessary. The aircraft was big enough to probably carry up to ten people, not including the crew.

There was a hundred feet between the line of posts and the building, or, as Ash saw it, a hundred feet between him and his children. They had to be there. It was the only possibility. To think otherwise would be pointless.

He continued down, following the odd-looking fence until he could see the front of the building. There were still no windows, but there was a door, and in front of it sat two cars.

He was contemplating walking all the way around to get a look at the east side of the building, the only part they hadn't seen, when two people stepped out the door.

"Get down, get down," he whispered as he crouched into the brush.

They watched the two men walk over to one of the sedans, get in, then drive toward the front of the property. Along that end was a traditional fence with a gate across the entrance road that opened automatically as the car neared. A few seconds later, the vehicle was heading down the half-asphalt, half-dirt road.

That was a problem.

Figure a mile and a half on a bad road would take them two to three minutes tops to reach the highway. If they turned right, no problem, but if they turned left, once they drove another thirty seconds, they'd pass Ash's car parked suspiciously off the side of the road.

So, two and a half minutes plus the time it took to call back to the building, and those inside would know someone was there. He and Chloe had to move before then.

He was pretty sure the posts were motion detectors, perhaps triggered when something passed between them. But while breaking their invisible beam would betray his and Chloe's presence, it would come as a surprise to those inside, and they would be on the defensive as opposed to being on the hunt because they'd been warned by their friends in the car.

A hundred feet. In college, Ash could run the forty-yard dash in four-point-seven seconds. He'd been younger then, and in slightly better shape, but he thought he could still do it in five and a half. And forty yards would actually get him all the way to the front door. Even if there wasn't any kind of delay before the alarm went off, he should still be able to get there before anyone inside had the time to react.

"How fast can you run?" he asked Chloe.

"Fast enough."

"Then that's what we're going to do."

He moved over to the imaginary line of the fence.

"Wait," she said. "What's the plan?"

"The plan? Get my kids back."

He put his head down, then started to run.

43

Their new room wasn't that much different than their old one. There were two beds and a bathroom, just like before. The only difference this time was that the door was locked.

Brandon knew the people watching over them had done something to put him and Josie to sleep before they switched rooms, but he had no idea why. The thought that the room they were now in was in an entirely different building in an entirely different state hadn't even crossed his mind. He thought they were still on his dad's base, just down the hall from the room they'd been in before.

His biggest concern at the moment was his sister. She had yet to wake up. He, on the other hand, had been awake for at least a couple hours, maybe even more.

The same guy who'd been bringing them food from the beginning had brought in dinner a while ago. He was the nice one, the guy who always smiled, and seemed to really care about them.

When Brandon asked him if he knew why Josie was still asleep, the man had said, "Because she's still getting over her illness."

That only made Brandon more worried. What if she was getting sick again? That happened sometimes, didn't it? He was sure he'd heard that before. Would she be even sicker this time? Would she even…die?

Thinking that terrified him. His mom and dad were already gone. What was he going to do if Josie wasn't around, either? He'd have no one. No one at all.

He sat on the edge of her bed, wiping her head with a damp towel from the bathroom. He didn't think she had a fever, but he wanted to make sure it stayed that way.

"It's okay, Josie. I'm here."

Ten minutes later, he fell asleep beside to her.

NB7 was not considered a high-priority location for project security. Its isolation was believed to be its best defense. That did-n't mean there wasn't a security staff on hand, but it did mean other resources such as constant satellite observation were considered unnecessary. It was, by design after all, mainly a storage and backup shelter facility.

What additional security the building did have consisted of a state-of-the-art motion sensor grid surrounding the perimeter, video surveillance along the road that led to the property, and a car recognition system set up on the highway.

The way this last item worked was that cars traveling on the highway would trip an electronic beam twelve miles either to the South or to the North. This would trigger a hidden camera to take a picture of the car and its license plate, then, in a completely auto-mated process, determine the make, model and year of the car. The vehicle would then be checked off when it crossed the opposite electronic eye on its way out of the area. There was leeway built in to the system to account for slower drivers, and for those who might stop to take a few pictures—something that happened more often than those at NB7 may have expected. But once these items were taken into consideration, if a car failed to trip the second beam in the allotted time frame, an alarm would be activated, and a team would be sent out to check.

Just such an alarm went off at 12:58 a.m. for a 2009 Honda Accord with Florida license plates. It was probably nothing, the head of security thought. He bet the driver had just pulled to the side of the road to take a nap. That had happened, too.

Still, protocol was to dispatch a team.

So he did.

Dr. Karp was feeling particularly pleased with himself. He'd been in touch with his research team, and was told all indications were that the new vaccine would work exactly as they'd hoped.

This was the fifth time they'd tested KV-27a, and only the first in which they'd run across someone with immunity. What a bonus that had been. They'd been working on a synthetic vaccine to that point and having multiple problems, but the blood running through the veins of Captain Ash and his children had proved most useful, and the previous problems quickly disappeared. Even the issue of how females versus males reacted was on the cusp of being solved.

The doctor had all but given up hope that they'd find someone like the three surviving members of the Ash family. Between the tests in Tanzania, Bangladesh, Tajikistan, Alaska, Barker Flats, and the unintentional victims of what the media was calling the Sage Flu outbreak, there had been 3578 subjects, of which 3575 had died. That was a success rate of 99.9%, even better than their targeted goal of 99.85%. Which would mean there should be even fewer genetically immune survivors when the official implementation occurred, and thus making it easier for those survivors chosen by the project to control those chosen by nature.

Of course, thinking like that was getting ahead of the game. There were still many obstacles to overcome. But his part was all but done. He was sure of it. Once the vaccine was in production, he could relax and act as consultant for the others as he waited for the great day.

His most immediate task was the children. What he had to do wasn't pleasant, but he was smart enough to understand this was not a task he could delegate. These children would be giving their lives so that he and the others could make things right. In many ways, they were as important to the future as he was. Well, almost.

He would take care of them first thing in the morning before they woke—that would be best. Right now, he was content to let them have one more night of dreams.

Why not? Everything was going so well. Even the outbreak in California had given them more data to back up his work.

Yes, very well, indeed.

44

"What time is it?" Tamara asked.

Bobby turned the camera back on, its display screen lighting up their tiny room. It was the only clock they had. His cell phone was sitting on the editing console in the van, while hers was in her purse along with the wristwatch she had for work but seldom wore.

"Eleven fifty-three," he said.

He switched the camera off to save its battery, plunging them back into darkness.

Tamara dropped her chin to her chest. Eleven fifty-three p.m. They'd been in the truck's secret compartment for over five hours. And who knew how much longer they'd have to stay?

After the first ten minutes in the box had passed, she'd had a moment when she started to think that maybe Chavez was wrong, that maybe the soldiers weren't there to kill them. But then an image of her brother's face appeared in her mind. Gavin looked confused and unsure at first, then suddenly his eyes went wide and he started to scream. The bullet. It had been fired by one of the soldiers who were now chasing her.

"Should…should we check?" Bobby had asked. "Maybe they're gone."

"No," she said quickly.

Another silent minute went by, then, as if to confirm Tamara's response, the sound of several boots running on asphalt could be heard approaching the truck, then stopping at the back.

"Clear!" one voice called out.

"Clear!" a second one chimed in.

There was some scuffling around, then a new voice said, "Team one, recheck the buildings along that row. We'll take these over here. They've got to be in one of them. Say whatever's necessary to get them into the helicopter, but let's get this done now."

Several voices replied, "Yes, sir," then immediately there was the sound of at least half a dozen people running off.

Say whatever's necessary to get them into the helicopter...

The words stuck in Tamara's mind. Any lingering doubts that the soldiers just wanted to talk to them were gone.

As the hours passed, they could hear groups of people running by the truck on five separate occasions. Whether they were the soldiers or not, it was impossible to tell, but it was more than enough to reinforce the idea she and Bobby were better off in their box than anywhere else.

Then an hour passed with no one running by. It was the longest gap there'd been yet. Tamara hoped the others had finally left, and that the next sound she and Bobby heard would be the three knocks on the side of the truck, telling them it was safe to come out.

But the night remained silent.

"Why don't you stretch out on the floor?" Bobby suggested in a whisper.

Their hidey-hole was set up with cushion-topped metal boxes they could sit on at either end. In the boxes, as they'd found out by touch, were food and drink, and on the floor near Bobby's side had been the pot for relieving themselves. So far both of them had been able to avoid the need to use it. Between the two metal makeshift seats was an area plenty long enough for either of them to lie down, just not both at the same time.

"I'm fine," she said softly. "You can use it."

"I know you're not fine, because I'm not fine. Now get some rest. The sooner you're done, the sooner I can lie down."

"Bobby, seriously. You can go first."

"Absolutely not. You first, or neither of us go."

Even though she knew he couldn't see her, she rolled her eyes, but as soon as she lay on the floor, she was thankful he'd forced her to do it. She was completely drained. The time since they'd arrived outside the roadblock at Sage Springs seemed to have blurred into one long, living nightmare.

"We probably lost our jobs," she said as she closed her eyes.

"They won't fire us. They'll make us stars. 'The reporter and the cameraman forced into hiding by...' "

" '...a rogue military force,' " she finished for him.

"Oh, that's good. I like that."

They fell silent for a moment.

"Who do you really think they are?" he asked.

"I wish I knew."

He asked her another question a moment later, but though she could hear his voice, she couldn't make out the words as exhaustion took over, and she fell into a deep sleep.

45

The low tone of the motion sensor alarm suddenly pulsed out of the speaker in the security room right off the lobby at NB7. The head of security had been sitting at the monitoring desk, talking to one of his men. The moment the alarm went off he whirled his chair around and looked back at his computer.

His first thought was that the two men he'd sent out to check for the missing car on the highway had somehow triggered the motion sensors.

By the time he took a good look at the warning screen, six seconds had passed.

Cameras covered the entire grounds, but there was no sense in constantly watching them since the system would alert security to any problems, at which point the video could be reviewed.

Though he immediately saw the others weren't there, the head of security wasn't worried. They'd had these alarms in the past, and all had turned out to be animals wandering in from the desert. The beams were supposed to be elevated high enough to cut out this kind of false alarm, but it still happened.

As he tapped the link to the video, he said, "Luke, go out front and check."

The other man got up from his chair and went into the lobby.

By the time the head of security was looking at the video feed from the west side of the building, ten more seconds had gone by.

There was nothing on the screen but the same monotonous desert he'd been looking at since he'd been assigned to this post. Apparently whatever had triggered the alarm had wandered back out. As he hit the button that would take the video back a full minute, he heard Luke open the front lobby door and go outside.

He almost called out to stop him, but realized he was too late.

He shrugged—no big deal.

Eight more seconds passed.

The video started playing again. He watched in real time for several seconds, then tapped on fast-forward, making the footage go at double speed.

Suddenly, he slapped the keyboard, pausing the image. "What the hell?"

Just then, out in the lobby, the front door opened again.

Ash didn't have a stopwatch, but he was pretty sure he reached the sidewalk near the front door in less than six seconds. Not as good as he hoped, but good enough. As he stopped, he looked back and saw that Chloe was still right behind him.

The entrance was actually a double metal door that opened outward. It was taller than normal and a little bit wider, obviously designed to accommodate large items. There was a security card reader mounted on the wall next to the door, which was a pretty good sign that the door was locked.

The wear marks indicated the right half of the door was the one used most. Ash moved over to the hinges, then pulled the box of little bangs out of his pocket. His intent was to use one of the white crackers along the edge, and hoped it was enough to blow the door loose. But just as he was lifting the lid off the box, the knob turned and the door swung out.

There was no way Chloe could get out of sight, so she froze in place.

The man who stepped through the doorway saw her immediately, but hesitated for a second, caught off guard. That was all the time Ash needed to put the barrel of his gun against the man's back.

"Nothing stupid, agreed?" Ash said, giving his gun a nudge.

"You shouldn't be here," the guy said.

"Is that a yes or a no?"

"Sure. Nothing stupid."

"Good." Ash glanced at Chloe. "Check him."

Chloe stared at the man, not moving.

"You said you wanted to help," Ash said.

She took a breath, then nodded. She first took the man's gun from the holster on his belt, then frisked him quickly as if he might explode at any second.

"Just the pistol," she said when she was done.

"What's inside?" Ash asked the man.

"Lobby," he replied.

"Anyone there?"

"No."

"You're lying."

The man hesitated. "Not in the lobby. In the security office next to the lobby. One guy."

Ash shoved the man toward the reader on the wall, then pulled the guy's security card from his belt and touched it to the pad.

The latch clicked, and Ash pulled the door open.

"Let's go."

The head of security activated the general alarm then jumped out of his chair. His hand was moving to the gun at his side as he pulled open the door to the lobby.

"On your knees."

A woman with milk-chocolate skin and fire in her eyes stood just on the other side of the door, a pistol in her hand pointed straight at his chest.

"Now," she said.

Beyond her, he could see Luke kneeling on the floor. Standing behind him was a man with a bandaged face, and a gun very much like the one the woman was holding.

"This is private property," the head of security said, buying time. NB7's security force was small, but more than adequate to handle the man and the woman, even given the fact that twenty percent of his force was out on the road at the moment, looking for the lost car. "I'd advise you to put your guns down and lie on the floor."

"Your. Knees," the woman said again.

He moved his hands in front of him, holding them palms out. "Hold on. I don't think you fully appreciate the situation you're in. There's more than just the two of us. It would be best if you'd—"

"Chloe, switch," the man holding the gun on Luke said. "I'll deal with him."

"No," the woman, Chloe, replied. "I got this." Her gaze bore into the man's eyes. "Knees."

He grinned and started to shake his head. "Now that's not going to—"

The bullet tore through his leg just above his knee. The pain was so intense he didn't even realize he'd fallen to the ground.

"That wasn't so hard, was it?" she asked, as she removed the gun from his holster.

Dr. Karp had just started to drift off when the general alarm began to pulse. In his half-asleep state, it had at first confused him. He reached for the clock he assumed was on the nightstand to turn it off, but there was nothing there. That's when his eyes popped open and he sat up.

The alarm.

NB7 had always been considered a safe location, its whereabouts known only to a handful of project members. The only reason Dr. Karp and his team were there was because the outbreak in California meant there was a microscope on the state, and the Directors had felt moving the assets—the Ash children—out of state was a good idea. NB7 was the closest and most logical location. Since the doctor had used the facility a few times in the past, he had no problems with the plan.

But now the alarm was going off. Why?

He grabbed the room phone and pushed the number for Security. After the fifth ring, he hung up. His confusion was now turning to concern. He hoped it was just a false alarm, but what if it wasn't?

He pulled his clothes on as quickly as he could. If this was real, and the facility had somehow been breached, then he knew exactly what he had to do.

The children. He had to dispose of them.

Now.

"Well, if they didn't know we were here before, they do now," Ash said, as the low pulsating alarm droned through speakers in the lobby.

"Here," Chloe said.

She tossed him a couple of long, plastic strips she'd taken out of a pouch on the wounded man's belt. They were ties that could be used as handcuffs. As Ash bound his man's wrists and ankles, Chloe did the same with her guy.

"My leg," the man pleaded. "I'm going to bleed to death."

"Yeah," Chloe said. "You probably will."

Ash came over and looked at the man's leg. It was a mess. "You want me to tie that off?" he asked.

"Yes. Yes, please!"

Ash crouched down. "Then tell me where the children are."

"The…the children?"

Without hesitation, Ash placed the muzzle of his gun against the man's other leg. "I'm not going to ask again."

"They're inside. Bottom level."

"How many kids?"

"Two," the man said quickly. "A boy and a girl."

They're here, Ash thought. *We found them.*

He ground the muzzle into the man's leg. "Where on the bottom level?"

Behind them, a door that led into the rest of the building flew open, and several men poured out, opening fire. Ash was in a poor position with his back to them, so he dove through the doorway into the security office. Chloe had been better situated, and was able to get a couple of shots off before she joined him.

"How many?" he asked her.

"I counted four."

He was tucked right up against the doorjamb. "Hit any?"

"One down for sure. Maybe two."

"You're pretty good with that."

"Yeah. Bet you're glad I came along now, aren't you?"

Instead of answering, he peeked around the edge, his gun ready. Apparently, the men who'd come rushing in hadn't known exactly in which direction to fire. There was plenty of damage all over the room, not the least of which were the two now dead men Ash and Chloe had just tied up. Wherever the others were, though, they were staying out of sight.

"Here," Ash said, handing Chloe his gun.

He retrieved the box of little bangs, pulled out four of the gray crackers, and checked their numbers. He then activated the controller.

"You in the office," a voice called out. "There's only one way out of that room and we've got it covered. Toss your weapons out here, then step out with your hands where we can see them."

The man had asked for weapons to be tossed out, so that's exactly what Ash did. He threw the four crackers into the room, trying to arc them around so that they wouldn't all fall in the same place.

"You have ten seconds to toss your guns out here," the voice said.

"We're not going to wait that long," Ash told him.

He set off the little bangs, mentally crossing his fingers that they did what Pax had promised.

They did, and then some.

Even from behind the wall where he was, the bangs were so loud Ash immediately threw his hands up over his ears. Chloe tried to do the same, but was holding the two SIGs so was less than successful.

"Gun," he yelled.

She didn't seem to hear him, so he grabbed his pistol from her and raced through the door.

While the lobby looked basically untouched, the four men who'd been there were all on the ground. Two were unconscious, while one looked like he wanted to be. The fourth guy still had enough wits about him to try to aim his weapon at Ash, but Ash's bullet hit him in the forehead before the guy had a chance to pull his trigger.

Chloe found some more ties and secured the other three men.

"You all right?" Ash asked her.

She touched her ear. "Ringing. But I can hear you now."

Ash grabbed a security card off the nearest man's belt, then used it to open the door to the rest of the building.

Dr. Karp had just left his room when a loud explosion reverberated down from the ceiling.

"What the hell was that?" someone said.

Several of the doctor's technicians were in the hallway because of the alarm. Now most looked truly scared. Although their jobs were ultimately concerned with death, they were not interested in putting their own lives on the line.

Neither was the doctor, but he knew he couldn't show that. There had always been the possibility his life might need to be sacrificed. It was something he understood from the very beginning. It was also expected that in the face of sacrifice, a full project member would still keep the goals of the project in mind, and carry out whatever tasks were necessary to protect it.

So, despite whatever the explosions on the floor above might mean, he knew he still had work to do.

"Learner, Ramos, I need you to come with me."

Two of the technicians broke from the crowd and followed the doctor to the elevator.

46

Most everyone at Cryer's Corner was asleep. The Flu Crew, as the segregated group had come to call themselves, was spread throughout the café. The only two who still seemed to be awake were Martina and Ben. They were lying on the floor next to the booth in the back corner.

Understandably, blankets were in short supply. The residences of Cryer's Corner had been able to scrounge enough so most of the girls had one, but the men had to sleep in jackets and whatever else they could find to wear.

Thankfully, though, the heater in the café worked well enough that no one had to dress like they were spending the night in the Arctic.

"Do you think this might be the last night we remember?" Martina asked.

"God, I hope not. I'm supposed to go to Europe this summer. I hate to think of all those Italian girls I wouldn't be able to meet."

"Ha ha. Funny. I'm serious. This flu is supposed to come on quick, and, and…that's it."

"Paul's still around," Ben said.

"Yeah, but he's sick."

"I'll bet you a glass of orange juice he's still here in the morning."

She couldn't help but smile. Ben had been optimistic since she'd watched him drive into the desert to get Paul. He was always trying to keep things light and put a good spin on what was happening. Too bad he was three years older than she was, and in college. Of course, she'd be in college in the fall…

Well, not of course, she realized. She wasn't likely to be anywhere in the fall.

"What's it like being on your own?" she asked.

He glanced at her. "You'll find out soon enough."

"Tell me."

He looked back at the ceiling. "Well, I'm not as good a cook as my mom. And you get bills every month from all these people for water and electricity and your cell phone and your rent. I don't like that part."

"Yeah, but you get to set your own schedule. Stay up as late as you want. Go wherever you'd like."

"True. That is nice. It's a balance, like everything else, you know? You just hope the side with the good things is heavier than the side with the bad."

She snorted. "Seems like the bad side's pretty heavy right now."

"It ain't light, that's for sure. But there are some good things."

"Doubtful."

"You learned how to use a CB. That's a skill you never had before."

Despite herself, she laughed.

"You got to climb up on top of a gas station."

"You saw me?"

"Of course. You got to meet me. That's gotta count for something."

She held her tongue, worried she'd say something stupid.

"I promise," he said. "Tomorrow won't be the last morning you wake up."

She looked at him.

"Second to last, maybe. But not the last," he told her, then smiled.

She knew he was just trying to make her laugh, but suddenly an image of her mom's face appeared in her mind. Her mom who'd been so proud of her, such a big supporter of everything she did.

Martina couldn't help the tears that began to flow, nor could she stop them.

Ben immediately moved over to her, putting his arms around her. "Hey, it's okay. I'm sorry. It was a bad joke."

"No," she said, her head tucked in his shoulder. "It was funny.

I just…I just started thinking about…home."

She continued to cry as he stroked her hair, whispering, "Everything's going to be okay."

Her strength drained way with her tears, and she could feel sleep taking hold. Maybe it would be all right. Maybe it would all be fine.

She heard a noise right before she fell asleep. It didn't completely register, but somewhere in the back of her mind she knew what it was.

A cough.

47

Ash was under no illusion that the six men they'd left in the lobby were the entire security contingent at NB7, but he also didn't want to waste time tracking down the other ones. He'd deal with them as they showed up.

The lower level was where he needed to get to, but how?

The hallway on the other side of the lobby door seemed to run from one end of the building to the other. To the left there were four doors, and to the right, two.

"This way," he said to Chloe, heading left.

Three of the four doors were on the same side the lobby was on. The first they came to was one of these. Ash tried the knob, expecting it to be locked, but it wasn't. The space inside was dark. He reached around the jamb, located a light switch, and flipped it on. The room was about twice as wide as the lobby. Set throughout were rows of heavy wide shelves that went all the way to the ceiling, but were all empty.

They checked the other two rooms on the same side and found identical spaces.

They then went to the door on the right. It was locked, but clicked open as he touched the security badge to the pad on the wall.

This time they didn't find a storage room with empty shelves. They found a spacious warehouse that took up the entire back two-thirds of the building. It was clean and empty, with only half the lights on, probably so that security could walk through without running into anything.

"My God," Chloe said. "It's a depot."

"A depot?" Ash asked.

"Matt said they're set up all over the place for, you know, after. To store whatever the others think they're going to need. Probably a good thing it's not full yet. Humanity's got a little more time before the plug gets pulled, I guess."

Ash wasn't sure what to make of the space, or what Chloe had said, but he'd save that for later. "Do you see a way down?" he asked.

They both scanned the warehouse.

"What's that?" she asked, pointing across the room.

There was another one of the security pads mounted on the wall, but there didn't seem to be any doors in the vicinity.

"I don't know."

They ran over to it, then Ash touched the ID to the pad. Nothing happened. He touched it again. Still nothing.

"Whatever it's for, I don't think it can help us," he said. "There's got to be a way down some—"

The sound of an electronic motor caused Ash to whip his head around. The floor just to the right of the ID pad lifted into the air like a blast door. It was thick and heavy, and had fitted so seamlessly into the floor that neither Ash nor Chloe had noticed it.

He stepped over, getting there before the door was halfway up, then smiled.

Below it was a set of stairs.

Dr. Karp and the two technicians, Learner and Ramos, took the elevator to level four, the lowest level of the facility.

Since their arrival the previous afternoon, Dr. Karp had requested that two security guards be stationed on level four at all times. He really didn't think there would be a problem, but with the escape of the children's father from Barker Flats, and the earlier experience a colleague had had with Lauren Scott's disappearance, he didn't want to take any chances.

The two security men were standing just outside the elevator, guns drawn, when the door opened. As soon as they recognized the doctor, they dropped their weapons to their side.

"Do you know what's going on?" the doctor asked as he stepped out of the elevator car.

"No, sir," one of the guards said. "No word from up top yet.

They're probably busy dealing with whatever the situation is."

"Did you hear the explosion?"

The men glanced at each other.

"What explosion, sir?"

"Maybe three or four minutes ago, on the top floor."

"Do you think one of us should go up and check?" the second guard asked.

"I'd rather you both stay here," the doctor said, which made it an order.

"Yes, sir." The first guard paused for a moment, then said, "With your permission, sir?"

"Yes?"

"When the alarm went off, per procedure we stationed ourselves here. But if it's okay with you, one of us could go to the substation down the hall, and bring up the security cameras so we can determine what's going on."

The doctor thought for a moment, then nodded. "Good idea. Report to me as soon as you know. I'll be with the subjects."

"Yes, sir."

The stairs ended in a brightly lit room, approximately fifteen feet square. The only things there were an elevator door and a call button. As soon as Chloe joined him, Ash pushed the button.

Almost immediately, the heavy door at the top of the stairs began swinging down again, closing them in.

"I'm not sure I like that," Chloe said.

"They're probably designed so both doors can't be open at the same time," he guessed.

"I hope you're right."

The door thudded shut.

Chloe stared at the elevator, then glanced nervously at Ash. "I don't think it's coming."

"It'll be here."

She began rocking slightly back and forth. "Are you sure? Maybe this is just a trap."

"Too elaborate for a trap."

She looked around, her gaze darting from one spot to another.

"What's wrong?" he asked.

She said nothing for a second, then, "I don't like enclosed spaces."

"You were fine in those tunnels at the hospital."

"There was always a way in and out. We're locked in here." Her breathing began to increase.

"Are you going to be okay?"

She gave him a single nod, but he could see it was an effort for her. Then, soundlessly, the elevator door opened. With a relieved gasp of breath, she raced in.

"This is an enclosed space, too," Ash said as he entered.

"Yeah, but it's going somewhere."

There was a row of five buttons, and another security pad on the control panel. The top button was lit up. Ash touched the one on the bottom, figuring that would take them to the lowest level, but nothing happened. He tapped the security pad with the badge, then touched the button once more. This time the button flashed red, and the car remained stationary. He used the badge again, then tried the fourth button down. Flashing red, no movement. The third button down received the same response. He did it once more for the second button.

This time it lit up green, and the car began to move.

Great, he thought. He'd taken the badge of someone limited to only the first lower level. He hoped to God he'd find something there that would get him to the bottom.

As the car began to stop, he said, "Move to the side and get ready."

She went left, and he went right, positioning himself so he could see out but duck quickly for cover if need be. He raised his gun, then tensed as the doors began to slide open.

There were half a dozen people just outside. None, though, was holding a weapon. They froze as a group. All, that was, except one in the back who started running down the hall away from them.

Ash stepped out quickly. "Stop!"

The man skidded to a halt.

"Don't hurt us!" one of the others shouted.

"Walk back here now, and I won't shoot you."

The runner turned around, then began retracing his steps back to the group, his arms in the air.

"Who are you?" a man standing in the middle asked.

Ash moved his gaze quickly over them. "How many of you have access to the bottom level?"

No one moved.

He pointed his gun at the guy who ran. "How many?"

"We...we all do," the man said.

"Good. You have your badge?"

The man nodded. "Yes."

"Then you're coming with us."

The man's eyes widened as Ash reached out and grabbed his arm.

"No," Chloe said.

Everyone looked at her, including Ash.

"I want that one." She pointed at the man in the middle who'd asked who they were.

"Why me?" he said, sounding frightened.

"Sorry, buddy," Ash said. He moved over and grabbed Chloe's choice. "You're with us."

Dr. Karp stood in the entrance to the room, watching the children. The boy had fallen asleep beside his sister, his arm lying protectively over her shoulder.

Such a waste, the doctor thought.

In the morning, he had planned to take sections of their vital organs before their bodies were disposed of, but now there would be no time for that. They needed to disappear to prevent any potential connection to the project.

Like most of the project's facilities that Dr. Karp used, this one had something that could handle just such a problem. There was a biosafe level-four laboratory on this very floor. It had three specialized chambers for the most delicate work. In the case of an emergency, a code could be entered into the system, and the chamber in question would go through a series of events designed to render whatever was in the room harmless. First, fire would be blasted into the room at temperatures exceeding 2,370° F. Though this would ensure nothing survived, the project Directors didn't want to take any chances, so next a quick hardening polymer, stronger than most metals, would be pumped into the room, filling it to capacity and sealing away forever anything that was in the room.

The chambers were not meant to serve as tombs, but the doctor knew the Directors would approve of his improvisation.

In the hall outside the patients' room, he heard two gurneys being rolled in his direction. He moved to the side just as Ramos brought the first one in. Learner followed right behind him with the second.

The doctor watched to make sure the children didn't wake up while they were being transferred, then said, "I'll meet you in the lab."

He had to stop by the medical supply room first to pick up something that would let the children slip away before the first flame licked their skin.

Such a waste.

48

As soon as the elevator doors closed, Ash said, "Take us all the way down."

"No problem," the man said.

He touched his card to the pad, then pressed the button for the bottom floor.

Ash shoved the man against the wall. "Where are the children?"

"Your kids are in one of the rooms in back. I can take you there."

It took Ash a second to realize the man had not said "the kids," but "your kids."

"You know who I am?" he said, pressing his gun against the man's stomach.

"You're Daniel Ash, right?" The man shot a quick look at Chloe. "You got my note."

Note? Ash took a step back.

"Yes," Chloe said. "Thank you."

Ash stared at the man. "You're the guy who—"

"Why do you think I picked him?" Chloe said.

Ash dropped his gun to his side. "Sorry. I didn't know."

"It's okay. I get it," the man said.

"What's your name?"

The man hesitated for a moment, then said, "Winger."

"Thank you, Winger."

Matt's inside man nodded uncomfortably, then glanced over at Chloe. "They did a good job on you. But I still recognized you. It's your eyes. They can't change that."

Chloe said nothing.

"Are my kids all right?" Ash asked.

"Last I saw them, yes. But Dr. Karp headed down here when the alarm went off. I don't know what he's planning on doing."

Ash's anxiety rose as he considered the possibility that he might still be too late.

But before anyone could say anything else, the elevator began to slow.

On sub-basement four, the arrival of the elevator was always preceded by the soft *whoosh* of air moving around the car as it reached its lowest point. Unlike when Dr. Karp arrived, there was only one of the security men standing in the elevator lobby, a guy by the name of Montrose. Wyle, his partner, hadn't returned yet from checking the surveillance footage.

As soon as Montrose heard the *whoosh*, he drew his gun and tensed. From down the hall he thought he heard footsteps, but his attention was focused on the door, so he paid them little attention.

The elevator settled in place, then paused for half a second before the doors slid open.

Montrose let out a breath and relaxed a little. It was just one of Dr. Karp's orderlies. He'd probably been called down to give the doctor a hand.

"They're back with the subjects," the guard started to say, but the only thing he got out of his mouth was, "They're back—"

It seemed unnecessary to go on, given the two guns that appeared from either side of the open door, aimed directly at his chest.

"Gun on the ground," Ash said softly.

The security guard dropped his pistol by his foot.

"Kick it over here."

The man seemed reluctant, so Ash wagged the SIG's barrel to remind the guy who was in charge. The gun skidded across the floor a moment later.

"Now on your knees."

Again, there was a hesitation, but before Ash could repeat the command, the man complied.

Carefully, both Ash and Chloe came out from the protection

of the elevator. Ash motioned for her to bind the man's hands and legs while he stood back a few feet. Once she was done, he put a foot on the man's chest and pushed him all the way to the ground.

"Where's Dr. Karp?" he asked.

"I don't know," the man replied.

Ash put his foot on the man's neck and pointed his gun at the guy's head.

"I *will* kill you."

"He...he said he was going in back. To the holding rooms."

Ash glanced at Winger. The orderly nodded once, confirming that's where his children were.

"You here alone?" Ash asked the guard.

"Yes," the man said quickly.

Ash immediately knew he was lying. He leaned down and put the SIG's muzzle against the man's forehead. "Those kids your Dr. Karp has back there? They are *my* kids."

The man's eyes widened in surprise.

"Don't think for a second I won't pull this trigger," Ash continued. "How many other guards are there?"

"One."

Ash pressed the gun into the man's skin.

"I swear! Only one."

"Where is he?"

"He...went with the doctor."

Ash stood, then looked at Winger. "Which way?"

Montrose's partner Wyle heard most of the conversation from just around the corner. Though only one person other than Montrose had done the talking, Wyle could tell there was another person with him.

"Where is he?" the voice said from the elevator lobby.

"He...went with the doctor," Montrose said.

Wyle couldn't help but smile. Montrose had held it together, and given him a chance to deal with the situation.

As quietly as possible, Wyle took several steps backward.

"Which way?" the voice said.

"Around and to the left." This was a new voice, confirming that there was definitely more than one unfriendly.

Wyle raised his Beretta, his finger poised on the trigger.

Ash walked to the edge of the lobby. Just beyond was a corridor that went left and right. He listened, but the only thing he could hear was a steady hum of the ventilation system.

"How far down?" he asked Winger.

"About thirty feet. Then we take the hall on the right. That'll get us all the way back."

"Okay. Stay close behind me." He glanced at Chloe. "Ready?" She nodded.

Leading with his gun, Ash ran into the hallway.

He saw the other guard a split second before he heard the double tap of the man's gun. Just as Ash pulled the trigger of his SIG, searing pain flashed up his arm as a bullet pierced his skin. The hit caused him to twist to the side, sending the shot from his gun well to the left of its intended target.

Not missing a beat, though, Ash pulled his trigger again, moving his arm in an arc and sending five quick shots in the direction of the guard. Chloe, kneeling around the corner from the lobby, fired several rounds at the same time.

The guard was only able to get a single wild shot off before he was caught in the barrage and tumbled back onto the floor.

Ash rushed forward, his gun ready if the man even twitched. But it was unnecessary. The man wasn't going to move, not now, and not ever again.

Ash allowed himself to look at the wound on his left arm. The bullet had grooved his skin a couple inches below his shoulder. It was painful, but not debilitating. He turned back to the others.

Chloe was helping Winger off the floor. There was blood on the man's shirt, concentrated mainly on the right side of his abdomen. A gut shot.

"I'm okay," the man said once he was on his feet. But he clearly wasn't. His breathing was labored, and he was doing a lousy job of keeping the pain off his face. "Let's keep moving."

"Maybe you should stay here," Chloe suggested.

He shook his head, then locked eyes with Ash. "We need to get to your children. Now."

Ash moved up next to him, draped Winger's arm over his

shoulder, then put his own carefully around the guy's waist.

"That hall?" he asked.

"Yes."

A series of airtight rooms led into the biosafe level-four lab. Each had a greater and greater negative airflow from the room before it, meaning air would always move toward the lab, not away from it. This would ensure that any accidentally released airborne pathogen would be unable to escape the lab.

It also meant that each door not only sealed the atmosphere in, but it also greatly reduced any noise from the other side. Dr. Karp and his technicians were already two rooms in out of the three. Though there was no need to take the extra precautions they would have had to take if a level-four pathogen had been present in the lab, they still had to close each door before the system would allow them to open the next. So when the gunfight near the elevator took place, they heard nothing.

As they finally entered the lab, Dr. Karp said, "Put them in number three."

Chamber three was in the corner, and the most logical one to turn unusable.

Ramos wheeled the gurney carrying the Ash girl into the lab first, then Learner tried to follow with the boy. Unfortunately, doing so pretty much clogged up most of the usable space.

"Roll those back into the airlock," the doctor said impatiently. "Just carry them in."

As they did this, the doctor set the supplies he'd picked up earlier on the counter. There were two sealed and empty hypodermics, and two small glass bottles, each with more than enough Beta-Somnol to put a grown adult into a final sleep. The children would pass peacefully. Given what would happen in the world soon enough, the doctor couldn't help but feel he was doing the humane thing, something most would be denied.

He opened one of the hypo kits, stuck the needle into the bottle, then started drawing the drug out.

Yes. Very humane.

"That door there," Winger said, his voice weakening. "Those

are the subject rooms. They're in there."

"I think it's best if we leave you here," Ash said. "Do you want to lean on the wall? Or sit on the ground?"

"I...don't know if I can...stand on my own."

"Okay, no problem."

Ash tried to ease the man to the floor as gently as possible, but the orderly still sucked in his breath and winced.

"I'm sorry," Ash said once the man was down.

"It's okay." Winger tried to smile. "Go get your kids."

Ash gave him a pat on the shoulder, then he and Chloe moved down the hall to the door Winger had pointed out.

"What's the plan?" she whispered.

"Play it by ear."

"Oh, okay. So the same plan as before."

Ash didn't bother to respond.

He turned the knob until the latch was all the way out, then he inched the door open just enough so that he could see inside. The space appeared to be set up similarly to the wards back at the Palmer Psychiatric Hospital—central corridor and doors off to the sides.

He eased the door open some more. No shouts, no sounds of movement, nothing.

With a quick warning glance at Chloe, he pulled out the door wide enough to get through, then rushed inside. No one was there.

"Check the doors," he whispered.

They worked from opposite sides, opening each door and looking in. Every room Ash checked had beds, but all the mattresses were bare and appeared unused.

"Ash!" Chloe called out.

She was standing in the doorway of a room near the back wall. He rushed over and looked in.

There were two beds inside. Both had blankets and sheets but were unmade. He moved in quickly, put a hand on one mattress, then the other. The bed on the left still had the warmth of a body.

He ran past Chloe out of the room, through the outer area and back into the hallway.

Winger's eyes were closed as Ash reached him.

"They're not there!"

"Wha...what?" Winger said, his eyelids barely peeling apart. "They're not there. No one is. Where are they?"

"Not there?" The orderly looked confused. "I don't..." He stopped, then his eyes opened wider. "No. Oh, God, no."

"What?"

"Okay," Ramos said as he stepped out of chamber three, where he'd just laid Brandon Ash next to the girl on the floor.

At that very moment, the indicator for the door to the first airlock switched from closed to open on the lab's computer screen.

Dr. Karp almost missed it. He had just finished activating the controls for chamber three, and had turned away to retrieve the hypos of Beta-Somnol when one of his oldest habits, his need to double-check everything, caused him to look back.

Not for one second did he think whoever had entered was one of the project members there to help him.

This was it. The end. Unless there was some kind of miracle—something he didn't believe in—his own life would soon be sacrificed.

Before it had been just a possibility. Now, the harsh reality was numbing.

Five seconds passed without him moving at all. Then he remembered his oath, his promise to the project. The job he still had to do.

He grabbed the needles, and was halfway to chamber three before he realized there wouldn't be enough time. He'd have to start the sequence without administering the drug. Hopefully, the children would remain asleep and feel no pain as the intense heat quickly took their lives. Not quite as humane as he'd hoped, but still better than nothing.

When he got back to the monitor, the indicator for the door between the second and third airlocks was already in the open position. As soon as it closed, the door to the lab would open.

He started punching in the code.

49

Ash pulled the door between the second and third airlocks shut, then jammed down the handle that created the final seal. Already having positioned herself at the door to the lab, Chloe began pulling up its handle the second he finished. Ash got there just in time to grab the edge of the door as it released and yank it open.

"No one move!" he yelled as he and Chloe rushed into the room.

There were three men inside. Two were standing next to a wide window that looked into what appeared to be another room, while the third was at a counter along the right wall in front of a computer. Ash knew this third man. He'd seen a picture of him at the ranch. He was the man responsible for the hell Ash's family had gone through.

"Dr. Karp, where are my children?"

The doctor's head tilted slightly to the side, then his eyes narrowed. "Captain...Ash?"

"Where are my children?"

"I'm impressed, Captain. I didn't know you were this resourceful. Unfortunately, I'm afraid you're too late."

"What do you mean?"

"They died in the outbreak at Barker Flats," the doctor stated matter-of-factly. "You were told that before."

"We both know that was a lie."

Dr. Karp lowered his hand, his fingers now resting on the edge of the counter. "Why wouldn't we have told you the truth?"

Ash took three quick steps forward, closing the gap between them to less than ten feet, and pointed the SIG at the center of the doctor's face. "Where are they?"

"Seriously, Captain. They're dead. There's nothing you can do."

Dr. Karp's fingers tapped nervously against the counter.

Without looking at her, Ash signaled Chloe to check the rest of the room. As she moved past Dr. Karp, he eyed her nervously.

"Where are they?" Ash asked the doctor again.

The ends of Dr. Karp's mouth went up and down in a quick smile. "It doesn't really matter, you know. You'll all be dead soon enough. Well, maybe not *you*, but everyone else. The whole world will be different then."

"They're in here!" Chloe yelled.

Ash turned to look. Chloe was standing next to an open door that appeared to lead into the room the window looked in on. Before Ash could react, he caught movement out of the corner of his eye, and turned back just in time to see the doctor hit one of the keys on the keyboard.

Ash wanted to run over to Chloe, but he sprinted to the doctor instead, grabbing the man by his collar.

"What did you do?" Ash demanded.

"It's closing!" Chloe yelled.

"I told you," the doctor said. "There's nothing you can—"

Chloe screamed out in pain. "Stop it! Stop it!"

Ash looked over. She'd put her leg between the door and the jamb, preventing it from sealing shut. But whatever was closing it was keeping the pressure on her.

"Help her!" Ash yelled at the two men cowering by the window. They hesitated a moment, then jumped up when Ash pointed his gun at them, and moved quickly over to Chloe.

"I'm not sure you want them to do that," the doctor said.

"What are you talking about?"

"Look for yourself." Dr. Karp nodded toward the window.

Ash wasn't about to leave the doctor behind, so he manhandled him across the room, then looked through the window. Josie and Brandon were on the floor. While his son looked like he was asleep, Josie was sitting up, her eyelids only half open.

"Oh, that's too bad," the doctor said. "The sound must have woken her. I was hoping they'd both just sleep through it."

Ash turned on him, and leaned in so that their faces were only inches apart. "What did you do?"

"Once that door seals shut, they die. Moving your friend's leg will make that happen all the sooner."

"Open it!"

"Sorry."

Ash jammed the gun into the side of the doctor's head. "Open it!"

"If you're going to shoot me, then shoot. It doesn't change the fact that once the sequence is initiated, I can't undo it." He grinned. "Oh, and if the door remains jammed for more than three minutes, this entire lab will be sterilized at a nice toasty 3000 degrees."

"Three minutes?"

The doctor shrugged. "Sorry I can't be of more help."

"That's where you're wrong."

Ash moved the gun from the doctor's head, and shot the man in the hip. The doctor's face went slack in surprise. Before he could fall to the ground, Ash caught him and dragged him around to the doorway.

The two men had made no progress in getting Chloe free. The moment they saw Ash they started to back away.

"You're going to help me, or I swear to God I will shoot both of you, but not kill you. Do you understand what I mean?"

Apparently, they did.

Ash directed them to grab the edge of the door and pull back as hard as they could.

"More!" he said, as he watched the gap.

At first it didn't grow at all, then suddenly it moved a quarter inch, a half. When it reached three-quarters of an inch wider, instead of pulling Chloe's leg out, Ash shoved the doctor's injured leg in.

Dr. Karp screamed in pain, then yelled, "What are you doing?"

Ash felt no need to answer as he then eased Chloe's leg out. Once it was free, he said to the two other men, "All right. Let go."

The doctor screamed out again as the door smashed against him.

"You going to be okay?" Ash asked Chloe.

She clenched her teeth, fighting off the pain. "Don't worry

about me."

He knew her leg was probably broken, the bone perhaps even crushed. But she seemed to be in control. "Cover them," he said.

"My pleasure." She pointed her gun at the two men. "Sit down. Both of you."

Ash didn't stay to see if they cooperated. He knew if they didn't, she'd shoot them. He moved back around to the window. It was the only other way in, but it wasn't something he could just break through with a chair.

He pulled out the little bangs, choosing the four special white squares. These were the ones Pax said did more than just cause noise. He quickly removed the projection sheets off the adhesive backs, and placed the crackers near each corner of the window. He thought about adding a couple of the noisemakers just in case they might help, but decided against it. He pulled out the controller, then moved back around to the side where the door was. As expected, Chloe's two friends were sitting on the floor.

Ash stepped over the doctor, then said into the gap, "Josie! Josie, can you hear me?"

"D...dad?"

"Yes, sweetie, it's me."

"Dad? But...but...they told us—"

"Josie, I don't care what they told you. I'm here and I'm going to get you out."

"Dad!" She crawled toward the door. "Dad! Oh, my God!"

"Sweetie, you need to listen to me. This is very important. We don't have any time, okay?"

"Dad. Please get us out of here."

"That's what I'm trying to do. Now, listen, I need you to grab your brother and take him against the wall that the window's on. But in the corner, off to the side. Not in front of the window. Do you understand?"

"Um...uh...I think so."

"Please, baby. If you don't do it, none of us are getting out."

"Okay, Dad. I can do it."

"Excellent. Do it now. And be ready. There's going to be a loud bang."

He moved back around, and watched Josie through the window as she pulled Brandon into the front corner. Once they were there, he returned to the door.

"Cover your head," he said.

He didn't look to see if Chloe and the others did the same; he just hit the button.

The two security men who'd been sent out to check for the missing car came back after fifteen minutes. They'd found the car ten minutes earlier, abandoned at the side of the highway not far from the road to NB7, but when they called it in, no one had answered. After being unable to reach anyone for five minutes, they decided to come back.

Everything looked the same out front as it had when they'd left, so they were starting to think their boss had just gone on a bathroom break without feeling the need to have anyone fill in for him. That was, until Collins, the younger of the two, opened the front door.

"Oh, Jesus," he said.

His partner, Edwards, started to push by him, but pulled up short when he caught sight of the scene inside. "What the hell?"

The lobby was riddled with bullet holes. And there were five bodies that they could see. The two men moved in and checked for pulses. Two of their colleagues were still alive, their hands and ankles cuffed with the same ties the security team used.

"What happened?" Collins asked.

Edwards shook his head, then headed over to the security room. That's where he found their boss sprawled across the threshold, cuffed and dead.

"Do…do you think whoever did this is still in the building?" Collins asked.

"I have no idea."

The younger man hesitated, as if he didn't want to say what was about to come from his lips. "Should we check?"

Edwards looked down at his boss, then at the other men strewn across the lobby. "I'm not sure that would be a good idea."

Four minutes later, with the pair of unconscious men slumped in the back seat, Edwards and Collins pulled out of the compound then headed south on the highway as fast as they could go.

Even though Ash had covered his ears, the noise was deafening. Debris flew across the room, smashing into the wall where the counter was, and destroying the monitor the doctor had been using.

Ash immediately jumped back to his feet and returned to the window. However strong the glass had been, it wasn't strong enough to stand up to the little white squares. He climbed through the opening and went to the corner where Brandon, awake now, clung to his sister.

Ash couldn't believe it. He was looking at his kids. They were alive.

He grinned broadly and held his arms out, but instead of hugging him, they drew back.

"Who are you?" Josie asked, sounding scared.

"It's me, baby. Dad."

"You're not my dad," she said.

The bandages. The surgery. Even the contacts. He must look like a stranger to them.

"It's me. I swear. I've just had…an accident. We can talk about it later. We need to get out now."

Reluctantly, they let him guide them out of the room.

He had no idea how much time they had left, but he knew it was probably less than a minute.

"You see that door?" He pointed at the airlock.

They nodded.

"Go in there. I'll be right behind you. I just have to help my friend."

They both looked over at Chloe, then back at their father, more confused than ever.

"Go!" he said.

That got them moving.

He knelt down next to Chloe. "Put your arm around me," he told her.

Once she did, he started to lift her, but then remembered there was one more thing he had to do. He moved over to the doctor.

"I hope you enjoy your trip to hell."

The doctor forced a smile. "You can't stop anything, you know that. Your kids would have been better off to go now instead of being alive to witness the world they know melt into nothing."

"I have a feeling you're the only one who'll be doing any melting in the near future."

"Humor's not one of your best traits, I'm guessing."

Ignoring him, Ash said, "Before I go, I have a message for you from an old friend."

The doctor looked at him, a smirk on his face.

"Olivia says hi," Ash said. "I got the feeling from her she wasn't too happy you left her to die. Pointed out something about the irony that you'll be dead before she is."

"Olivia? But she's—"

"Goodbye, Doctor."

Ash lifted Chloe off the floor and headed for the airlock. Just before he passed through the door, he yelled to the other two men, "Once we clear this airlock, I suggest you get in it, if there's still time."

It turned out there wasn't.

50

It wasn't the starting of the truck that woke Tamara and Bobby. It was the pothole they hit sometime later. According to the clock on the camera, it was 7:12 a.m.

"Do you think whoever's driving knows we're back here?" Tamara asked.

"I don't know," Bobby replied. "I would think so, though. Wouldn't you?"

The world seemed to have flipped on its end, so she didn't know what to think anymore.

"I wonder where we're going," Bobby said several minutes later.

"Can't be far." The quarantine would prevent any long travels.

But either they drove around in circles or she was wrong, because six hours passed before the engine was turned off for the first time. After a few moments, they could both hear fuel flowing into the tanks.

"Maybe we should get out now," she suggested.

"We haven't heard the knock."

"Maybe there's not going to be a knock. We're not on the base any more."

But neither of them made a move to open the door, and soon they were on the road again. Nearly seven more hours passed before the engine cut out once more. This time, though, there was no sound of tanks being filled. In fact, except for the opening and closing of the cab door, there wasn't much sound at all.

After thirty minutes of not moving, Tamara said, "I'll bet we're in another parking lot."

"If nothing else, we're going to get a great story out of this,"

Bobby said.

"If we have a job."

Bobby was quiet for a second, then, "Do you...do you really think Joe is dead?"

She was silent for a moment. "They killed Gavin, didn't they? And those kids in the desert. So..."

A few silent minutes passed.

"How far do you think we've come?" she asked.

"Impossible to know."

They broke out some food, and had a dinner consisting of apples, bread, and some kind of deli meat. As she'd done all day, Tamara only took a couple sips of water. Even though it was dark in their hiding space, the idea of peeing in front of Bobby had zero appeal to her.

Tap-tap. Tap.

The knock had been on the side of the truck, right behind her head. Tamara nearly leaped forward in surprise.

Tap-tap. Tap.

She wanted to scream, "We're here! We're here!" But she held her tongue.

She could hear Bobby already working the door latch. As he opened the door, they could see that the back of the truck was still open, and outside it was night.

"You wait here. I'll check," Bobby said.

"Hell, no. You wait here. *I'll* check."

She pushed past him and walked stiffly to the back of the truck. It was cool out, much cooler, in fact, than it had been when she and Bobby entered their sanctuary, making her realize that the box had actually been heated. She crossed her arms and ran her hands up and down her biceps as she stepped onto the back bumper, and then hopped to the ground.

They seemed to be parked on a small grass clearing in the middle of an evergreen forest. Pine trees encircled the part of the clearing she could see. One thing was for sure—they were certainly not in the Mojave Desert any more.

She looked over her shoulder as Bobby stepped down to join her.

"Where the hell are we?" he asked.

She was about to say she had no clue when a voice from near the front of the truck called out, "Hello?"

Tamara and Bobby exchanged a look, then walked over and peeked around the side.

Standing by the cab were a smiling man and woman.

"Oh, good," the man said, taking a couple steps forward. "I was afraid you guys might have wandered off. I wasn't looking forward to hunting you down."

"Hunting?" Tamara said.

"Oh, no, no, no," the man said with a chuckle. "Bad choice of words. Searching is more what I meant. Come on. You probably want to get out of here."

Still leery, Tamara and Bobby stepped around the side and walked halfway up to the cab.

"Who are you, exactly?" Tamara asked.

"Me? I'm Mike." The man closed the distance between them and extended his hand.

Bobby shook it automatically, while Tamara did so with more reluctance.

"And that's my wife, Janice."

Janice waved, but didn't come closer. She looked as cold as Tamara felt.

"So what are you doing here?" Tamara asked.

Mike shrugged. "Offering you a ride."

"I hope you don't mind," Janice called out. "I'm going back inside. It's too cold out here." She started walking around the front of the truck. "Coffee should be ready by now, so whenever you're ready."

"Coffee?" Bobby said.

Mike smiled. "Sure. Janice makes the best on the highway."

When Bobby gave him an odd look, Mike smiled and motioned for them to follow him to the front of the truck. From there, they could see an old Winnebago RV parked fifty feet away.

Bobby glanced at Tamara. "Come on. They're obviously here to help us."

Tamara looked at the Winnebago. "Do you have a bathroom in that thing?"

"We do," Mike said with a smile.

She could feel her tension ease. "Then a cup of coffee sounds great."

"Excellent," Mike told her. "After you."

51

It was a struggle for Martina to open her eyes. When she did, the brightness of the new day made her shut them almost immediately. She could feel the congestion in her nose, and the rawness in her throat. When she'd fallen asleep, she'd felt fine. Now, not so much.

Her last morning. She was sure of it.

She worked her eyes open again, then rolled over and looked at the spot where Ben had been sleeping. He wasn't there.

Probably decided to move when he realized I was sick, she thought.

She raised herself up on her elbows. She could hear sniffling elsewhere in the dining area, and even a couple of coughs, her friends all dying with her.

"You're up."

She looked over her shoulder. Ben was standing behind her. He must have been in the kitchen. Though he was smiling, she could tell by his red nose that he was sick, too. That depressed her even more. She liked him, and had been hoping that maybe he'd be the one to survive.

"What's wrong with you?" he asked.

"What do you mean?"

"You're all sour face."

She lay her head back down. "I guess I was kind of hoping we wouldn't get it."

"Right," he said, his smile widening. "You've been asleep."

"What's that supposed to mean?"

"Come on. I'll show you."

With more than just a bit of effort, Ben helped Martina to her feet, then led her to the front of the café. Most of the others were there, all but one or two showing signs of the flu. The TV on the counter was on, tuned to PCN. At the bottom of the screen was a banner that read: *Quarantine Partially Lifted.*

"Lifted?" Martina said. "But we're all sick here."

"Yeah, and we're still in the quarantine zone, but not for long," Ben told her.

"What are you talking about?"

"Maybe he can tell you," he said, nodding at the next booth over.

She turned and saw Paul sitting on the end of the bench seat. He looked tired—exhausted, actually—but what other signs of the illness he'd had seemed to be gone.

"You owe me a glass of orange juice," Ben said. "I believe that was our bet."

"He's all right?" she asked quietly.

"He's recovering from the illness, but I don't think he'd say he's all right."

Of course. His brother and his girlfriend.

"They're saying on the news that there have been over five hundred new cases in the last thirty-six hours, but most haven't resulted in death. People are being asked to voluntarily stay home until the flu has disappeared, but the quarantine is expected to be fully lifted by tomorrow night."

"So…what? It just stopped killing people?"

"Apparently."

She couldn't believe it. "We're going to live?"

Ben smiled again. "Didn't I tell you this wasn't going to be your last morning?"

52

"Would you like me to play it again?" the Director of Preparation asked.

There were head shakes all around the table.

"Do you really think she's alive?" the Director of Facilities asked.

"How would Captain Ash have known her name otherwise?"

They had just watched Ash and an unidentified woman rescue his children from NB7. The video had lasted right up to the point when the flames flared up. Ash had clearly stated the name Olivia and mentioned she'd been left for dead.

At the end of the table, the Principal Director leaned forward. "I think it would be unwise to assume Olivia is still alive based solely on a single brief conversation. But I also think it would be unwise not to try to find out more."

"Yes, sir," the DOP said. "I'll get a team right on it."

"There are several things, though," the Principal Director went on, "that concern me more at the moment, lapses of security on this operation that were totally unacceptable. The loss of the NB7 facility, in particular, does not make me happy."

"Yes, sir," the DOP said. "I agree with you one hundred percent. Though it should have been unnecessary, we will definitely learn from these mistakes. To that end, if I may…" He glanced at the Principal Director, who gave him a nod. "Bring up channel four, please."

The monitor came back to life, this time showing what looked like a conference room.

Sitting on one side of the table was Mr. Shell, and on the other, the soon-to-be former Director of Recovery. Ostensibly, the meeting was for the DOR to critique Shell's performance during the out-break. That in itself was highly unusual, given that project members almost never met face to face with the Directors, but it was not entirely unprecedented. Given the gravity of what had just played out over the last several days, neither man questioned its necessity.

The DOP used the remote to turn up the volume.

"...more. You must understand that," the DOR said. "These kinds of slips are completely unacceptable."

"Yes, sir," Mr. Shell said. "I understand. There were problems that were unforeseen."

"Nothing should be unforeseen!"

The DOP couldn't resist the opening. He touched the button for the microphone that was clipped to his collar. "You're absolute-ly correct. Nothing *should* be unforeseen."

Both men on the screen looked up toward where the voice must have been coming from.

"The Directorate would like to thank the Director of Recovery and Mr. Shell for their contributions to the project," the DOP went on. "It is our unanimous decision that neither of your services will be further required."

"What?" the Director of Recovery said. "Wait. You can't—"

The DOP hit the mute button. "Terminate," he said.

He waited until the two men in the other room started chok-ing as the air to their room was cut off, then had the monitor turned off. He looked back at the group.

"Even with these unfortunate incidents, there is much good news. From Dr. Karp's own calculations, we know that the effec-tiveness of KV-27a exceeds our hopes. Even the safeguard that he encoded into the virus of turning it into a simple flu after the fifth or sixth host worked perfectly. And with the discovery of the Ash family's immunity, we should have a working vaccine within weeks. It is unfortunate that the doctor isn't with us anymore, but his work still goes on. I think we can safely designate stage one of the deliv-ery agent complete. That is, unless anyone has any objections?" He looked around the table, but no one said a word. "We will concen-trate on stage two now, which is already well on its way. At this time, I see no threat at all to the implementation timetable."

The Principal Director leaned forward again. "What about

Captain Ash? He's still on the loose."

"He is, sir. But I don't believe he's any kind of problem. He only wanted his children."

"And these missing journalists?"

"We believe they were scared off, sir, and will resurface soon. When that occurs, they will be dealt with."

"Yes, but who is helping these people? They couldn't have done this all on their own. And if Olivia is alive, where is she?"

"We're looking into all of that, sir, but, again, we don't think any of it is a serious threat. The boulder is running downhill. It's too late for anyone to stop it."

53

As they sped away from NB7, Chloe called Matt, requesting a safe house and a doctor. They were directed to the home of an elderly woman in a small, Western Idaho town. Despite the fact the sun had yet to come up when they arrived, she smiled at the children and told everyone to make themselves at home, then disappeared into a room in the back.

Ash hunted down some aspirin for Chloe, then found a couple of bedrooms upstairs and told Josie and Brandon they could use them. But instead of separating, they chose to share a room. He could tell they were still unsure if it was really him, but he didn't want to push himself on them.

After they were settled, he cleaned out his wound again. The first time he'd done it had been in a gas station restroom, not exactly the most sterile of places. This time he found some rubbing alcohol in the medicine cabinet, and poured it into the groove on his arm. It burned worse than when he'd actually been hit, but he knew he had to do it, and dumped nearly half the bottle over the wound before he stopped.

When he returned downstairs, he found Chloe propped up on the couch.

"Why don't you get some sleep," he suggested.

"I tried, but this isn't going to let me," she told him, touching her leg.

He wished he could do something more for her. The pain seemed to be hitting her in waves. She'd be fine for a bit, then, with no warning, would close her eyes tight and cringe.

Just short of an hour after they arrived, there was a knock on the door. It was Pax and Billy. Billy quickly checked both patients, then gave Chloe a sedative that allowed her to fall asleep. As soon as she was out, he dealt with Ash's wound.

"Clean this yourself?" he asked.

"Yeah."

"Remind me not to use you as a nurse."

More burning, then a bandage to cover the gash. When he was through, Billy examined Ash's face, looking at the scars of the surgery from what seemed so long ago.

With a simple "It looks like nothing's going to fall off," Billy went to see what he could do about Chloe's leg.

"You got 'em," Pax said, once he and Ash were alone.

"Yeah, I did." Ash knew he should be happy, but the worry he'd had for his kids' safety had turned into worry for their mental well-being. Sometimes being a parent sucked. "Thanks for your help. Those mini-explosives you gave me, I couldn't have done it without them."

"Don't even worry about it."

They talked a little longer, but at some point Ash fell asleep. How Pax and Billy got him into a bed upstairs, he had no idea. But that's where he woke to an afternoon sun shining through the window.

He showered, put on the new clothes someone had laid out for him, and headed downstairs. He found Pax and the old woman in the kitchen, laughing and having a cup of coffee.

"Where's Josie and Brandon?" he asked, alarmed.

"Your kids are fine," the old woman said. "They're out back, playing with the dog."

Ash walked over to the open back door and looked out the screen. Josie was sitting on a picnic bench, petting the head of a golden retriever while Brandon was trying to coax the dog away with a ball. It seemed so...normal.

"And Chloe?" Ash asked.

"Billy took her back to the ranch," Pax said. "Said she needs surgery on the leg, but that she should be fine."

Ash hadn't told her thank you. He should have done it already, but he'd been too drained to even think about it.

"Can I get you a cup of coffee?" the woman asked.

Ash shook his head. "Not right now, thanks."

He opened the screen door and stepped into the backyard. Both his kids looked over and stared at him. He wondered if their uncertainty would ever go away, if they'd ever truly believe he was their dad.

As he walked toward them, the golden retriever ran to him. Ash knelt down and petted the dog's head. "Hey, buddy." He looked over at his children. "What's his name?"

Neither of them said anything for a moment, then Brandon took a step forward. "Strider."

"Hello there, Strider," Ash said to the dog.

Strider wagged his tail and licked Ash's hand.

"He likes to play catch," Brandon said.

Ash stood up. "You have a ball?"

Brandon nodded and showed him the tennis ball in his hand.

"Throw it for him," Ash said.

Brandon tossed the ball across the yard, and Strider took off after it. As the dog was bringing the ball back to the boy, Ash casually walked over.

"Can I try?" he asked.

"Sure," Brandon said, handing him the ball.

They played toss with the dog for several minutes, alternating turns, with neither of them really saying anything. While they did this, Josie sat quietly on the bench watching them.

As Ash was about to throw the ball again, Josie said, "Why did they tell us you were dead?"

Ash paused for a moment, then let the ball fly. "I don't know, sweetheart. Because they weren't very nice, I guess. They told me you were both dead, too."

"They did?" Brandon said.

Ash nodded.

Strider returned with the ball and dropped it at Brandon's feet, but the boy didn't seem to notice. Brandon looked at his father for a moment, then glanced at his sister and whispered something just low enough so Ash couldn't hear it.

Josie seemed to be lost in thought for a moment, then looked up at their dad. "Is...Mom alive, too?"

Ash could feel his heart suddenly break. He sank down to his knees so he was closer to their height, tears forming in his eyes.

"No, sweetie. She's not."

"But you're here, and they said you were dead," she countered.

Ash could hear Brandon's breath become ragged as he fought his own tears. "I know, Josie. But your mom was gone before they even took us out of the house."

"But…but…are you sure?"

He nodded.

Brandon was the first to fall into his embrace, sobbing into Ash's shoulder, but Josie wasn't far behind him.

"I love you guys," Ash said, then repeated "I love you" over and over.

"I love you, too, Dad," Josie said, once her tears had finally lost their strength.

"Me, too," Brandon added.

The hug that followed seemed to last for hours.